A Prisoner of Dreamland

and Other Oneiric Terrors

A Prisoner of Dreamland

and Other Oneiric Terrors

Garrett Boatman

WEIRD HOUSE

ISBN: 978-1-957121-81-9

Text © 2024 by Garrett Boatman

Cover Art © 2024 by K. L. Turner

Interior and cover design by Cyrusfiction Productions

Copy-Editing F. J. Bergmann

Editor and Publisher, Joe Morey

Weird House Press
Central Point, OR 97502
www.weirdhousepress.com

For my sister
Vicki Lynn McCarthy
R.I.P.

CONTENTS

"The machinery for dreaming planted in the human brain was not planted for nothing. That faculty, in alliance with the mystery of darkness, is the one great tube through which man communicates with the shadowy. And the dreaming organ, in connection with the heart, the eye, and the ear, compose the magnificent apparatus which forces the infinite into the chambers of a human brain, and throws dark reflections from eternities below all life upon the mirrors of that mysterious camera obscura—the sleeping mind."

—Thomas De Quincey, *Suspiria de Profundis*

OF CONSCIOUSNESS
AND CHAOS

"The mind, in short, works on the data it receives very much as a sculptor works on his block of stone. In a sense the statue stood there for eternity. But there were a thousand different ones beside it, and the sculptor alone is to thank for having extricated this one from the rest. Just so the worlds of each of us, howsoever different our several views of it may be, all lay embedded in the primordial chaos of sensations, which gave the mere matter of the thought of all of us indifferently. We may, if we like, by our reasonings unwind things back to that black and jointless continuity of space and moving clouds of swarming atoms which science calls the only real world. But all the while the world *we* feel and live in will be that which our ancestors and we, by slowly cumulative strokes of choice, have extricated out of this, like sculptors, by simply rejecting certain portions of the given stuff. Other sculptors, other statues from the same stone! Other minds, other worlds from the same monotonous and inexpressive chaos! My world is but one in a million alike embedded, alike real to those who may abstract them. How different must be the worlds in the consciousness of ant, cuttlefish, or crab!'"

The lecturer, Dr. Liam Wilkins, an alienist by profession, a spiritualist by enthusiasm, paused to survey the diverse audience that filled the steeply tiered benches of the Wandsworth Institute of Psychical Research Lecture

Theatre. The hall was packed for the evening's topic, the metaphysical being as much in demand as the scientific in this modern age. Apprentices and mechanics in corduroys sat alongside London gentry in flannels and tweeds. Quite a few ladies, including housewives, shopgirls, and switchboard operators, gazed down with attentive faces. The free lectures afforded even a couple of the Leviathan's homeless respite from the cold. One of these was snoring softly to the annoyance of his neighbors.

"Thus, the American alienist and philosopher, William James, eloquently describes the process by which each of us forms our perception of reality out of the superfluity of sensory data and associative thoughts vying for our brains' attention. James' general law of perception applies here." He consulted his notes. "'Whilst part of what we perceive comes through our senses from the object before us, another (and it may be the larger part) always comes out of our own head.' That 'larger part' is our capacity to reason, which is shaped, in turn, by our cultural mindset. In England, for example, rich or poor, educated or not, our citizens share a commonality of ideas, of values, of concept of an orderly world. Denizens of Malay or of New Guinea, or the aborigines of Australia, may share very different ideas about the shape of reality.

"Consider the visual perception. We see something: a boat on the Thames, a portrait in the Tate. We see the same thing again at a later date. Both times, the only real data are the physical picture on the retina. However, each time the state of consciousness is different. Perhaps you've argued with your employer, or your lunch doesn't agree with you." He paused for a laugh. Getting none, he continued. "Let us agree, as Kant does, that a reality exists outside the mind, and that when a tree falls within the forest and there being no one to hear its fall, yet it makes a sound. Because we perceive the world through our sensory apparatus and cannot empirically prove that our perception accurately represents the world around us, we cannot empirically know the world exists, but, as its existence presupposes the entirety of theology, science, and philosophy, we must accept its existence. Common sense is not so demanding as science or philosophy. As Dr. Johnson, refuting Bishop Berkeley's theory of subjective idealism, struck his foot against a stone and replied, 'I refute it thus.'"

That brought a murmur of laughter.

"So our perception of reality—the *truth* of reality, if you will—is relativistic, determined by what we select from the plethora of sense data clamoring for our attention and our personal and cultural preconceptions. What if, however—" Here he paused for dramatic effect. "—the human consciousness was unlimited? What might that perception be? Would we, at last, overcome the barriers between the individual and the Absolute which is the great mystic achievement?"

The lecture over, the attendees filed out, some wishing him a good evening as they passed. One lingered to speak with him. The fellow was perhaps in his later thirties or early forties. His weathered face marked him as an outdoorsman, as did his Norfolk jacket and hiking boots, a choice more suitable for a country hunt than a London lecture. Something about the man disturbed him. He couldn't put his finger on it. Perhaps it was the glow in his gray eyes that raised a flag of disquiet. Was the man a zealot, one of the ardent promulgating the new religion of spiritualism? One of those who made the rounds of mediums anxious for a glimpse beyond the veil? He didn't look the type; with his hard figure, tanned features, and sun-bleached hair, he was obviously more inclined to the active life than the sedentary. His grip was firm; he didn't squeeze, but Wilkins imagined he could break bones if he wished.

"I enjoyed your lecture, Doctor." His voice was deep, with a bit of the rasp of one who did not often converse. "What you said about our overcoming 'the barriers between the individual and the Absolute'?"

"Yes?"

"What if I told you I have found a way to overcome the barriers between the individual and the Absolute? A way to expand the consciousness and, in one blinding glory of perception, perceive the entirety of reality. To gaze with infinite clarity upon the face of the Absolute?"

Wilkins raised his brows. Did the man refer to an opium dream? He saw nothing of the addict's lethargy in the man's countenance; indeed, he appeared focused, his eyes clear, his pupils undilated. Despite his apprehension, Wilkins warmed to the topic. It was November out, yet the man's tan and sun-bleached hair proclaimed he had recently come from a tropical land. Perhaps in his travels he had come across something to unlock the mysteries. Wilkins, an armchair traveler, conceded the world abounded in mysteries awaiting discovery. Still, professional skepticism bade him to be pragmatic.

"That would be wonderful," he said in a voice he hoped conveyed good humor. "Alas, the brain is what it is. Perhaps after a million years of further evolution …" He let his tone imply there was nothing further to discuss.

"Aye," the man said. "'The brain is what it is.' But how well do we understand it? Your field of psychology, as well as that of neurology, is in its infancy. Even your esteemed Professor James is as a babe in the woods when it comes to the mysteries of the mind. Perhaps the brain is limited, but is the mind? The localists make progress in isolating the cerebral sites responsible for our various functions. I've even heard of one neurologist who claims he has found the seat of dreaming in the cerebral cortex. But has anyone discovered the seat of mind?"

Wilkins was tempted to launch into an explanation of mind as a product of neurological activities involving cerebral centers for perception, memory, and reasoning, but he had not had his supper and his stomach looked forward to a steak dinner at his club. He refused the bait and said nothing.

He was surprised when, as if reading his mind, the man said, "Ah, where are my manners? I'm keeping you from your supper. If I may … I would be honored if you would be my dinner guest so we could—" He paused to smile. "—further discuss the 'great mystic achievement?'"

As the man, who introduced himself as Adams, wasn't dressed for his club, they settled on steaks at the Hotel Continental, where Adams was staying. If Adams was to be believed, he came with serious credentials, being a member of both the Anthropological Society and the Royal Geographical Society, the latter of which had partially funded his journey to the Peruvian Upper Amazonian where he had lived with and studied the indigenous Quechuas.

After dinner, over cigars and brandy, they continued their conversation.

"What you said in your lecture about truth, for humans, being relative because of the limitations of their sensory apparatus."

"Yes?"

"Your thesis is that if we could process the flood of sensory data in its entirety, then we might perceive absolute reality and, therefore, absolute truth.

"Well ..." Wilkins swirled his brandy. "In theory, yes. But there are drawbacks that make such a superhuman leap unlikely."

"Such as?"

"Take the dementia praecox paradox, for example. Victims suffer from an avalanche of sensory information. But because their brain's sensory systems are unable to filter out unnecessary information, simple tasks become unbearably difficult. The human brain is just not capable of processing all the information coming through our sensory pathways as well as our thoughts. Then look at the dilemma of modern man. The overload of information assaulting the brain in the industrial age is debilitating. The epidemic is spreading fast. Progress as a virus."

Adams tapped ash. "That's true for man in the normal state. But isn't it posited that in the mystic state we become one with the Absolute and become aware of our oneness?"

"Go on."

"If you were able to become one with the Absolute and perceive the Absolute in its entirety, then truth would no longer be relative but absolute."

"Unless different mystics had different perceptions of the Absolute. Then you're back to relativity."

"This is precisely why I approached you, Doctor." Adams rolled his cigar between thumb and forefinger before flashing a smile. "I have seen what lies beyond the veil. I have looked on the face of the Absolute."

"That, sir," said Wilkins, "is a bold statement."

"It is. And I would not make it were it not true."

"And what, may I ask, did you see? Understand that I am skeptical, but as you have been an excellent host, I will hear you out." He did not add that, despite his skepticism, he was curious. There was about the man an aura of mystery, and Wilkins wondered if, perhaps, Adams was truly on to something. He decided he would make an effort to attend Adams' upcoming lecture at the Royal Geographical.

"That, sir, I will keep in reserve. Understand that I am not trying to bait you. I have my reasons for withholding certain information until you hear my proposal."

At the word "proposal," Wilkins pursed his lips. He disliked solicitors whether ideological or mercantile. "Before you begin," he said, applying humour rather than outright rejection; after all, the man had bought him supper, "let me assure you I have no interest in buying a rubber plantation on the other side of the planet, no matter how lucrative you make it out."

Adams laughed and tapped ash in the pewter tray embellished with the hotel's logo. "No, sir, I've not brought you here to sell you real estate. I have a much larger proposal, a request, if you will."

"Go on."

Adams reached into his jacket breast pocket and withdrew a flask-shaped bottle. "I brought a quantity of this back from my travels," he said.

Wilkins could not tell the color of the liquid through the brown glass. It might have been whiskey. "What is it?"

Adams studied Wilkins a moment before answering, as if appraising his worthiness for the knowledge. "It is a ritualistic potion used by an indigenous people far up off the beaten path, which, considering where I've traveled, is far off indeed."

Gazing at the bottle with its supposedly shamanistic contents, an errant draft, like a spectral breath, stirred Wilkins' neck hairs. With a mental smile of amusement, he found he wanted to believe.

"You've heard of ayahuasca," Adams said, "the conscious-altering tea the indigenous tribes have imbibed for ritualistic purposes since before the coming of the Spaniards?"

"Vaguely. It's not my area of expertise. I understand it alters one's thinking and produces intense visual and auditory hallucinations and gives one a sense of being one with the universe."

"Quite right. But this—" Adams shook the bottle. "—is far more potent."

Gaslight shone through the glass. The liquid moved sluggishly. "What's in it?"

"I confess I'm not certain. A chemist is investigating its properties, but I have been given to understand it contains, like ayahuasca, a decoction or tea made from the *Banisteria caapi* vine and leaves of the *Psychotria viidis* shrub, as well as the flowers of a certain rare vine that grows deep in the rain forest. One backwoods shaman I questioned suggested it contains a hallucinatory secreted by the glands of a rare toad."

Wilkins' frown expressed his distaste. "Not particularly appetizing."

"Oh, I assure you, the taste is quite dreadful. I'm told honey is added to make the tea more palatable." Adams returned the bottle to his pocket.

Having finished his cigar, Wilkins sipped his brandy. "And your proposal, sir?" he asked after dabbing his lips with his napkin.

"I propose you take the concoction. I will take it with you and be your guide. Afterward, you will relate what you saw, and then open an envelope which I will give you beforehand. Enclosed, you will find a description of what I encountered during my visit. My purpose for enlisting your participation is to see if each of us sculpts the same reality from the experience or if our experiences differ." Adams smiled as he signaled the waiter for the check. "I'm sure you are not convinced, Doctor, but you are curious."

Wilkins returned the smile. "I am indeed."

It was no great feat for Adams to convince Wilkins to take the air after their meal. His curiosity urged him to concede to Adams' experiment while caution admonished that it was a bad idea. Secretions from a rare toad sounded downright toxic. But the man would be accompanying him on his journey; there was that. While he doubted any visions gained under the influence of a hallucinatory would be reliable, the advantage of an agent allowing greater processing capacity might open new avenues for the investigations of the metaphysical.

Electric lamps lit the long gray curve of the Embankment. Below, a ferry, lit up like a birthday cake, passed on the greasy brown Thames. Few stars were visible through the hazy London smog. Lights glowed in the distance on the Surrey side. Upriver a boat horn sounded and was answered by another.

"Do you, sir, consider yourself a mystic?" Wilkins asked his companion.

Adams had lighted another cheroot. He took a long pull and blew the smoke out before answering. "I consider myself an explorer. My curiosity has carried me into the mystical side of things, it is true. However, I've had more than a passing acquaintance with the pragmatic as well, as my encounters with malaria and mosquitos of the Amazon attest. But yes, once you have seen what I have seen, how can you not be thenceforth other than a mystic?"

Wilkins thought a moment, then said, "Godhead, or whatever might be the equivalent of godhead—or the utter absence of any conscious progenitor of the universe, as the mechanistic materialists would have it—ought to be the litmus for the Absolute. The One, the Original, the Source. But as mankind's opinion of what this godhead constitutes—Jehovah? Allah? The elephant-headed Indian god of creation? You say you have looked upon the Absolute. Yet no two persons looking at anything ever see precisely the same image. Therefore, if human perception is relative, and man goes to war equivocating about which god rules the cosmos, how can truth ever be other than relative?"

"That, my dear doctor, is what I propose to find out. Humans find succor in the absolute. And while they can't prove God's existence, they base the truth of His existence in belief. I propose to bypass belief and look directly on the mystery. I'm not saying we will ever be able to empirically prove what we see is the ultimate truth of the cosmos, but I would value your opinion. And who knows? If our observations match, perhaps you will find an empirical way to verify the absolute."

"You are an interesting fellow, Adams. I— Are you looking for something?"

Adams appeared to be distracted. His gaze swept the Embankment. "Yes," he answered. "We need one more ingredient to complete the potion."

"What?"

"There."

Ahead, a boy no more than nine approached, head down, shoulders hunched against the night chill. He was dressed in dirty cords. A flat cap angled rakishly upon his narrow head. He carried a shoeshine box. Wilkins surmised he was hurrying home, probably heading for the Blackfriars Bridge and across the river to Surrey.

Adams stopped. As the boy made to pass, he said, "Come here, boy."

Throwing his shoulders back and pasting a smile on his face at the unexpected prospect of employment, the child approached, obviously thinking the tall man wanted his boots shined. "What ken I do fer ya, guv?" he said in the cheerful voice of the successfully self-employed.

Adams passed a hand before the boy's eyes. The lad's mouth went slack, and he stood like an automaton gazing dumbly at his solicitor.

Adams reached in a pocket and passed Wilkins a pen knife. "We will need blood."

Repulsed, Wilkins stepped back. "You didn't mention anything about human sacrifice?"

Adams smiled. "I didn't say *kill*. You must think me a monster. Truth is I've been so long among the native tribes it's broadened my way of thinking. A drop or two will do. A nick in the neck. A drop in the bottle."

"I can't. It's not right."

"You must. The blood is merely symbolic, cementing your resolve, confirming that you have the necessary will to penetrate the veil."

Wilkins took the knife. It felt wrong, and yet ... Though the blade glinting in the lamplight was small, it transmitted a thrill of empowerment.

"Just a scratch, mind you," Adams said. "A pinprick. You'd never forgive yourself if you cut the lad's artery."

Wilkins steadied his hand and made the slightest incision just above the mouth of the bottle Adams pressed to the boy's neck. A scarlet drop welled from the cut, fell into the bottle.

Adams wiped the knife on the boy's collar. "Scat."

The child wandered off as if in a daze.

Not a peep out of him. Was Adams a mesmerist as well as a mystic?

Adams pocketed the bottle.

"Well, Doctor? In for a penny ..."

"How's that?"

"Do you feel like gazing upon the beating heard of creation tonight, or would you rather put it off until tomorrow?"

Exhilarated yet appalled, Wilkins' heart raced. He felt energized, excited. He had cut the boy. The tiniest of pricks, no more than a drop or two of blood, yet his hand had done a deed he would have thought himself incapable of committing.

"Tonight" he said. "I doubt I'll sleep a wink anyway."

Back at his Bloomsbury apartment, it was all Wilkins could do to suppress his excitement until he got his guest comfortably seated by the hearth.

"Tea?"

"No, thank you." Adams withdrew the bottle from his jacket and set it on a side table. "But you might bring two cups."

Wilkins brought these. Adams poured a couple inches of thick tea-colored liquid into each and passed him one. Taking the armchair opposite Adams, with the low embers glowing in the fireplace between them, Wilkins looked into his cup.

To gaze with infinite clarity upon the face of the Absolute.

Was it possible? Did he hold in his hand the key to the great mystic achievement?

Adams set his cup beside the bottle on the table, crossed his legs, and smoothed his trouser leg. "As I said, I will be your guide ... your spirit guide, so to speak." He smiled. His teeth and the whites of his eyes shone in the fire light. "If you have a question during the session, ask and I shall answer."

"So we will be able to communicate?"

"You and I are right here. Do we not have mouths to speak, ears to hear? However, the farther you go into the ..."

"Hallucination?"

"No. You will think you are hallucinating, but what you will see is real. Otherwise, what would be the point of our experiment?"

"The face of the Absolute."

"Precisely. As I was saying, the closer you approach the Absolute, the less you will need your voice to communicate."

"Telepathy?" Wilkins raised his brows. "I've heard such was possible. And you insist you would rather not give me a hint as to what I might see?"

"I would rather not. I don't wish to prejudice your experience. You will see what you will see." Adams withdrew a sealed, white envelope and laid it upon the table beside the bottle. "When we return, you will compare what you have seen with what I have written. Now, let us drink."

Wilkins sniffed the tea. The smell was slight. Perhaps a hint of an exotic flower. They drank. The brew was bitter. It bit into his tongue and coated his throat. It didn't seem to affect Adams, so he drained his cup and set it aside, maintaining as stoic a face as he was able.

The mantel clock ticked. The flames played along the half-burned log. The embers glowed. Presently the room grew less distinct. No less bright than before, but as if he viewed the fire, his companion, through a haze of afternoon light, such as he might see walking in Regent's Park on an autumn day. The ticking of the clock, the crackling of the burning log faded. A blissful quietude settled over him. A lightness and sense of well-being uplifted him. A thrill rippled through his nerves. The narrow portals of his thought expanded so that he was aware of every facet of his being. He counted his heartbeat and processed a thousand sensations in the passage of a breath. His mental acuity had not been this sharp since boyhood. He recalled with startling clarity how he used to focus to the exclusion of all else as he listened to a birdsong or examined in rapt fascination the structure of a descending snowflake as it drifted toward his face. His chest swelled. His anxious shoulders relaxed. He sighed and was about to comment on his newfound beatitude when he caught movement out of the corner of his eye. He mentally held his breath as he strained to see what approached. When it came it came from everywhere at once.

The room dimmed, as if a fog had rolled in obscuring the autumn afternoon glow, and in the diminished light he observed a myriad shapes, elongated, ovoid, flagellated, multi-tentacled, reminding him of plates in the biologist Thomas Farquhar's book on plankton. Drawings of life forms viewed through a microscope. Only these were big, macroscopic instead of microscopic. They flowed and swirled around him translucent and quivering, like jelly fish in an aquarium. At first, he likened these to the ubiquitous shadows that floated on the retina. What ancients called *muscae volitantes,* flying flies, imperfections in the eye's vitreous fluid casting shadows on the retina. But these were large and outside of him.

"What are these?" he asked.

"The seeds of life," Adams responded. "Observe."

He watched and the flagellated ovate elongated tentacled quivering menagerie passed around and through him as if they were unreal images in a magic lantern show, except for the gelid cold where they passed through him.

The last vestiges of the room vanished, replaced with a scintillant darkness. He was suspended weightless in a soup of utter night. He laughed as a familiar floral scent tickled his nose. Without any empiric evidence, he understood the floral notes were those of the rare, unknown flower Adams had mentioned. The flower whispered to him.

"It is the plant speaking," Adams said, as if he was hearing it, too. "Its language is unique to its species. I have listened long often enough to understand it. It is not a language of phonetics and alphabet. It cannot be transcribed. Open yourself up to it and you will understand what it asks of you."

Wilkins opened his heart to its urges. The telepathic flower spoke in a vocabulary of impulses. He understood. It was telling him to follow where it led.

He felt himself moving. A great distance in fact, though he was enveloped in darkness and had no reference point by which to judge. And as he flew—for that was the sensation he felt, the sensation of flight which he had experienced in his dreams as a boy—he experienced a sensation of swelling, as if he was growing larger, or as if his spirit or higher self was leaving his body and he felt reborn, euphoric, his youth restored. His heart raced. His mind expanded, as he opened to the Divine.

And now he heard a sound ahead as of many thinly piping flutes. The piping grew louder. The melody was eerie and multitudinous, as if a thousand discordant flutists were playing a thousand unharmonious tunes. The notes fell on his skin like icy rain.

And now the blackness was not absolute but seemed full of invisible entities that whispered as he passed. Or, if not entities, emanations from—

From what?

His eyes adjusted, as if he had developed a new sense that could perceive in this mystic dimension. Ahead, a point of dim light appeared. From thence came the fluting.

He advanced. The shape grew huge. He shivered in the chest-heaving throes of numinous awe. The creature—monster or god he knew not, but from his human perspective both—reared mountainous into the infinite. A throbbing bastion of gelatinous gray from which a myriad protean mouths formed and reformed, the breathing of which transmitted the piping he had heard. A sea of eyes, as numerous and vast as the reflection of starlight on ocean, boiled in and out of being, staring in all directions. Beneath this polymorphic manifestation of primordial chaos, this cosmic sentience, he cowered less than an ant.

Adam's voice echoed in the corridors of his transubstantiated mind: "Behold the Absolute! Here is no abomination. Neither good nor evil. Neither compassionate nor antagonistic nor indifferent. Gaze upon Truth. The Absolute. Chaos, not anthropomorphized into a supremacy man only in his most hideous nightmare might realize, but the everlasting Original. The eternal Source engendering all semblance of what man conceives of as Order. Behold!"

A rift appeared in the mountain. A great black fissure, devoid of eyes or stars. A monumental mouth in the engines of chaos. Without intention and to Doctor Wilkins' great horror, he glided toward and vanished into the insatiate orifice. The mouth closed behind him when he had passed.

In Doctor Wilkins' sitting room, Adams rose from his chair where he had been observing the litany of his host's responses—wonder, awe, dread, and abject horror. Adams snapped his fingers under Wilkins' nose. He got no response. He knew he would not. None ever responded after they had gone over. Wilkins would sit like this, awake yet not awake, his involuntary muscles performing their functions, breathing, heartbeat continuing until his body shut down, unless someone discovered him, in which case he might exist in a vegetable state at St. Thomas or University College Hospital.

The being who had introduced itself as Adams dissolved, became a scintillating globe of writhing eyes and minute mouths from which an eerie fluting keened. The messenger vanished, leaving the bottle for anyone who wished to sample its contents.

A Cure for Insomnia

The bell over the door jingled as she entered the Apothecary. Old Mr. Phelps, who had been old when she was a girl, was at the counter. He smiled as she approached.

"Good afternoon, Miss Cooper," he said. His expression was commiserative. It was not faked. He had worn the expression so long it had taken root and was as much a habit as the way his arthritic right hand clutched and unclutched absentmindedly on the marble counter. "How may I help you?"

Encouraged by Mr. Phelps' professional empathy, she wanted to respond, "Fine." But she was not fine. She was ill. Her guts were cramped. Her head buzzed. Her hand shook as she resisted the urge to grip the counter for support.

Jars of fudge, marzipan, jelly babies, liquorish, lemon drops, pear drops, peppermints, toffee, fruit pastilles, fruit gums, and a variety of other colorful sweets lined shelves behind the counter. As a child, the kaleidoscope of confections fascinated her when she and her sister accompanied their mother to the Apothecary. Farther back, where Mr. Phelps practiced his pharmaceutical art, more shelves supported jars of herbs and salts and bottles of tinctures and medicinal chemicals. A large mantel clock ticked atop the mahogany cases. Its ticking was inordinately loud in the quiet shop. A large balance scale at one end of the counter reminded her that life is brief, each moment weighed before dropping into oblivion.

"I'm not sure," she said. "It's just that ..." She could not think how else to say it, so she blurted it out: "I haven't slept since my sister died."

"Ah." He shook his balding head. "Please accept my sincere condolences for your loss. Your sister was a fine young lady."

Though the Coopers had used Mr. Phelps' services for as long as she could remember, she doubted he knew her sister well enough to make such a judgement. Again, his response was habit, part of his professional vocabulary. She did not fault him for it. It was soothing really. Much like a good family physician's bedside manner. "Say *Ah*. Does this hurt? Have a candy."

"Thank you." Now she did rest a hand on the counter but refrained from fidgeting with her jacket collar. Though it was November and she had just come in from the cold, she felt unnaturally warm. "I'm exhausted." She did not go into detail. Did not tell him that when she retired to her bed and closed her eyes, she smelled the cloying sweetness of the flowers crowding the viewing room at the funeral home and saw her sister's coffin lowering into the grave. Neither did she bore him with the details of how she spent her insomniac nights, reading poetry by candlelight but hearing her sister's labored breath and seeing her eyes glaze over as death's shadow crept over her countenance.

"If I may presume," Mr. Phelps began by way of preamble.

She interjected, "Please do, Mr. Phelps. I'm at my wits' end."

"The funeral was...?"

"Monday, four days ago. But I haven't slept since Saturday, the evening of Elspeth's passing. Nor did I sleep much for most of the week during her decline."

"And what measures have you taken to alleviate the condition?"

She described the chamomile tea, warm milk, and warm baths she had self-administered in the hopes of a restful night. "I even took a little of my father's wine last evening, though I normally do not indulge, to no effect. Might," she asked with some timidity, "laudanum help me sleep?"

"I should say not," he said, and, in a tone that allayed her fear of admonishment, explained, "It is obvious you are suffering from a prolonged irritability of the nervous system, which invariably produces an augmented accumulation of blood in the cerebral vessels. Laudanum, as well as tea and coffee for that matter, only worsens the condition. An evening walk taking fresh air, preferably cool, to the point of slight exhaustion, followed by a light meal, will prove a better soporific than any tonic. Have you taken any exercise?"

She shook her head. "My sister and I often walked in the park, but I haven't gone out of my room much since her passing."

Mr. Phelps nodded sagely. "You're not a stomach sleeper, are you?"

"No."

"My advice is to take exercise in the open air and to sleep with your head elevated so as to lessen the flow of blood to the brain. Excuse me just a moment."

He went into the back. The ticking of the clock grew louder in his absence. When he returned, he handed her a small bottle.

"This is bromide of potassium. It will do much to lessen the irritability of the nervous system and to diminish any hyperemic condition of the brain. Take thirty grains at six o'clock in the evening. Repeat the dose at ten, then go to bed half an hour afterward. The first dose will produce a decided sedative action. The second will be effectual in calming any mental excitement."

She thanked the apothecary and left, feeling as if an anvil had been lifted from her shoulders.

She was back two days later. Mr. Phelps, in his habitual starched white shirt, black bow tie and frock coat, was at his station behind the counter, as if he had not moved since her last visit.

"Ah, Miss Cooper," he said. His brows were raised in inquiry. His shoulders slumped ever so slightly, as if conceding failure to cure her insomnia. That her condition had worsened was obvious. Had not her mirror revealed her sallow skin and staring eyes? "No improvement?"

"I haven't slept," she said.

"None?"

She shook her head.

"You followed my prescription?"

"I've gone for walks, not overtaxing but sufficient that I felt the exertion. I've dined on salads, some soup, a bit of roast chicken, buttered scones. Cold water only for my refreshment. No stimulants of any kind. And fearing stimulation from literature, I'm reading *The Stones of Venice*."

She caught the nervous twitching of her fingers on the cuff of her jacket. She stopped, but in a moment the effort was forgotten, and she returned to tracing the paisley brocade.

"You've kept your head elevated?"

"Yes."

"And the potassium of bromide had no effect?"

"I grew drowsy, briefly. But I kept remembering times spent with my sister and I would grow agitated and wakeful. You must have something...."

"Stronger? Ah, there lies the problem. You will recall sleeplessness is caused by an increased flow of blood to the cerebral vessels; in other words, a cerebral congestion. This in turn is caused by anxiety or too-strenuous mental activity overtaxing the nerves. That is why I discourage the use of laudanum or belladonna, as these increase the flow of blood to the brain rather than decrease it."

"So there is no cure for my condition?"

Mr. Phelps massaged his arthritic knuckles for a moment while he considered. "Short of using ether, which would be only a temporary solution ... Wait. Perhaps I do have something. Excuse me for a moment."

She watched the elderly chemist go into the back. He returned some minutes later with a small amber medicine bottle, which he sat on the counter.

"A merchant mariner who sometimes brings me medicinal plants and other useful pharmaceuticals from foreign ports brought me this." He tapped out a few grains of white powder onto a folded piece of paper.

"What is it?" she asked, her heart quickening at the sight of possible salvation.

"I confess I'm not sure. It isn't an opiate. Nor is it from any plant like foxglove or lotus that I'm aware of. I presume it is derived from some unfamiliar eastern plant. I tried it on two dogs. To one I administered ten grains. This one grew lethargic for a space of two hours. The other I administered twenty grains. It slept a deep sleep, but its heartrate decreased by half. Yet I concluded the sleep was restful because when it awoke there was none of the drowsy transition to a full awakefulness such as I experience each morning." Mr. Phelps smiled, as if sharing a witticism.

She stopped fraying her cuffs and reached for the bottle, her spirits buoyed by the possibility of sleep.

But Mr. Phelps held onto the bottle. "I must advise caution, however. Though this powder may be the solution to your insomnia, I have not tried its effects on a human subject, and I have no idea what its side effects might be."

"Mr. Phelps, I am desperate. I must sleep."

He relinquished the bottle. "You will start with ten grains. The dogs succumbed to sleep within twenty minutes, so you must immediately retire to bed. If sleep is not forthcoming within the hour, take another five, and so on until you sleep. But by no means take more than twenty-five the first night. The effects may be gradual, and dogs are generally less anxious than humans."

That evening, after a warm bath and a cup of warm milk, she self-administered her ten grains. She lay in the center of her bed with her head and shoulders elevated on pillows and her hands folded across her midriff for the better part of an hour, then rose and took another ten, thinking she would rather not waste the night experimenting.

She was asleep within minutes.

She dreamed she was at the seaside. She and Elspeth wore summer dresses—Elspeth in yellow and she in white—and wide straw sun hats. The sun was warm, the wet sand cool beneath their bare feet. The surf rolled in with a relaxing monotony. They had walked this same brown strand more than once in their teens. They had not vacationed here for several years.

"Elspeth, I've missed you more than I can say." Tears welled in her eyes with the joy of walking in the sun beside her beloved sister. They had always been so close, separated in time by less than two years. She had grown up in her sister's shadow. Seldom had she needed to determine what they should do: whether to play with dolls or jump rope or bring out the tea set, she was always content to let Elspeth choose.

"Silly goose," Elspeth said, taking her hand. "I haven't gone anywhere."

But Elspeth *had* been away, hadn't she? She couldn't recall and pushed the troubling notion aside to concentrate on enjoying their walk.

The warm sun on her shoulders and Elspeth's cool hand in hers combined with the ceaseless murmur of the sea to soothe her spirits.

All was blessedly and contentedly perfect in the world … except for the sour whiff of the rotting fish that now rolled ashore in droves.

⚜

She woke with the dim roar of the sea fading in the darkness and the image of rotting fish washing ashore. Her nose wrinkled at the memory.

She pushed back her comforter and sat up. No dawn showed at the curtained window. It was still night. She lit a candle. The clock on the mantel read 3 a.m. She had slept four hours! And dreamed!

It all came rushing back. She and Elspeth walking on the beach, Elspeth's hand in hers. Her heart soared. Her sister's body lay in her wooden coffin beneath the green sward of the church cemetery, but Elspeth could still be with her in dreams. And now she could sleep.

"Thank you, Mr. Phelps," she whispered and hugged herself, as much on account of the cold as to recapture the warmth she had felt walking on the beach beside her sister. She could still feel Elspeth's hand in hers. She marveled at how beautiful consumption had made her sister. The pale translucent skin, the sparkling dilated eyes, the unnaturally rosy cheeks and carmined lips caused by fever. It was a look so many women emulated with corsets and rouge. The romantic allure of wasting beauty.

She blew out the candle and settled into her bed. But the stink of corruption kept the dreams away.

⚜

The following night, she had to rein in her excitement. Mr. Phelps' powder not only gave her sleep but glorious time with her sister. It was as if the medicine and its gift of dream erased time, or at least suspended fate so that she could be with Elspeth and for the duration of the dream forget the coffin entombed in the hungry earth. Since it would not do to overstimulate herself, she spent an hour reading more of Ruskin's treatise, which she was discovering seemed to be as much about history, politics, and philosophy as about aesthetics.

After her bath, she tapped twenty-five grains of the white powder onto a folded paper, then upended the contents onto her tongue. The taste was bitter, but she looked forward to the elixir's sweet effects.

This time she and Elspeth strolled in a park. It was not their local park with its quadrangle of intersecting paths, open lawns, and central fountain, but a marvelously convoluted pageantry of twisting lanes that wound through shifting visions of the landscaper's art. Here beds of eyebrights bordered the path. Now roses, chrysanthemums, purple clematis, and nodding peonies greeted their gaze. A lily pond shimmered as they rounded a turn. And like a parasol shading them from the afternoon sun, branches of elm and sycamore, oak and maple arched above their heads. It was hard to conceive that their surroundings were real. Not that she doubted the solidity of the flagstones under her feet or the sweetness of the Jasmin-scented air, but she had the queer sensation of walking as if in a dream, so perfect was the moment.

They talked little, each enjoying the other's companionship. At least, she believed Elspeth, whose smile was an ornament more lovely than rose or lily, shared her contentment. Elspeth's hand was cold despite the day's gentle warmth. She rubbed her thumb over the back, hoping to transmit some warmth into it.

"Do you remember," Elspeth said, "when you were eight and I was ten, our Aunt Alma came to visit?"

"I remember. She brought Cousin Wesley along."

"I'm not surprised you remember him."

Elspeth was teasing, but only a curl at the corner of her lips betrayed her humor.

"That was my first kiss," she said, refusing to let herself be embarrassed.

"There have been others?" Elspeth's smile had spread.

"Maybe."

"He kissed me, too," Elspeth said, bending to pluck a pansy.

Her brows went up. "He didn't!"

Elspeth nodded, and they both burst out laughing.

A moment later, she glanced up. Perhaps they had strayed under a denser canopy. The light had dimmed, as if a cloud had passed over the sun. But no; she saw no clouds through the lattice of limbs. Rather the sky had darkened, as if day was waning and night approaching much too soon. Still, there was beauty in the leaf-filtered primrose light.

When she turned back to Elspeth, she gave a start. Her sister's eyes were dry, sunken berries, her lips chafing rust stretched over soil-speckled teeth. A curl of gray flesh hung from her cheek.

She woke shaking and perspiring, her guts threatening to disgorge. For a moment, she thought she was having an attack and took deep breaths to calm herself. But even as her heartbeat slowed, she smelled the cloying sweetness of decay. Despite the coldness of the season, the air was close and fetid. Was some corrupting foulness lingering in the darkness beside her bed? Shivering, she lit a candle with palsied hands. She was alone. Still, the olfactory hallucination continued, as if rancid meat had been left to fester beneath her bed.

She cursed her luck. She had found sleep and a means to be with Elspeth, to cheat the finality of the grave, yet the devil toyed with her and ruined her happiness.

The following nights were a kaleidoscope of chthonic horrors, a descent into the corruption of the grave. No longer were her reunions with Elspeth joyous. Nor did the dreams begin in vibrant sunlight. Where before colors had been startlingly vivid—the blue of sky, the red of rose, the green of fresh cut sward—more gorgeous than the mundane light of waking day could ever paint, the air of a purity and freshness seldom encountered in city—now the dreams began in a dun dimness like light filtered through moldering curtains. Colors were faded like those of ancient parchments seen in museums, the air a miasma of malarial mists.

Elspeth, too, had undergone a ghastly change. Though still hauntingly beautiful, enhanced by the softening shadow of death, she grew thinner each night, her cheeks hollower, the circles under her eyes starker against the ashen pallor of her face. Soon, as light fled and darkness bloomed, colors drained to the loathsome gray of rotted meat. A mist the color of soap scum and reeking of the charnel house coiled about their ankles. Worms writhed beneath their feet. Dreading what she knew she would see, she faced her sister. Elspeth's skull was almost visible through the veined translucent skin. Her luxurious hair, the darkness of which complemented the beauty of her alabaster face, had lost its luster and clung to her head like cobwebs. A leprous hand stroked her face. She endured her sister's touch, ashamed of her instinct to withdraw.

She no longer fled from the dream, starting awake in darkness, swathed in perspiration, the lingering stench of the grave embalming her pillow, but clasped her sister's hand as she had those final weeks of Elspeth's illness. The hand was slimy, and, again, she felt guilty for feeling repelled. This was her sister. Howsoever horrible the dreams became, she must be grateful for their nocturnal reunions.

Embracing the darkness and her sister's decaying flesh, she hugged Elspeth. Her sister's dress crumbled like the rotted cerements of the long-buried dead, and her body collapsed in a shower of ashes.

She woke into darkness and the reek of decay. She tried to rise and bumped her head. She struck out at the barrier and encountered satin quilting. In the clutch of horror, she realized where she lay.

"Oh, Elspeth," she moaned. But she did not blame her sister for wanting to walk in the light and breathe the air of day.

Fingers brushed her hair. "Sleep well, my darling girl." Her sister's voice. And despite the utter blackness of her prison, she saw Elspeth's face floating before her. She had regained her former beauty, not the malingering lily of the consumptive but the rose of vibrant youth.

"I would wish you a pleasant sleep," the vision said, "but it won't be. I should know."

Elspeth smiled. No longer did grave mold speckle her teeth; they glowed like pearls in moonlight. Through the cloying atmosphere of the coffin, she smelled Elspeth's lavender cologne. She held onto the scent, savored it, as her sister's apparition faded. She closed her eyes against her tears. Her one consoling thought was that she and Elspeth would someday reunite in the moist embrace of the grave.

SOMNIPHOBIA

She groaned, opened her eyes. She'd been dreaming of falling. She didn't pursue the dream. She had more pressing concerns. She was leaning downhill backward, her head lower than her legs. A weight like a trunk pressed her chest and pinned her legs.

The seat in front of her had broken. The big man who had been sitting there now lay in her lap, his head just below her chin. His dark curls glistened in the starlight that made its way down the aisle from the bus's big front window. She smelled lemon-scented pomade.

She tried to move. Pain exploded in her legs. She panted until the agony subsided to a harrowing throb. She tried to reach the phone in her pocket but couldn't.

How long had she lain here? Where was *here?*

Her head hurt. Her temple was wet. She was bleeding. She was sweating despite the cool breeze coming in through the—

Beyond the woman beside her, head tilted back, eyes and mouth open as if surprised, a mass of vines pushed in through the broken window. Her gaze returned to her neighbor. It was hard to tell in the near dark, but the dead woman looked familiar. Had they just met? Were they traveling together?

In the dark behind her, someone groaned.

"Hello?" The word came out a barely audible croak. Her tongue was thick, her mouth dry. She felt dizzy from dehydration. She must have been out a while. She tried again.

"Hello?"

A child's tearful voice answered in Spanish. "My momma needs help. She's not breathing."

The Spanish wasn't the Castilian she'd learned in college but had the singsong quality of Mexican … or …

Memory flooded back. She'd come to Bolivia for vacation and to do research for her master's dissertation. Much had been written about Western society's erosion of South America's indigenous people's "traditions." Her thesis sought evidence to refute what she had read. So far, she had found that Aymara and Quechua traditions were thriving: not just kept up for their pageantry and entertainment, but because they were intrinsic with people's beliefs. She'd celebrated *Día de los Muertos* in Coroico. Afterward, she'd visited the countryside where she'd interviewed the deeply religious and, some would say, superstitious inhabitants who did not associate the Day of the Dead with sports bars, horror movies and Halloween as they did back home in Leeds or in the U.S., as they did in most of the First World, but honored and communed with their dead.

"Can you move?" she asked.

"I think my leg is broken. It hurts. My momma isn't breathing." The child—boy or girl, she couldn't tell from the voice—began to cry. She felt helpless, pinned by a corpse and unable to help the child. Was no one else alive?

Her scalp crawled. Reality hit her. She was trapped in a bus surrounded by corpses at the bottom of a ravine, probably not visible from the road, and no one would come looking for them until the bus was missed. That wouldn't happen until after sunrise. No one was crazy enough to venture onto the Death Road at night.

She fought to calm her racing heart. Panic wouldn't help and would only wear her out.

"Hello?" she yelled. "Can anyone hear me?"

Someone coughed. The sound of someone trying to move followed by a grunt. "Hello?" The voice was weak, an elderly man's perhaps, and rattled as if he had blood in his lungs.

"Are you hurt?" she asked, desperate for him to come and lift this weight from her chest.

"Feels like something's broken inside." She heard him spit. "Blood," he said, more matter-of-factly than in surprise.

The woman beside her gasped and shook her head. *Luz*, that was her name. They'd met at the Coroico bus terminal where there was no set schedule, the bus departing when the driver decided it was full. Luz had been visiting relatives in Coroico. She said she had to get back to La Paz for the *Día de las Ñatitas* festival, where hundreds of human skulls, wearing colorful knit *ch'ullos*, baseball caps, Panama hats, and sunglasses, all topped with floral wreaths, would be paraded to the *Cementerio General*, where celebrants would place lighted cigarettes between their smiling jaws and regal them with music, dance, food, and liquor.

When Luz learned of her master's thesis, she had invited her to join her in celebrating the Day of the Skulls. She was surprised to learn Luz kept four *ñatitas* in her household shrine, one of which was the skull of a great-aunt with whom she maintained a close relationship. According to Luz, it didn't matter if the skulls were of family members passed down for generations or those of strangers taken from the communal paupers' grave or purchased from medical students, what mattered, as it did in any relationship, was that you got along with your skull. "All *ñatitas* are skulls," Luz had pointed out, "but not all skulls are *ñatitas*."

"You're alive."

Luz moved her mouth as if her jaw were injured. "What happened?" She blinked, trying to see in the darkness.

"We went off the cliff. I remember the bus sliding. I hit my head." She touched her temple. The abraded skin along her hairline was wet and tender.

Though the North Yungas, known as the Death Road, claimed nearly three hundred fatalities every year along its forty-three miles of switchbacks that climbed to 15,000 feet with perilous two-thousand-foot drops at every turn, the scenery was said to be spectacular, and taking it appealed to her sense of adventure. She'd been skeptical when she saw the old blue vintage sixties bus waiting at the terminal, its roof top-heavy with the bundles and boxes lashed to its luggage rack, and she'd tried to ignore its near-balding tires. But Luz, who had ridden the route many times, said most fatalities were people driving drunk or too fast or who had been struck by others driving drunk or too fast. "Emanual," Luz pointed out a stout, short-legged man smoking a cigarette by the bus's open door, "is an excellent driver. Very careful. Knows the road well."

Apparently not well enough. But she didn't mention it to Luz.

The child was crying. The man's breathing sounded labored and moist. She worried help would arrive too late for him. And perhaps for others who were unconscious but not dead.

A scratching caught her attention. At first, she thought it was the vines stirring in the open window and worried something might be prowling in the dark. Then she heard it again. Claws advancing down the aisle, stopping, then starting. The hair on her scalp lifted at the thought of some predatory beast sniffing among the dead, seeking live meat. Except for jaguars and llamas, her cultural studies had not equipped her with a knowledge of the local wildlife. Imagining claws and teeth, sleek fur, and red eyes, she shuddered.

The child's scream broke the quiet.

"*Deos mio!*" the man shouted. The terror in his voice chilled her to the bone. "Something's got the boy! Help!"

But she couldn't help. She could only quake with fear. She wanted to call out to the boy but clamped her mouth tight lest she alert whatever was attacking the child to her presence.

Then the man was shrieking, "Get off me! No!"

His struggles ceased. In the following quiet another sound drove new terror into her brain. It was not the sound of rending flesh or crunching bone. The sound was as gentle as a sigh, as if someone was taking a long inhalation.

While the predator was feeding or whatever it was doing to the man, another set of claws scratched down the aisle. There was more than one of them, and one was coming her way.

Something landed atop Luz' seat back, startling a gasp from both of them. A face appeared. She saw it in profile as it leaned over her neighbor. She mistook it for a monkey, but though its head and shoulders were covered with a silvery fur, its pale, hairless face was all too human. She was reminded of a woodcut she had seen in an old bestiary: the manticore, the body of a lion with the head of a man and a predator's sharp teeth.

"*Devorador de Almas,*" Luz moaned, as the thing swung over the seat and crouched on her chest.

The creature, under three feet tall, gazed hungrily into Luz's eyes. Its claws were long and black. It weaved its head like a cobra before a mongoose. Then it stopped and licked its lips. Its tongue was forked, its teeth a double row of spikes.

She would have run. Shoved the gentleman off her and run. But she couldn't. She was pinned, helpless to aid her fellow traveler.

Another of the creatures appeared before her, a twin that climbed over the man in front of her and smiled across the glistening, lemon-scented curls. Its nose was bulbous, its ears big, its fingers long and taloned. Its face drew close to hers. Its breath smelled of cloves or cinnamon, something fragrant and soporific. Heavy with the need for sleep, her eyelids fluttered closed as its mouth opened and it leaned to kiss her.

The monitor was spiking when the nurse ran into the room. Heartrate 140, blood pressure 150 over 90. It was happening again. As it did every night in each of the four rooms in which the survivors of last month's fatal bus crash lay. The young woman was thrashing, her upper body convulsing. The nurse hurried to calm her. Not that she was going anywhere. Both her legs were in casts.

The woman started awake, bug-eyed and panting.

"*Devorador de Almas!*" she said between ragged breaths. The nurse had heard it every night for the past three weeks. The woman held her hand before her face, as if fending off something that had pursued her into the waking world. "It's here!"

The nurse, who had one eye on the monitor, held her gently by the shoulders, as much to comfort her as to make sure she didn't further damage her legs. "Shh. You were dreaming. You're safe." Her heart rate dropped.

A young doctor entered the room. His black hair gleamed with brilliantine. His stethoscope was tucked under his smock. "How's our patient?"

The nurse indicated the monitor. Her pulse was still high, her heart rate down to 130. "She's good," she said for the patient's benefit. "Had another dream."

The doctor took the woman's pulse. It was an old trick, unnecessary because of the monitoring device, but it helped to put the patient at ease.

"Same dream?" He addressed the woman.

She nodded, her eyes pleading. "*Devorador de almas*. That's what Luz called them. Soul eaters. It took her soul." She shook her head, her eyes wide with terror, as if seeing something horrible taking place in her mind's eye. She looked at the doctor. Her eyes grew even wider. "Maybe mine, too. I'm not getting better, am I?"

"Well ..." The doctor gave her a reassuring smile. "Your legs were badly broken. Give them time and you'll be back on your feet. For now, it's late and you need to rest. Nurse."

Anticipating the doctor's request, the nurse had prepared the syringe. She handed it to the doctor.

The woman cringed. The lines on the monitor grew erratic. "Don't send me back!" she pleaded. "I can't! It's waiting!"

"Now, Miss Channing. We've talked about this. You survived a terrifying ordeal. Two hundred fifty feet. No wonder you're having bad dreams. You're suffering from post-traumatic stress syndrome. Rest is the best medicine."

The nurse held her while the doctor administered the sedative. Miss Channing fought, but she seemed to have weakened in the past weeks.

"*Devorador de Almas*," the nurse said when the woman was asleep and the monitor stable.

"What's that?" the doctor asked, preparing to leave.

"*Come Almas*. Soul Eaters. My grandmother used to tell me bedtime stories about them. How they steal a person's soul and the body wastes away."

The doctor looked at her disapprovingly. "You're an educated woman, Nurse. Doesn't PTSD make more sense than 'Soul Eaters'?"

The nurse looked at the woman. The patient's face was gaunt, her lips bloodless. She had lost weight since the accident. She took a little broth, a little bread. She wouldn't eat meat or anything that took energy to chew.

The vitamin B shots hadn't helped. She was always tired, but she fought sleep.

"Yes, Doctor. Of course. But she's not getting any better, is she?"

He favored her with a frown before answering. "No, I'm afraid she's not."

That the health of all four of the accident survivors was deteriorating, they left unspoken.

The doctor left. The nurse turned down the light so only the monitor and a night light illuminated the woman in the hospital bed. She was about to leave when blood pressure, heart rate and respiration began to spike on the monitor. She started to take a step toward the woman. She froze. Gooseflesh rippled up her arms, swept over her back. The room was suddenly cold. Something was happening in the bed. A gray mist rose from the woman's open mouth. The mist took shape. In a moment, a small, hideous man-like creature squatted on the woman's chest. Her breathing labored, as if the illusion had weight. The monitor spiked, began to beep. The nurse was torn between seeing to her patient and running. The apparition leaned forward until its grotesque face was an inch from the woman's. Its lips brushed hers. It inhaled. The beeping stopped. Her vital signs grew stable.

The nurse backed out of the room, the crepe soles of her shoes silent on the tiled floor. She closed the door softly behind her and fled, terrified *el Devorado* had marked her presence and would come for her in her dreams.

THE WITNESS

The bullet—a 9mm round traveling at 1,200 feet per second fired from a Glock 17 clutched in the hand of a robber named Deshawn Jenkins, recently paroled after a ten-year stint for armed robbery—struck *Knoxville Star-Sentinel* reporter Adrian Fellows in the temple at 10:20 p.m. on a Friday night. Adrian, responding to the report of a liquor-store holdup on his police scanner, arrived in time to witness the ongoing hostage standoff and was videoing the incident on his cell phone from a doorway down the block when the bullet hit.

Tonight was Deshawn's unlucky night. The end to his robbery spree. The end of everything in the repeat offender's violent, unhappy life. Deshawn's hand twitched as a policeman's bullet punched a hole in his hoodie and chest. His finger jerked. His weapon fired. The stray bullet struck Fellows. Robber and reporter hit the ground at about the same time.

But it was not the end of Adrian Fellows, who woke in a Knoxville intensive care unit seventy-three hours later.

⚜

The advent of the prophetic dreams started some two weeks after Adrian's hospital discharge. The dream was exceptionally vivid, and he woke excited, as he always did when a story got his nose up. Realizing it was a dream, he went back to sleep and forgot about it. Until he saw the story on the six o'clock news. A Jeanette Rollins, twenty-eight, was stopped at a South Knoxville red light when a man pulled her out of her car and jumped in. Her sixteen-month-old son was in the back seat. As he took off, she threw herself onto the hood. The man accelerated. Jeanette was thrown off a block away, sustaining minor injuries. The car and child were found in Old Sevier. Police were looking for the carjacker.

Adrian was flabbergasted. Still, coincidence couldn't be ruled out. Or maybe seeing the news story reshaped his memory of the dream. After all, he'd forgotten the dream for most of the day.

The headaches didn't make his thinking any clearer. He was up to four twelve-hour Tylenols a day by the time he went by his doctor to get the stiches out. "You're a very lucky fellow, Adrian," the doctor said, not for the first time. Adrian agreed he was. The bullet, which struck at an angle, didn't penetrate the temple but glanced off his skull, traveled between bone and scalp, and exited behind his ear. He had a little bald spot back there that might not grow back but would make a good conversation starter when he got back in the dating game.

"Hard head. Good genes," Adrian joked, also not for the first time.

The next time he had a special dream, he held a Tennessee Cash ticket. He had added Quick Cash to his playslip, and when he scanned the ticket with the lottery app, he found he'd won $50. On impulse, on his drive to work he bought a ticket and, sure enough, he won fifty bucks.

Interesting, he thought. If only he could dream a bigger jackpot. Or, remembering the carjacking, dream crimes before they happened. Now there was a thought. Wouldn't hurt his career.

The next day, he had lunch with his old friend, Knoxville Police Detective Felix Dawson. They'd gone to high school together, even dated some of the same girls, and pretty much knew each other's quirks. He told Felix about the carjacking and lottery ticket, even bought lunch with the fifty bucks. Amused, Felix looked at the prominent scar on his temple and said, "Let me know if you dream anything bigger. I'd like to get in on the action."

Two nights later, Adrian did just that.

"Felix," he said into his cell. It was 3 a.m. and, friendship notwithstanding, he imagined Felix would be pissed getting wakened at that hour. But the dream had been compelling.

"Adrian? Do you know—?"

"Yeah, I know. Listen up."

"Another dream?" Felix suddenly sounded more awake.

"Yeah. A homicide."

There was a pause, then, "Nothing's come in over the scanner."

"It hasn't happened yet."

Another pause, then, "Right. Tell me. And it'd better not be bullshit. Scratch that. You said homicide?"

"Yeah, sometime late in the day. It was overcast, lightly sprinkling. A car repair down the block on the other side of the street. Sign might've said Manny's. Anyway, it started with a 'Man.' There were a few tenements. Lights were on in a grocery store on the corner. You know one of those small mom-and-pop stores. Girl comes down the block. Dark hair. Short, the hair I mean. She was about average height. Some sort of tattoo on her neck. She passes right by me. Doesn't see me, and I'm standing right in the middle of the sidewalk. She passes. There's a white laundry van parked at the curb. 'Prestige' I think the sign said. Blue letters."

"'Think'?"

"I wasn't paying attention to details. Felt something terrible was about to happen. Side door slides open. Guy jumps out. Late twenties, early thirties. Dark hair. Average height."

"You're describing yourself."

Adrian grinned, ran his hand through his sweat-damp hair. He was sitting on his bed in pajama bottoms. He'd taken the top off. The room was chilly, and the nightmare-sweat was cooling.

"Yeah, maybe you're right. Dreams are funny like that. Anyway, he pops out, grabs the girl, puts a rag over her face, and shoves her in the van. A moment later, the van takes off and I wake up."

"License plate?"

"Didn't think of it. Woke up shaking, called you. And here's the kicker: I wanted to do something, but I couldn't move. It was like I was paralyzed, my shoes nailed to the sidewalk."

"Yeah, well, like you said, 'Dreams are funny.' Get some sleep. And Adrian …"

"Yeah?"

"No more dreams tonight.'

Felix called the next night. When the sun set and the street lights came on, Adrian figured the dream was just a dream, and nothing bad was going to happen to some girl with a neck tattoo. Or maybe it wouldn't happen, if it happened, till the next night, or the next. Felix proved him wrong.

The girl's body had been found in a dumpster in Marble City. Nude, raped and strangled. No ligature marks or fibers. The killer had used his hands. Finger marks but no prints. She had a butterfly tattooed on her neck. A call to Property Crimes identified a Ford Transit stolen earlier that day. No cleaning-service sign, though.

"Contacted a Prestige Cleaners. Their two vans were accounted for, but one was missing a sign. Vinyl stick-on type."

After Felix hung up, Adrian went into the bathroom and threw up the Chinese he'd had for supper. Afraid to sleep, he watched old movies till two in the morning, or rather, he gazed at the television and watched the dream over and over trying to remember any detail he'd overlooked. He finally passed out, woke two hours later. No dreams.

Adrian got himself assigned to cover the investigation. When he explained to his editor his detective friend was on the case, his boss was only too glad to hand the job over to him.

"Found the scene you described." Adrian was at his newsroom desk when Felix called. "Up North Central in the twelve hundreds. You were right: the repair shop sign is Manny's and there's a bodega on the corner. No traffic cams. We're checking if anyone has a doorbell camera."

Adrian didn't dream that night. Nor the next. At least none he remembered. For which he was thankful. But sleep was a restless bedfellow. His body was in a state of near-constant anxiety, as if he so much as dozed at a red light, he would witness another abduction. Or worse.

Worse came the following Wednesday.

This time it wasn't an abduction but a drive-by. The sign over the club entrance read "TJ's" It wasn't one of those downtown clubs with a line down the block and well-dressed greeters at the door. The wide street was poorly lit and there was litter in the curb. The club was a white-painted cinderblock bunker with a steel door painted red. Two beefy guys in black sweats and do-rags guarded the door. Several people milled about on the sidewalk in front of the club. Though the door was closed, heavy bass from the subwoofers pounded into the street. There wasn't much traffic. A car went by. Adrian felt the breeze of its passing, but, again, he was rooted.

Adrian knew the area. Not the precise location, but he was in East Knoxville where poverty and crime held hands.

A moment later a black Escalade screeched around the corner and automatics shoved through an open window hosed the pedestrians. Incredibly, instead of diving for the concrete, several pulled weapons and returned fire. The Escalade ran a traffic light and disappeared.

Three bodies sprawled on the sidewalk didn't get up.

Adrian called Felix.

"This is getting to be a habit, Ad." Felix sounded sleepy but alert. He didn't question the veracity of the dream but had a few inquiries. No, he didn't get the license plate. No, he didn't remember any faces. They were all black, young, mostly male, a few females.

"You got the name of the club. That should be enough."

"No idea what time it was?"

"No. But it was late. Traffic was light. You're the detective. What time is most common for drive-bys?"

"Good point. Most crime takes place ten to midnight."

Adrian looked up the club on the Internet. The following night he was parked down the block with a camera he'd borrowed from the paper. Felix and his driver, Sergeant Highsmith, were parked around the corner where they would have a view of the club. Felix had told him no way the captain would order the club closed on a tip from a dream.

"You could tell him you heard it on the street."

Felix looked at him as if he had multiple heads. "You know me better than that. Start lying and next thing you know, I'll be fleeing to Venezuela with a suitcase full of evidence cash."

Adrian smiled. "You been thinking about that long?"

At 12:05 the drive-by went down just as he'd dreamed it. He was ready. His arm ached from repeatedly raising the camera to his eye, but his vigilance paid off. The video caught the Escalade rounding the corner, the shots fired, the bodies dropping. When the big SUV sped off, the detectives pursued. They caught the perps, but a local gang was short two members by the time the ambulance arrived.

Felix called shortly after Adrian's edited video broke on the Knox News app.

"You were there, weren't you?"

"I've got a living to make."

"A little morbid, don't you think?"

"You got the perps. I spelled your name right, didn't I?"

Over the next two weeks, Adrian had three more prophetic dreams, two of which paid off in news stories and arrests. A third was particularly fortuitous. Adrian dreamed a car would plunge off the Henley Street Bridge at 1:07 a.m. He'd been studying up on lucid dreaming and had willed his dream self to wear a watch. He had no idea how accurate the time piece was until the officer Felix requested watch the bridge pulled over a tan Jeep weaving down the road, its driver intoxicated and half asleep. The Jeep matched the one in his dream.

"Buddy, you're a one-man crime stopper," Felix said the next time they lunched.

"Naw. I just report. You make the arrests."

The partnership paid off for them both. Adrian got a raise and first dibs on whatever story he wanted to cover. Felix got a citation.

October turned to November and the nights got cool and blustery. Meanwhile, the police made no progress in the dead girl's case. It was as if the Strangler—that was how Adrian thought of the dark-haired man who had abducted and killed the girl with the butterfly tattoo—had left town.

Adrian dreamed he was in an indoor parking lot. Hiding in plain sight, the Strangler stood just outside the circle of illumination cast by an overhead light. *Smart*, Adrian thought. Close enough to a light to appear harmless, but just far enough away to make identification hard. The man's left arm was in a cast supported by a white sling. He wore a University of Tennessee hoodie. The hatchback of his Civic was raised, and he seemed to be having trouble lifting a large bag of dog foot with his one good hand.

The killer bore more than a superficial resemblance to him. His dark hair was a little longer. His nose was sharper and straighter than his own. His mouth was wider, his lips thinner and curled ever so slightly up at the corners as if locked in a perpetually bemused smile. The effect was charming, like one of those old-time British actors you might catch on a late-night black-and-white romantic comedy. The man wore charisma like a chameleon displaying false colors. Only this lizard was deadly.

Adrian checked his watch: 7:25 p.m. Earlier than last time.

A young lady came along pushing a cart. She wore an orange-and-white University of Tennessee jacket with a big orange T over her heart. With a jolt, Adrian realized where he was: the parking lot of the Publix near the University of Tennessee campus. The coed slowed as she neared the Strangler, as if debating whether to help. He noticed her, gave her a charmingly embarrassed smile, and went back to his task, getting the bag on one knee and making it halfway to the hatchback before it slid off his leg to the ground.

"Let me help," she said, parking her cart.

Adrian couldn't have been standing more than ten feet away, but, again, he couldn't move. Nor could he cry out. He opened his mouth and tried, but his vocal cords refused to cooperate. It was as if he was fated to observe. In no mood to appreciate the irony of the dream world, he tried harder, but no sound escaped his open mouth.

The Strangler spoke. "That's very kind of you. This is embarrassing really." His voice was not much deeper than his own. More of a northeast accent.

"Not a problem," she said. Her smile and tone of voice told Adrian she was mildly attracted.

She did a half squat, came up with the bag, and pushed it into the hatchback.

While she leaned forward, the top of her body half inside the vehicle, the man pulled a sap from his hoodie and slammed the weighted leather into the back of her skull. Before she could slump to the concrete, he hooked his free arm between her legs, lifted, and shoved her into the hatchback atop the dog food. He slammed the hatch and hurried to open the driver's door. Before he got in, he turned to Adrian and smiled.

Adrian woke. His heart hammered. He swallowed hard. Had that just happened? Had the Strangler smiled at him? Did the man know he was being watched?

With a shaking hand, he reached for his phone and called Felix.

Felix took Adrian's warning to his boss. Captain Tanner was skeptical but, based on Felix's arrests, assigned two officers to assist Felix and his sergeant.

Felix refused to let Adrian accompany him on the stakeout.

"No, Adrian. And that's final. Stay out of this. I believe you, but Captain Tanner's going out on a limb. If Command learns where he got his intel, he'll be a laughingstock, and there goes all hope of his making Commissioner. Besides, I don't want to see a case thrown out of court because I authorized the presence of a reporter prior to an arrest. We're doing this by the book. Capiche?"

He did capiche, but the Strangler didn't show. Neither the next night, nor the next.

Felix phoned him the third day. "Captain's pulling the detail. You know, it's possible the dream was a result of your anxiety."

Adrian admitted Felix might have a point. But he wasn't convinced. Was the Strangler playing with him? Was it possible for the dreamed to be aware of the dreamer?

No more impossible than to dream something before it happened, he told himself.

Meantime, while Felix lurked for the Strangler, Adrian had two more prophetic dreams.

One was a bizarre auto accident. He was sitting in a booth in a Kentucky Fried Chicken when a Silverado crashed through the storefront, killing one person and injuring four. He noted the time and location, and the next afternoon was sitting in his booth when the truck came through the store front. The accelerator had gotten stuck, and the driver had lost control. One dead, four injured. He got the truck coming through the window on video. The clip went viral. His editor called him into his office wanting to know how he'd gotten the video. He'd lied, said he had his phone out flipping through some pictures and must have accidently pressed record. Lucky, I guess. His editor didn't press. Ratings were up.

Felix wasn't so happy. "You didn't think to share that information? Or at least to warn the people in harm's way?"

"You can't be everywhere, Felix. And your captain isn't too pleased with my prognostications."

The second was a six-car pile-up on I-40.

The night was foggy. A speeding truck plowed into the pea soup and struck a car which struck another car and the next three cars plowed into the first three. Trusting his dream, Adrian parked his car well off the shoulder and videoed the collision. The squeal of tires and screech of twisted metal was unnerving, but the clip got more hits than the Kentucky Fried.

Adrian got a call from Nashville Fox 17 wanting to know how he did it and would he consider coming to work for them. Adrian said he was flattered, but he just happened to be in the right place at the right time. What he didn't say was he was entertaining bigger ambitions, like working for television. Fox News maybe. Or CNN.

The Strangler showed up in his third dream.

It was the same dream as before right down to the cast, the girl in the Tennessee varsity jacket, and the time on his watch. Again, the killer smiled at him before getting into his car.

He woke, heart hammering, but figured Felix was right. Anxiety caused the dream. He debated calling Felix, but eventually decided not to and lay in bed until dawn lightened his bedroom window and he drifted back to sleep.

He was wakened before seven by a knock at his apartment door.

"Hold on," he grumbled, scratching his head as he padded barefoot across the living room carpet.

He did a double take when he peered through the peep hole and saw Felix standing in the hall.

Felix pushed past him when he opened the door. Sergeant Highsmith waited in the hall, his craggy Irish and Cherokee face impassive.

"Felix?" Adrian said when he had closed the door. He was fully awake now. Something was very off.

Felix watched him with narrowed eyes as he rubbed his jutting chin.

"What gives, Felix?" Adrian said, annoyed at his friend's uncharacteristic scrutiny.

Felix stopped rubbing his chin. "Get dressed. I'll explain on the ride downtown."

"Downtown?"

"Captain sent me to bring you in for questioning."

Adrian's bowels gurgled at the mention of questioning. "What happened?"

"Get dressed."

The Strangler had struck after all. Just like in his dream.

Captain Tanner was a big man with enough years on the force to retire to a life of fishing and golf, but he had his eye on the commissionership. They sat in his downtown headquarters' office, Tanner in the big chair behind his desk, Adrian in one of the two chairs facing the desk. Felix stood with one elbow on a file cabinet where he could watch the proceedings.

"Where were you yesterday evening between six and eight o'clock?" Tanner asked after thanking him for coming down to "clear up a few things." Adrian had hit the man up for comments several times and Tanner had always been professionally polite if gruff. His bland expression gave no hint of suspicion. His searching eyes told a different story.

"Home." Adrian tried to maintain an equally dispassionate tone, but his guts were rumbling, and his palms were sweaty.

"Any witness to verify that?"

Adrian glanced at Felix, who stared at a point between his boss and Adrian, avoiding eye contact. "None. I picked up a meatball parm from a pizzeria down the block, took it home, ate, watched some TV. You thinking I had something to do with the girl's abduction?"

"What makes you say that?" Tanner's watching eyes didn't blink. The man was letting him sweat. It did feel warm, despite the November chill.

"Look, I've been an investigative reporter long enough to know you wouldn't bring me in if you didn't have good reason, so spill it."

Tanner tapped his blotter. "We have a person of interest on security footage."

"And this person of interest looks like me." Adrian breathed a sigh of relief. Glanced at Felix again. "When I described the Strangler to Felix, he said it sounded like I was describing myself. I admit there's a superficial resemblance, but …" Adrian snapped his fingers. "The image isn't clear, is it? Otherwise, I wouldn't be here."

Tanner glanced at Felix. Felix took his arm off the file cabinet and moved closer.

"You're right. The image could be better, but it looks enough like you to bring you in for questioning. Standard procedure. You understand."

Adrian nodded. "Yeah, I understand." He addressed Tanner, letting Felix know he knew he was just doing his duty. No offense taken. He stood. "If you've no further questions, I need to get to work."

Tanner didn't stand but continued to scrutinize him. "No further questions—for now."

By the time Adrian arrived at work, the newsroom was buzzing with the latest homicide. On the drive to the *Star-Sentinel*, Felix refused to divulge anything about the homicide or the investigation. "Captain's orders not to discuss the case with you so long as you're a person of interest," Felix said. Adrian was annoyed but understood. Felix was doing his job.

Back in the newsroom, he learned the woman—a University of Tennessee student named Melony Fredericks—had been found in a dumpster, nude, raped, and strangled.

The Strangler liked dumpsters, and Knoxville had plenty of them. Every restaurant, bar, alley, and construction site had at least one. As with the first victim, no prints, fibers or semen was found on the victim. The absence of restraining marks on either of their wrists meant the women must have been unconscious or dead while the perp violated them. If they had been conscious and their hands free, there would have been evidence under their nails. None was found.

Adrian's chief rival at the paper, Suzie Kurtz, had covered the story. Adrian was tempted to ask her about the security footage but reflected the police wouldn't have allowed her access to it and the less she knew about his visit downtown the better. Let sleeping dogs lie.

Two days later, the Strangler visited his dreams again. It was Saturday. He had dozed off in his recliner after two beers while watching the Volunteers take on Vanderbilt. The scene was a parking lot next to a restaurant made from a converted church. He'd eaten at the restaurant before. 71 South if he remembered correctly. On the edge of Knoxville's Urban Wilderness, a system of Wildlife Management Areas and hiking and biking trails on the southside of the Tennessee River.

A woman in bike shorts, long-sleeve jersey, and backpack was taking her mountain bike off her car rack. Adrian recognized the hatchback that pulled in beside her, not too close, not crowding her. There were three other cars and a pickup in the lot. A few cars up the lot near the restaurant. No people.

The Strangler got out and stretched. He smiled at the woman. She smiled back. He looked the lot over. Satisfied, he came around and opened the hatchback. She was lowering her Trek to the ground when he stepped up behind her. She half turned, and he bashed her across the skull with a length of tree limb. Blood and bark splattered her trunk. She collapsed over her bike. He scooped her up and folded her into the back of his car, closed the hatch. He wore gloves. He lifted her bike onto her rack without securing it, turned, and smiled at Adrian. As if the man saw him clearly, he tapped his wrist. Adrian looked at his watch: 4:15 p.m.

The Strangler got in his car and drove away.

Adrian woke, snapped his recliner upright, checked his phone: 3:46 p.m. The killer had smiled at him, insisted he check the time. Seized with the certainty the man was telling him the abduction would happen that afternoon, that the monster was, even now, on his way to commit atrocity and was daring Adrian to beat him to the scene, Adrian grabbed his keys and bolted out the door. He drove toward the James White Parkway Bridge as fast as he could without risking a ticket. He pushed the Talk button on his steering wheel. "Call Felix." Felix answered on the third ring.

"Felix! Just listen! The killer's fixing to strike. Now! In a few minutes! Send cops to the 71 South restaurant parking lot. You know the place?"

"Yeah, I know the place. I'm on my way. You're sure—?"

"Yeah, I'm sure."

He ended the call, sped up.

The Strangler was gone when he pulled into the parking lot. The woman's car was there, her bike on the rack. He stopped behind her car, got out. A length of branch maybe three inches thick lay on the ground. He picked it up. There was blood at one end and a few strands of hair. A woman swung into the parking lot on her bike. Not the woman he'd seen abducted. An older woman in a red hoodie. She looked at him. He looked at her.

A squad car pulled in. A policeman got out. Seeing him wielding the branch, he drew his service weapon, yelled, "Drop it" and ordered him to lie face down on the ground.

The woman picked him out of a lineup. A couple who had seen a man wearing a cast the night the University coed was taken from the Publix parking lot identified him from the security footage. His fingerprints were the only ones on the limb. A jury of his peers convicted him, and, for the heinousness of his atrocities, a Tennessee judge pronounced the death penalty.

Years of appeals ensued. To no avail.

During those years he had prophetic dreams. Winning lottery numbers (he wasn't allowed to play himself, but he passed the news to one of the guards in exchange for chocolate and chewing gum, and one time a kaleidoscope that amused him for a while). An occasional accident, robbery, or homicide: these he passed on to the warden who made a call. Sometimes an accident was prevented, a victim saved, or a criminal apprehended. Felix visited him from time to time. His chin seemed to grow more prominent as he put on weight and lost his hair. But in all those thousands of nights he never once dreamed of the Strangler. According to Felix, the Strangler had retired. No similar modus operandi turned up on the FBI's database. Sometimes, Adrian would catch Felix rubbing his chin and looking at him wonderingly through the glass partition.

Sometimes he wondered if maybe the doctors were right, that he had imagined a surrogate killer, his conscious mind, horrified at his actions, foisting guilt onto an imaginary doppelgänger.

Nineteen years after his conviction, he was asked what he would like for his last meal. He chose two bacon cheeseburgers, onion rings, a chocolate shake, and a pack of Wrigley's Doublemint.

At seven o'clock the following evening, Adrian was led to the execution chamber.

The state of Tennessee, along with Alabama, Arkansas, Florida, and

Kentucky, authorized lethal injection for execution with the option, should an inmate so choose or if lethal injection drugs were unavailable, of electrocution. Adrian opted for the chair. Neither was appealing, but the thought of going prone on his back while witnesses observed from the gallery was humiliating.

Nashville's Riverbend Maximum Security Institution's execution chamber was spartan and antiseptic, its walls and vinyl-tiled floor white, its door and rubber baseboard brown like the chair itself. The chair was straight-backed, uncomfortable looking, and ugly. Its back was padded but the seat, Adrian observed with morbid amusement, was perforated with a shallow sliding pan underneath. He was glad he'd relieved himself prior to the long walk.

The guards sat him down, fastened the straps to his arms and legs. Adrian looked at the glass of the witness gallery. The curtains were closed. They would open soon so the witnesses—media, victims' families, his own—could observe his passing.

His attorney, Martha Weldon, was struggling with her emotions. The left side of her face kept twitching. She'd been a lot younger when she'd taken his case. She'd seen him through several appeals. The later ones gratis—his bank account having long ago run dry. She spoke to him now. "I wish you well, Adrian …" She looked at the ceiling as if seeking a happier place. "… in the great beyond."

His mouth was dry. He mumbled thanks.

She glanced at the darkened window. "Your cousin Jamison requested permission to sit in the witness gallery at the last minute. Warden Mitchel granted the request."

That surprised him. He didn't remember any Cousin Jamison. Probably some slick operator trying to sneak snuff photos. Then he remembered phones and cameras weren't allowed.

Martha left to take her place in the witness gallery.

Standing on his right, looking solemn in his black suit, Warden Mitchel asked him if he had any last words. He'd thought about that. Quite a bit actually. Had tried to come up with something memorable, or at least amusing, without seeming hokey. Funny how someone who had made his living wrangling words couldn't come up with anything worth saying. He shook his head.

At 7:15 the witness gallery curtain opened. Adrian glanced over the faces. A few journalists: no one he had known from the Sentinel back in the day. There was Felix, looking solemn. His high school buddy dipped his head when their gaze met. Martha sat beside him. She mouthed something he couldn't make out. Didn't matter—there was nothing left to say.

Adrian's eyes widened when he saw who sat on her other side.

The Strangler was dressed in a black suit. He hadn't aged all that much. He looked trimmer than Adrian now. Of course, he'd been free to work out, go for walks, while Adrian had spent twenty-three out of most twenty-four hours in solitary confinement. He thought about saying something to the warden, decided it didn't matter. The Strangler had retired and there was nothing left to say.

He dipped his head in a single nod to Felix, Martha, Cousin Jamison. From where they sat, they would each think it meant for them. Each nodded back. His cousin's lips didn't move, but the charming curl at either corner gave the illusion of a wry smile.

The guards at either side fastened the helmet on his shaved head. The helmet contained a sponge soaked in saline solution to help conduct the electricity into his body. The excess liquid gushed down his face and soaked his beige Tennessee Department of Correction shirt. He'd held it together so far. Now his right leg began to jump uncontrollably.

A guard wiped his face and attached a gray shroud to the helmet. The shroud would prevent the witnesses from having to see his face convulse as two cycles of 1,700 volts passed through the helmet into his head.

He felt a guard soak the sponges strapped to his ankles, heard them leave the chamber, their gum-soled shoes swishing softly on the vinyl floor. A maintenance staffer plugged a cable into the chair. An exhaust fan kicked on, its low hum a warning the first wave of electricity was coming.

He took a deep breath and began counting backward from one hundred.

Ninety-nine, ninety-eight, ninety-seven—

He made it to ninety-six before the current seized him and all thought was wiped from his brain.

EVERY KID IN TOWN

"The kids were all dreaming. Every kid in town. All of us dreaming the same dream. An extraordinary occurrence, don't you think?"

I nodded. "Peculiar. How do you know every child was dreaming?"

"We talked about it afterward. The survivors, that is. I suppose those that died did too. Had the same dream, I mean. But I ain't heard the dead talk yet." The old-timer chuckled rheumily, took a sip of his cocktail.

We sat at a back table in a bar down a quiet block off the main drag. The old-timer was telling his story while I plied him with drinks. He was in no rush. He was a smart old coot, who knew if he spun his tale out sparingly, he would get more drinks. I didn't mind. It wasn't costing me much. The man liked his Seven and Sevens, and at four dollars a drink, I could afford to keep him talking a while. For happy hour, the bar was nowhere near crowded, nor was the atmosphere particularly lively. A few barflies watched sports news. The sound was muted on the mounted television, closed captions shuffling across the bottom of the screen. A sour-looking couple nursed their drinks at a table. Country music, not loud, burbled cheerily from some tinny speakers.

The place was depressing, really. The bar more a habit than a gathering place. Customers came to drink among familiar faces who wouldn't judge because they shared a common taste for liquor.

The old-timer finished his drink, rolled the empty glass around on its base. I got the hint and waved to the bartender. "Another drink for my friend here."

We weren't friends. I'd only met the man today. He was one of the last of the survivors I could find. Figured he might have the answer to some of my questions. I didn't have to prompt him much. He seemed in the mood to talk.

"You know," he said after the bartender left and he'd tasted his cocktail and nodded his satisfaction, "the memory of those times seems like a dream. Like the time itself. The laws of time and physics suspended, gravity upended, the moral compass skewed. You try describing them and you even sound crazy to yourself." He paused. "But they were real enough. You can go up to the cemetery and see all the tombstones reading the same date: October 31, 1977. Say!" His eyes widened. "That's today, ain't it. I mean Halloween. I've been retired eleven years, and I don't pay much attention to what day it is." The rheumy chuckle came again. He washed it down with a sip of Seagram's and 7Up.

"Tell me about what happened," I prompted. "In your own words, as you saw it happen."

After a minute in which he appeared to be collecting his thoughts while wiping condensation off his glass, he said, "It started with the dream. My kid brother, Dan, woke me. We shared a room at one end of our little ranch house. Dan looked frightened. 'Mikey,' he says, 'wake up. Somebody's on the roof.'

"That got me moving though I was still half-seeing the dream in the near dark. I swung my feet off the bed and cocked an ear toward the ceiling. I didn't hear anything but the wind—it was gusty out as it had been in the dream—and I told Dan as much. But then I heard it, too. Now, as I said, we lived in a ranch house. Construction typical of those post-war prefabs. The ceiling wasn't high and there wasn't a lot of insulation in them, so I heard the sound on the roof pretty clearly. It definitely sounded like someone walking up there, a soft thump thump, a scuffle like sneakers on grit, a pause. I mouthed a 'What the...?' without finishing the sentence. This went with my dream. I tell you the hair on my neck bristled like a porcupine when I heard footsteps on the roof. I ran to the window. It was October, Halloween, as I said, and it was pretty chilly out, but I pulled the blind and raised the window lickity split and stuck my head out. I had to blink because the cold wind was gusting and struck me in my eyes. Dan squeezed in under my arm. We both craned our heads toward the sky.

"For the moment, I forgot about the roof and watched the show overhead, convinced that I was still dreaming."

The old-timer paused to sip his drink before continuing. I thought he was being dramatic, a born storyteller keeping me in suspense, knowing when to pause and leave you hanging, taking his time getting to the "good stuff." Then it came to me that he was lonely, and it wasn't often he got the chance to talk to anyone. Looking around, I didn't see a whole lot of good listeners. If I came in next week, I'd probably see the same faces. They'd probably told each other their stories so often they didn't bother anymore and had nothing new to share. So they read the captions on the television and listened to the tinny country music and nursed their drinks, probably only raising their voices at anything resembling good cheer on one of their birthdays or if one of them won a few bucks playing the numbers and bought a round of drinks. I suddenly felt a chill and warned myself to never grow old.

I digress. Back to the old-timer, Mikey, and his story.

"What I'm saying is, what I was seeing in the sky was exactly the same as what I'd been dreaming. Despite Dan's urgency waking me and informing me of trespassers on the roof, I was still seeing the images from my dream superimposed on the outrageous images in the sky. The moon was less than full but it was plenty bright. As I said, it was gusty, and the wind was herding long shoals of purple-gray clouds across the sky. The clouds' shadows swept across the yard, so it seemed the earth and sky flowed with synchronized motion. But there was something else up there, too. Not just clouds. And not birds either. That's what I first thought: that my eyes were playing tricks on me and what I thought was something else was really just birds taking advantage of the wind to sail by without having to flap their wings much."

The old-timer took a drink, set his glass on the paper coaster, looked at me. He opened his mouth, closed it. I waited.

"Look," he said. "I thank you for buying me drinks and taking an interest in what happened in this town—" He did some math on his fingers. "—thirty-some years ago. Nobody talks about it. Haven't for a long time. Treat it like it never happened. Like you would a nightmare your kid told you and you forgot about it the next day. People don't forget though, especially not those that lived it. They just don't talk about it. Like it was all a bad dream. But it happened. You'll probably think I'm crazy after you hear my story. Crazy old coot's brains rotted from all the booze. But I ain't crazy. No more than you, anyways." He smiled at this. He could have used a shave, but his thinning gray hair was combed, and his teeth were white, unlike some of the patrons in the place.

"I won't think you're crazy. Tell me." I tapped my wrist though I gave up wearing a watch years ago. "I've got nowhere else to be."

He nodded and took a drink, as if preparing to unburden something long buried. He didn't finish the glass but saved about a quarter of the amber liquid for later. He was obviously a slow and steady drinker by habit. The bar wasn't a Hemingwayesque clean well-lighted place, but it was the next closest thing for him. At closing time, there would be no place to go but back to his lonely, rented room and nurse a bottle and stare at a television or at the wall until tomorrow came and he could shake off the night and amble down to the bar. The bar was stuffy, but I felt a chill drift over my back as I considered my own advancing middle years.

"They were flying," he said, getting to the nut of his story. I could tell it was hard for him. His expression was clenched, his eyes squinting as if into an ugly past. One hand gripped his glass, the other opened and closed. "Hordes of them. Like dark shadowy kites sailing over the roofs. Like flocks of ravens. Only they weren't ravens or birds of any kind but looked like silhouettes of children with their arms extended as if they were gliding on the night air and weighed nothing at all. Scared the piss out of us, I can tell you. Of course, I figured right off that I was still asleep in bed and I was dreaming. I mean, no way flocks of children could be sailing over the rooftops. Right?

"But then whoever or whatever was on the roof … I remembered I'd looked out the window to see who was on the roof … stuck its head over the edge and looked down at me, and I swear if it wasn't like looking into a mirror. Dan saw it, too, and said, 'Mikey, he looks like you.'"

"'Into a mirror.' You mean the person you saw on your roof was your mirror image?"

He nodded vigorously. "Even wore the same pajamas. Only ..."

I waited. He wanted prompting. I wasn't playing that game.

"Only, it wasn't no person. Not human anyway. The thing's eyes were red." He tapped his glass as if remembering or maybe searching for the words to describe what he saw—or *thought* he saw. I had my reasons for wanting to hear his story, but I wasn't buying any of this without a heap of convincing. "Not just red," he went on, "but smoldering like coals. And its teeth were pointed. I could see this because it was grinning. As if it knew we were terrified and relished our fear. Then another, smaller, monster leaned over the edge, and darned if it wasn't the spitting image of Dan. I tore my eyes away from those burning peepers and looked at the sky and watched as those flying child silhouettes descended, presumably landing on roofs all over town. That's what I figured anyhow as I watched some of them land on nearby roofs.

"I looked back at my twin. It hadn't moved but continued to smile its pointy toothed smile and gaze at me with those hell-fire eyes. Then a powerful beam swept over the roof, and I heard Dad yell, "Who's up there?" And boy was I glad. He'd heard them, too. Up there walking around. The beam from Dad's flashlight passed right through our twins, as if they weren't real after all and I thought maybe somebody was playing a big hoax. Not just us but on the whole town. You know those Halloween and Christmas lights people project onto their garage door or the front of their house that look like snowflakes or witches and black cats moving around? I thought for a moment that somebody with a sick sense of humor was playing something similar with us. But no, I couldn't get that stare out of my head. Still can't." My guest shuddered. "Dad came around the corner of the house, his flashlight trained on the roof. When he saw us looking out the window, he asked us what we'd seen. Dan and I couldn't speak. We pointed. Dad raked his beam along the edge. Our twins hadn't budged. They were right there, grinning down at us, but Dad didn't couldn't see them."

I might've raised an eyebrow at that. "Your dad couldn't see them?"

"Nope. Turned out none of the grownups could see them, only us kids." He took a drink. His hands were trembling. "The next day I compared notes with my friends, Paul and Spliff and Zee, up top the water tower out on Farm Route 52. They had seen the same thing—kids' silhouettes sailing across the face of the moon, landing on roofs, kids that looked like them except for the burning eyes and pointed teeth walking around up there. Karen and her sister what's-her-name who lived three doors down saw it too. If you're thinking our comparing notes was a continuation of the dream, you're wrong. We were up there on the water tower in broad daylight, and we'd all seen the same thing, dreamed the same dream. So it wasn't just a dream, and none of us had gone back to sleep after the invasion. I mean, how could you? My heart gets racing just remembering." He shuddered. His glass was empty. I waved to the bartender.

"Your doppelgängers didn't follow you?" I asked while the barkeep prepared his drink. I was still nursing a beer.

"'Doppelgängers.' That's one of the names for a look-alike that follows you around. I didn't know that word then. At the time, we called them 'look-alikes' and 'twins.' Truth is we never figured out what they were or where they came from. The grownups didn't believe us, thought we were having nightmares, but as more and more of them compared notes, they thought the kids in town were having an episode of mass hysteria. Made sense, looking back on it as an adult. But at the time, it was a living nightmare to see monsters on the roof in broad daylight and to lie shivering in bed at night knowing they were right above you and your own parents, who you should trust to protect you, not believing you.

"But no, they stayed on the roof that first day. You could see them up there, just standing, watching us. Grownups wondering what we were staring at and not a single one of them able to see them. From top the water tower, you could see most of the town. And the only houses that didn't have one or more of those rug rats from hell on their roof were those owned by people who didn't have children. Later that first day, we learned that Franky Toomy, who lived over on Fourth Street, had disappeared. He liked to sleep on his roof. Fourth Street is a bunch of rickety old row houses with flat tarpaper roofs. Tar beach in the summer, patio the rest of the year. He liked to go up there with his sleeping bag and sleep under the stars. Said it made him feel like an outdoorsman. About as close to roughing it as we could get living in the city. He was never found. Didn't nobody sleep on the roof after that, I can tell you.

His drink arrived. "That wasn't exactly true," he said after taking a sip.

"What wasn't?"

"What I said about Franky. He showed up two days later, not saying squat to anyone about where he'd been. He showed up, but it wasn't him. His parents just thought he'd had some sort of traumatic experience, but we knew he wasn't Franky anymore. So did the family cat. That reminds me, grownups couldn't see them, but cats and dogs could. You never heard such a racket. Dogs howling and cats hissing twenty-four seven." He shook his head at the memory.

"I've got a theory," he said after another sip. I didn't let my interest show, but this was what I'd come for, more potentially useful information than reminiscences. "They came outta dreamland. Yeah, I know. But think about it. These things—I say things because I can't conceive of them being human, but sometimes they were three-dimensional like people, more like demons for all I know. When they flew, they looked flat as a sheet of construction paper and moved like animated shadows—like some sort of CGI special effects—but when they touched you or when their shadow fell over you, you felt it. Like dropping dry ice down your back. I mean you caught a wicked chill when that happened.

"Look, I wasn't any more superstitious than the next kid. I mean I wouldn't knowingly walk under a ladder, but I provoked plenty of sidewalk cracks and even petted Dominique DeSalvo's black cat, until it scratched me." He glanced at his hand where liver spots had replaced a long-ago scar. "Hell, my folks didn't hardly go to church except for Christmas and Easter. But think about it—it was Halloween, and we all dreamed the same dream. Something coming out of dreamland, following us back to the waking world, makes as much sense as anything."

"And the adults never caught on?"

"Well, they knew something was up. Ones who had kids had to. At first it was their own kids. I know my mom and dad were concerned. I tried to explain. Dan was too scared to talk, just kept looking up at the ceiling as if those things might come through the sheetrock. It wasn't long though before word got around and grownups all over town learned all the kids were suffering from the same delusion. That was a word that kept popping up. *Delusion.*

"Article appeared on the front page of local paper. Everybody read that, and then that was all anyone over eighteen could talk about. For a day. Yeah, it was a sensation for a day, then back to work, meal-planning, whatever. You see—and I know you do see, because I can see the skepticism in your eyes and the way the corner of your mouth hitches up now and then, as if it wants to smile but is used to being polite—the story was too ridiculous to waste time contemplating. Still, something was wrong with the kids. They had a meeting at the high school. Parents and teachers. Students weren't invited. Had some psychiatric expert come to tell them some mumbo jumbo about mass hysteria and mass hallucination."

The old-timer threw up his hands in disgust, almost toppling his drink. His countenance had grown dark. His pale-blue eyes squinted, as if trying to peer into a past clouded by years and drink. "'Mass hallucination," he mumbled. He looked me in the eye and tapped a finger on the table. "I tell you it was no hallucination. Those things followed us around."

"They followed you?"

"They did. On the second day they came down off the roofs and started following us around. It was weird … unnerving, really … riding on the school bus and everybody's twin crowded in the aisle. Same in school, kids sitting at their desks with their look-alikes standing beside them and the teacher not seeing a damn thing except a lot of frightened children staring everywhere but where they were supposed to. School was a waste of time. After that first day they started following us, most of us stayed out of school. Avoided going out of our rooms as far as I knew. Parents not believing you. Doppelgängers waiting outside.

"Over the next two days we knew something new was happening. There were significantly less of them on the streets."

"The doppelgängers."

He bobbed his head. "The herd thinned out. At first, we didn't know what was going on. Then somebody, I don't remember who, came up with the idea that some of us were being replaced. Those things were taking over our bodies … or worse, doing away with us and taking our place. Not that the replacements—*changelings*, somebody called them—had burning eyes or pointed teeth. They looked just like us. I imagine those who tried to warn their parents that their siblings weren't who they thought they were not only got disbelieved, but probably figured for looney tunes."

He took a drink. "Not all the parents were disbelievers. A kid on the other side of town drowned. Cops arrested his dad who swore the boy he drowned wasn't his son. That he'd been possessed. That caused another round of speculation. Parents looking at their kids and wondering if they'd been possessed. Things could have gotten worse if things hadn't progressed so swiftly."

He laughed. It was a bitter, humorless laugh. "Listen to me. 'Things could have gotten worse....' Things got a lot worse, only it wasn't grownups murdering their kids. A few days after the things started following us around, they took to the roofs again. There were still over half of them up there, which meant a lot of kids weren't the same people they'd been the week before. Some of the older kids posted fliers all over town to meet in the field behind Old Man Hendricks' barn. Used to be a cornfield, but the stubble was all worn down. Looked more like a rutted fairground after the carnival's pulled up stakes. It was a good place for a gathering. Old Man Hendricks was dead, and the place was for sale. It was out of eyesight from our peeping Toms and close enough to town that everyone could make it without too great a hike.

"We knew as we gathered in the field that some of us weren't really human but changelings, and everybody was eyeing everybody else suspecting them of hiding a monster. Several teenagers carried hammers and sticks. We hoped none of them were changelings. One of the older boys got up on a milk crate so he could be seen above the crowd and started talking, telling us to form a circle and look around and anybody you knew wasn't who he or she was last week, push them into the middle of the circle. He said we had to be tough. Neither our parents nor the police were going to save us, and if we didn't want to end up changed, we had to stop the sickness from spreading. We knew what he meant, and my stomach went sour just thinking about what had to be done. But I moved just like the rest to form a big circle. Already, some of the kids, presumably those that had changed, were being pushed into the middle of the circle. While others were running back toward town as fast as their legs could carry them.

"But before anyone could raise a hand, a great cloud of silhouettes boiled out of the sky from the direction of town, and a wind picked up where there had been hardly a breeze before. The horde was back, depleted but numerous enough to turn your legs to jelly. There were woods behind the field, and most of us took off thinking the trees would save us. I don't mind telling you I was in the mix.

"They were on us before we reached the tree line, tearing our hair. I saw two of the bigger creatures snatch one of the smaller kids out of the crowd, fly him up, and drop him from a great height. Not ten feet from me, one of the things landed in front of her twin, grabbed her, and—this is really gonna sound crazy, but in for a penny—and opened her mouth. And kept opening it, those pointy teeth yawning farther and farther apart. Then she clamped her expanding mouth over the girl's face, sucked air, and held her breath until the girl stopped struggling and slumped to the ground.

"I had paused to watch this, not because I wanted to see what happened, but because I was too shocked to move. But when I felt claws rake my scalp, I got moving. All around me these things were landing on top of their look-alikes and tearing into them tooth and claw. And here and there clusters of what could only be changelings were ripping apart some helpless kid. Some of the older boys who had brought weapons did what they could, battering a changeling to a bloody pulp or trying to pull a low-flying monster out of the air; but they were outnumbered, and the silhouettes were landing around them, turning into three-dimensional monsters as soon as they touched ground and attacking. I heard screaming and it must have been loud but all I could hear was the blood roar in my head and all I could think of was getting to the tree line before one of those things ripped my scalp off or smothered me.

"Then I remembered Dan. He had been right beside me. I looked back thinking he was gone, lying somewhere dead and mutilated in that bloody massacre. But he was right there. Only it wasn't Dan. Its eyes weren't blazing embers, and its teeth weren't pointy, but it wasn't Dan. The thing's lips were pulled back in a snarl that looked more like a mad dog's than a human's. And its eyes ..." The old fellow shuddered. I felt something of the horror of his tale and shuddered a bit myself, my imagination running riot with images of that bloody massacre. "Dan could never have looked like that. He was a sweet kid; not the brightest, but he meant well. He could be annoying when he wanted to play a game and I wanted to read a book or when he followed me when I wanted to hang out with boys my own age, but he was my brother and I knew him and no way my little brother could ever achieve that snarl or muster the hate pouring from those eyes: it was the gaze of someone who wanted to see the world burn. The creature launched itself at me. It bit me. Hard. I thought it was going to tear my arm off. I hit it with a rock. I must have hit it more than once. I lost it. When I realized what I was doing, the thing was dead. Its face was all smashed in. I killed my little brother."

A tear rolled down his cheek. I didn't think he was being melodramatic, and he didn't look the type to cry in public. I sipped the last of my beer and waited. He swiped the tear with the back of his hand and downed half of what remained of his drink.

"How'd you get away?" I asked to change the subject.

"Hmm," he snorted. "I ran. And kept running. I didn't go home. When they found me two, three days later, I was half-starved and covered with dirt and twigs from trying to burrow my way into the earth. I don't remember much of the time I was in the woods or the days after I was found. I was literally scared out of my wits and all I could see was that girl's face being swallowed and those things diving down and grabbing handfuls of hair. And Dan … not the happy kid face I had known but the raw pulpy mess I'd made of it with a rock. I still see that face every morning when I open my eyes and every night when I close them."

He finished his drink, pushed the glass away. When I offered to freshen it, he declined. "No, I've had enough. Thank you for your generosity." He pushed his chair back from the table but didn't get up. "Well, that's my tale, for what it's worth. Now you can tell me something."

I waited.

"Why did you want to hear my story? You must've known the gist of it before you contacted me."

I took my badge out of my inside jacket pocket and laid it on the table. Mikey stared at it a moment, then grinned. "Am I under arrest?"

I grinned myself. "No. Nothing like that. I told you I was calling from

Boswell. I'm sheriff in Powell County, and we're having a bit of a problem that nobody can wrap their head around."

The old-timer pursed his lips and nodded knowingly, as he'd suspected that was what I was here for all along. "Twins?"

I nodded. "That's what the kids claim."

"They would, wouldn't they?"

"I gotta confess, I do not want to believe any of this, but there are too many similarities between what happened in Talbot County in 1977 and what's happening in Powell County now. If—and it's a tough *if* to swallow—what you've told me is what's going on in Boswell, I need to know what I can do about it."

The old-timer's response surprised me. I guess I'd come hoping to learn something that would help, but all he had to offer was, "Nothing. Let it run its course like a virus. Of course, you could kill the kids. No, I didn't mean it like that. I mean if you could weed out the replacements, the changelings, you could kill them. But the parents won't believe you and will fight you if you try to take their kid. Either way, children will die."

He stood. I heard his knees pop. He picked his Totes hat off the chair beside him and clamped it on his head. "Thank you again," he said. "And good luck. I'd best get back to my room. I don't like to be out after dark, and I sleep with the lights on."

He left. I considered my options, saw I didn't have any. I ordered another beer.

CLARISSA

The mist was thick upon the river, the rising sun a pallid glow behind its curtain. The bench was wet with dew, but he didn't care. A sign by the River Walk read "Beware of Snakes," but he wasted no thought on lurking serpents. He'd be late for work, maybe get fired, but neither clock nor job held a candle to the rapture of Clarissa's embrace.

Holding Clarissa in his arms, her lips soft and responsive, her porcelain hand warm upon his stubble cheek, was everything. What mattered cold or serpent's coil when his senses thrummed, each heartbeat a fevered dream, his senses dancing a razor edge of ecstasy as joyful tears burned his cheeks.

She broke the kiss, gazelle eyes lifting to his broad face. "You're crying." Her voice was like the music of spring rain, as sweet as birdsong on a summer morn.

"Just the breeze." He wiped the errant drop.

She ran a hand up his arm, caressed his bicep. "You're so strong." She leaned against his chest. They fit together so naturally; it was as if his arms were made to hold her and for nothing else.

Otis Kretzer knew he wasn't particularly athletic or handsome. His job as a route driver delivering candy and soda to vending machines kept him active enough to stay fairly trim, but sampling the candy and soda—not to mention the beers he drank every night in front of the TV to make the long, lonely evenings bearable—were taking their toll. That was another thing he loved about Clarissa: she made him feel good about himself. Deep down, he knew she wasn't sincere; it was part of the program, but he happily put reality aside and wallowed in her adoration.

"I love the way you hold me," she said, snuggling closer.

He kissed her brow, her skin cool and moist from the mist, inhaled the perfume of her hair that smelled of summer breezes and reminded him with a nostalgic pang of sitting in a meadow picking wild flowers when he was nine.

Suddenly, Clarissa tensed and pulled away. His heart plunged with the unreasonable terror that she was about to reject him, as every woman he'd ever been with eventually did.

"What's wrong?" he asked, fearing the worst.

She offered a nervous smile, a wave of a sculptured hand. "It's nothing. I just had a sense of déjà vu. Like I've been here before."

Otis smiled, relief flooding his tortured heart. "I know what you mean. Though we've just met, I feel like I've known you forever."

He leaned in to kiss her upturned lips….

Otis woke, heart throbbing, lips parted to receive Clarissa's kiss, his senses electric with her scent, her yielding warmth … and found himself in a shabby store sitting in a worn vinyl lounge chair—the same lounger in which he'd succumbed to the puff of narcotic smoke from the dream dispenser.

Up and down the row of similar chairs, a scattering of patrons blissfully dreamt while coin-fed meters ticked, either puckering as if to kiss, arms twined about ghost lovers (*Ugh. Had he done that? He hoped no one saw.*), or scowling, arms jerking as if locked in mortal combat.

He frowned at his own meter: the red flag read "Expired." Had he been dreaming that long?

Eager to return to Clarissa's embrace, he dug in his pocket for coins, dropped them into the slot. A coiled spring inside the metallic box whirred with each added coin.

He settled back and closed his eyes. A smile of anticipation curled his lips as he waited for the grill beside his face to dispense the narcotic puff that would send him to dreamland.

He opened his eyes, looked at the vending machine. The "Expired" flag mocked him. He smacked the machine, settled back, closed his eyes. Opened them. Smacked the machine again. Muttering a stream of vindictive, he rose from the lounger and stomped up to the clerk sitting behind the counter in a mustard-stained tee-shirt, chewing a toothpick and eyeballing a porn magazine.

"Machine's not working," Otis said in a quieter voice than his approach suggested. Though annoyed with the delay, he was non-confrontational.

"Pick another," the clerk said without looking up from his mag.

"Don't want another." Otis was appalled at the idea. He wanted Clarissa. He'd been coming here for weeks and couldn't imagine being with anyone else. In his own peculiar way, Otis was loyal. Clarissa was the girl of his dreams. Literally, being a dream date, as the banner over the storefront advertised. And hadn't he sworn his undying love?

The clerk looked up, annoyed that Otis was interrupting his own dream date. He opened a drawer and plopped eight quarters on the counter.

"Try another. They'll all love you the same."

Despite his timidity, Otis smacked his fist on the counter.

"No!" he barked with as much menace as he could muster.

"What number?"

"Seven."

Leaving the coins on the glass, the clerk grabbed an "Out of Order" sign from under the counter, went over and hung it on the offending machine.

"Aren't you going to fix it?" Otis was flabbergasted.

"I just make the call," the clerk said without turning on his way back to his magazine. "I don't fix 'em."

A wave of insurmountable loss crashed over Otis as he stumbled into the sunlight. The machine wouldn't be fixed. Clarissa would languish in some dusty warehouse, his dream girl lost to him forever. Would she be as heartbroken as he?

The thought was unbearable.

Clarissa!

DEATH DREAM

DREAMIES HEALTH HAZARD?

PRINCETON, N.J (UPI) – Researchers at Princeton University today disclosed startling findings from a sleep study performed with the Madison Dream Imaging Transmitter.

The study—which consisted of having two hundred and fifty dreamie fans who had seen his or her favorite dreamie an average of twenty times sleep in the lab two nights and dream into the MDIT—showed that fans dreamed dreamie imagery and plot sequences seventy-six percent of the time. A computer breakdown of the findings further revealed that fans of Madison Blake's dreamies dreamt his imagery at an even higher eighty-nine percent of the time.

Dr. Rupert Ossing, Director of the Ernst Sleep Research Center, speculated on the potential dangers. "It's believed by many current researchers that the function of dreams is to solve the day's problems, or to rehearse for tomorrow's, to provide an outlet for frustrations. Generally, dreams are a lot like a computer program, a sort of symbolic code that processes your daily problems, flushes, solves, or files them.

"But since so much of the dreamers' subject matter

consists of preprogrammed repetitious images, the subject is deprived of this clearinghouse quality of normal dreaming. As a result, the dreamie abuser becomes irritable and quick to anger."

The Surgeon General's office is looking into reports of hormonal imbalance as a result of long-term exposure to dreamies, as well as the similarities between dreamies and brainwashing.

"Horror is a release valve, a temporary relief from that unfillable pit in the soul of modern existential man. We exist—but to what purpose?

"Horror gives us purpose. While some works just remind us that we have this void, this sense of purposelessness, Horror, temporarily, by firing the audience with purpose, fills the void. The purpose is ridiculously simple: it is to destroy the monster and, therefore, give us some measure of triumph, however transitory, over our boring lives and impending demise."

—Madison Blake, *Horror Blog* interview

"The purpose of horror is to scare the living bejesus out of the audience and to give them nightmares. The more nightmares, the better the horror."

—Madison Blake on *Late Night with Latisha Williams*

Selma brought the frosty pitcher into the library where the children were seated around the big table. Chilled glasses on coasters waited before each contestant. The drapes were drawn, the lights in the chandelier over the table dialed down so they were only halfway on and left the farther reaches of the room draped in shadows. Selma didn't like it one bit. With the lights dim and them all huddled around the library table, their headsets before them, wires snaking across the polished oak and plugged into Irwin's powerful gaming laptop, they looked like a bunch of Satan worshipers about to engage in unspeakable rites.

Of course, Selma knew nothing of the sort was going to take place. Irvin wasn't that kind of boy. He was too engrossed in his games to bother with the devil. As far as she knew, and she knew better than his parents, Irwin didn't drink, smoke, or do drugs. And hadn't she seen the same expression the children wore this afternoon half a century ago in North Carolina on the faces of old men sitting in the park playing dominoes or checkers? A competitiveness and a desire to one-up one's opponent?

No, not the same, she corrected herself. Those old men had been passing time; these kids were going to war. Even Irwin, normally aloof in his signature white linen suit, gazed about the table with a devilish twinkle in his eye.

Selma smiled, her wrinkled face gleaming like varnished mahogany in the half light. "Care for some fresh-squeezed lemonade?" she asked Lonnie, who sat next to Irwin.

"Yes, thank you."

Selma poured for each of them. *That Lonnie is such a sweet thing*, Selma thought. A mite skinny, but she had lovely blue-green eyes and pretty sandy-colored hair and good manners. She wondered when Irwin was ever going to notice her. Nora, on the other hand, the only other female contestant, was as swarthy as Lonnie was fair, and she had a mean-looking crease in her forehead that made her look like she was concentrating all the time—which she was: straight A's, president of two clubs. Irwin had informed her Nora wanted to replace him as President of the Games Club. That Nora was all business, as serious as any man about winning, but hadn't she felt the same way about beating her older brother Clark at tic-tac-toe half a century ago? As much as Selma admired the girl's gumption, she didn't care for her T-shirt. No sir, not one bit. White on black, it showed a vagina filled with shark's teeth. Selma doubted she'd get many dates wearing that.

Mike, the boy on the other side of Irwin, shy and quiet and, according to Irwin, not a particularly good player, seemed nice enough. But that Doren, who dressed in black with the silver chains and the turned-up collar and the sneer that never left his mouth was a pure-n-tee snot. Acted like he was doing a favor just to look at you. Selma's impression was Doren's daddy hadn't allowed him the taste of a good hickory switching often enough for it to have made any difference.

"Before I go, Irwin, is there anything else you'd like?" She sat the pitcher on the sideboard beside the tray of club sandwiches.

"No thank you, Selma. Have a pleasant evening." Irwin's smile was as charming and as insincere as his father's, God bless him.

"Any sandwiches left over, you cover 'em with plastic wrap and put 'em in the fridge, you hear. We don't want to see roaches running around your daddy's library, do we?"

Now Irwin's smile was more genuine—as it often was when someone said something he thought funny. More often, Irwin reserved his smiles for when he was doing the talking. As for roaches, there weren't any in this house. No rats or mice either. Selma Flowers didn't allow no roaches or mice, not in the twelve years since she'd been hired to cook and take care of Irwin.

"Don't worry," Irwin said. "I'll put the dishes in the sink when we're finished and the leftovers in the fridge."

Selma cast a disapproving glance at the headsets. Lonnie's was pink, Irwin's gray, the rest black. Virtual reality. Put them on and you were in whatever fantasy world or battlefield the game designer dreamed up for you. According to Irwin, they could all enter the same game world and play together—or against each other. It seemed unhealthy denying yourself the fun of looking in your opponent's eyes, sharing a laugh. Oh well, at least they were keeping out of trouble.

"All right, then. You kids enjoy your game. And may the best player win." She winked at Lonnie from the door.

Lonnie giggled. Doren rolled his eyes, but she didn't let on she'd noticed. "Night."

The door closed behind Selma. Irwin sat back and sipped his lemonade, sliding the chilled edge between his lips as he turned the glass. The table was rectangular. Theoretically, it had two places of prominence, but he had made sure it was clear that he sat at the head of the table. He had switched the dining room chairs for the library's. The dining room chairs were tall-backed and cushioned in red velvet—fitting the occasion. Two of them had arms, the other four did not. It had been a simple matter to bring in only five of the chairs and only one with arms and placing name cards in front of the four chairs lacking arms. As Game Master, it was his right that his place should show distinction; it also gave him a psychological advantage. But mostly he did it to piss off Doren.

Mike, Nora, Lonnie—they were all seniors at SCH and members of the Games Club—the three best players after him, in fact. Though he was the same age as Irwin, Doren was a sophomore at Drexel (having skipped the sixth and eleventh grades) where he was a computer graphics whiz. Doren planned to make a career out of game design. But though Doren was a savant when it came to weaving a tapestry of action with machine language, his first love was the same as Irwin's: total immersion virtual reality RPGs.

Irwin had met Doren at the PAX East convention. Neither of them saw all the exhibits because they both wound up entering a marathon, two-day *Semper Fi* tourney. He and Doren had talked during breaks, trying to size one another up, feel out each other's weaknesses, and had learned they were both from Philly. Neither of them won the tourney. Some kid from Eastern Indiana University had beaten the pants off all of them and returned to the Hoosier state a richer man. Doren had gotten killed off three quarters of the way through when he stepped on a claymore because he'd traded his mine detector and disarmer for a rock-eating tribble to escape a maze. He himself had bought the farm when, in the next-to-last battle, a Venusian spiderdragon wove a spell around him that conveniently immobilized him until a droid showed up and neatly decapitated him with a laser beam. Irwin had been more than a little pissed that no one had come along and saved him. It would've cost them only a couple energy points, and if they'd killed the spider, they could have scored ten points plus the rest of the spider's binding spells. Some guys wanted all the glory.

Calculating the odds, Irwin placed Doren as his toughest competition simply because he was a whiz kid, famous for figuring things out. Nora, of course, was the wild card. Sometimes he beat her badly, but she had whipped him twice, seeming to will herself to win, as if, having psyched herself up, she made it happen.She could get reckless, but sometimes that worked to her advantage.

Irwin took another sip of lemonade, set the glass down, and pushed the coaster farther away so he wouldn't spill his glass if he started waving his arms at something in VR land. He picked up his headset. "Are we ready?"

He could tell by the look in their eyes Doren and Nora were. Lonnie just kept smiling pleasantly. She liked to play, but she lacked the fire to be a fierce competitor.

Mike looked ill. He shook his head and pushed his headset centimeters away. "I don't know. Maybe we shouldn't."

Mike was a big guy, not exactly fat, but what people used to politely call "stout." There was muscle under the flab, and if he good-naturedly clapped you on the shoulder, you staggered under the impact. Tonight, he wore one of his signature checkered shirts—a red-and-white one that had the unfortunate effect of looking like a tablecloth and making the big guy look even bigger. The shirt was his idea of table dressing, a fashion it seemed the world had adopted since the Covid pandemic. Out of sight below table—or camera—level, he wore khaki cargo shorts with sandals and white socks.

"Wuss," Doren barked.

Nora gave Mike a withering look.

"What if we get caught?" Mike's voice had gone up a half octave. Was the chubso pleading?

"We're not going to get caught," Doren said as if he were lecturing an idiot. "I sneaked a peak. Security was minor, and I left a trap door for us to get back in."

"Look, Michael. We all agreed on this," Irwin said, trying to suppress his impatience. "Can you honestly say you don't want to check out

Madison Blake's latest creation? To see before anyone else what's going to rock the dreamie world next month?"

He was referring to the Dream Meister's upcoming Halloween concert at the Wells Fargo Center. A Blake dreamie was technically a full-dive, virtual reality massively multiplayer online role-playing game, or VRMMORPG, in which multiple players—thousands in Blake's case—vied against monsters, each other, or a hostile environment in a VR world. Only Blake had taken VRMMORPG to a whole other level by incorporating the gaming concept in a live, full immersion dreamie experience.

In a Blake dreamie, the audience, in a shallow but prolonged dream state, experienced the adventure from whichever viewpoint character they chose to role-play. Thousands attended multiple times to experience the dreamie through the eyes of different avatars. If last year's extravaganza were any indication, Blake's Halloween show was going to be gonzo. Not only was the man himself performing in their hometown—to which performance they all had tickets—but for the first time ever the event was being transmitted live around the globe via linked dreamatrons in select venues.

"I—" Mike wilted under their stares.

Nora shook her head. "If you're not down, go home."

Lonnie was more sympathetic. "I'm nervous, too, Mike. But—" She gave a smile and a little shiver. "—this is exciting."

Mike didn't seem convinced, but nodded as if he didn't want to appear less brave than Lonnie. "Okay, let's do it."

"Atta boy," Nora said.

Doren snorted. "'Bout time."

"We're just going in for a look-see," Irwin said. "Don't touch or interact with anything. We don't want to leave footprints. Okay?"

Lonnie and Mike nodded. Nora glared at him as she always did when anyone told her what to do. Doren smirked. Irwin looked him in the eye. "Okay?"

"Whatever you say, boss."

They donned their headsets. Irwin stabbed the return key.

※

They found themselves in what looked like the dining hall of an ancient Transylvanian castle. Rotting drapes hung like shrouds from tall lancet windows. A massive table that could easily seat twenty, flanked by tall-backed chairs, dominated the center.

Dracula's castle? Irwin thought with mounting excitement.

None of them were dressed for the bone-chilling cold. Lonnie's yellow summer dress was sleeveless, and she rubbed her bare arms. Irwin considered briefly offering her his linen jacket but turned up his collar.

At the far end of the table, a candelabra burned, the only light in the vast space. They made their way down the long hall under the glowering stares of the dimly seen portraits that lined the wall opposite the windows.

As Irwin drew near, he saw, to his delight, in keeping with RPG tropes, spread on the table, a map, and beside the map a sheet of foolscap.

Doren blew the dust off the map. Mike sneezed. They all glared at him for making noise, then leaned in to study the vellum. The top half showed a street map of a town. The bottom half mapped the subterranean maze beneath the town. Below this, a few branches of the maze ran off the paper.

"Arkham," Nora read the blackletter script in the upper right-hand corner. "1925."

"Cthulhu? Dagon?" Mike speculated.

"Nyarlathotep." Doren stroked his chin as if he sported a goatee: a sure tell that he was planning action.

Nora's brow furrowed in what looked like worry, but Irwin knew she was memorizing.

Irwin grinned despite himself.

"And where do these exits lead?" Lonnie tapped one of the passages that ran off the paper.

Irwin picked up the sheet of brittle foolscap and scanned its text. "Those, my dear," he said answering Lonnie's question, "are entrances into the dream world: minaret-studded Celephais ... the cold wastes of forbidden Kadath." He let the grin slide from his face. "But I warn you," he paused dramatically, "descend the slimed, time-eroded stair into nether dreamworld if you dare." His gaze moved from one to the other around the table. It was obvious from their fevered gaze they shared the thrill he felt. They had breached Madison Blake's defenses and were getting a preview of what was in store for his legions of fans come Halloween. How they would envy him ... if they only knew. He felt he couldn't have been more thrilled if they had broken into the Metropolitan Museum and were about to steal the Star of India. He continued reading: "Horrors. Indescribable horrors await those foolhardy enough to venture there, and heaven help the fool who enters unprepared." The latter he directed at Doren, who chose to ignore the slight. "Lest he—or she—" His gaze dropped to Lonnie's breasts. "—end up feeding Azathoth's fires, from which ..." He left the sentence unfinished.

Mike picked it up: "... there is no return."

"The name of the game," Irwin announced theatrically, "is 'Shadow Over Arkham.' The scenario: Arkham has been overrun by Lovecraftian denizens. They have gathered for the return of the Ancient Ones."

"Ohhh." Lonnie's eyes were bright with anticipation.

"Somewhere on the map is a gate. Your quest is to find the means to shut the gate before Cthulhu and his crew take over. The means to shut the gate may or may not be on the map," he finished mysteriously.

Nora regarded him suspiciously. "You mean we have to go through the dreamworld, don't we?"

Irwin was getting a kick out of this. Even ol' sourpuss Nora was hooked. He shrugged. "Maybe." He continued reading: "Your quest begins in the library of Miskatonic U. In the rare books section. Look around you." They did so, imagining the books, the curtained windows, the dark maw of the grand fireplace. "It is night, and every sane man left alive is locked in his house with all his candles burning. Power, incidentally, has been knocked out. I say *sane* because those victims not devoured by the ghouls or rats wander the streets, babbling mindlessly, their reason blasted by the revelation of monstrosities better left unwitnessed."

Lonnie rubbed her arms, looking goosebumpy and eager. Irwin went on.

"The librarian, the erudite Dr. Henry Armitage, opens a glass case and removes a huge and ancient volume."

"The *Necronomicon*," breathed Nora and Doren almost simultaneously.

"Yes, the *Necronomicon*. The blasphemous work of the mad Arab Abdul Alhazred, wherein is set forth the secrets of the Ancient Ones and the Elder Gods. Dr. Armitage lays the volume on a table, searches through its pages, then points to a passage scribed in Latin. Dr. Armitage, an authority in such matters, translates for the others."

Irwin passed the foolscap to Nora, who tilted the sheet to the candlelight and read:

> "They walk unseen and foul in lonely places where the Words have been spoken and the Rites howled through at their Seasons. The wind gibbers with Their voices, and the earth mutters with Their consciousness. They bend the forest and crush the city, yet may not forest or city behold the hand that smites. Kadath in the cold waste hath known Them, and what man knows Kadath? The ice desert of the South and the sunken isles of Ocean hold stones whereon their seal is engraven, but who hath seen the deep frozen city or the sealed tower long garlanded with seaweed and barnacles? Great Cthulhu is Their cousin, yet can he spy Them only dimly. *Iä! Shub-Niggurath!* As a foulness shall ye know Them. Their hand is at your throats, yet ye see Them not, and Their habitation is even one with your guarded threshold."

"Wow!" Lonnie said when Nora finished.

Irwin smiled to himself. Nora had left unspoken the next line, which said: "Yog-Sothoth is the key to the gate, whereby the spheres meet."

Whoever recalled the passage from "The Dunwich Horror" would be at an advantage. He suspected Doren would. Nora and Doren were too good at gaming to share the knowledge. Mike and Lonnie...? Well, you had to have cannon fodder.

Mike whooped, startling him from his thoughts. The big guy stooped and grabbed something off the floor. He came up beaming with what looked like a gold doubloon between his fingers. The coin glittered in the candlelight.

"Oh shit!" Irwin and Doren said at once.

In his Manhattan studio, Madison Blake, King of the Dreamies, Master of Disaster, Guru of Gore, icon of millions, noticed the amber light blinking in the upper right corner of his dreamatron's curved console. He sat his mug of Earl Grey down on a side table and walked over to his gleaming instrument.

The dreamatron's keyboard was ivory. The cockpit-like, mother-of-pearl console gleamed under the studio's recessed lights. Blake's right hand smoothed the fabric of his black silk pajama front. *Well, well. Someone wants to rock and roll.* A grin split his narrow, almost handsome face. He'd give the intruder a show he wouldn't soon forget.

Making himself comfortable in his custom Eames chair, he dialed down the lights and threw a switch activating the machine's automatic biofeedback unit. A red light so dark it appeared purple began to pulse at the top center of the console. At eight cycles per second, the strobe aided in putting the Dreamer into the alpha state necessary to project his dreamie.

The Dreamer's eyes fluttered, closed. Within moments, he entered REM and reached out to welcome his visitors.

A wind sprang up, extinguishing the candles and plunging them into blackness. The floor beneath Irwin's feet vanished and he tumbled ... landed with a bone-bruising *thump* on what felt like concrete. The grunts and *oomphs* of falling bodies told him the others shared his fate.

He felt along the cold, rough cement, gritty with sand, and encountered an ankle. A booted foot kicked him in the chest.

"Don't touch, lunkhead," Nora growled.

"This is weird," Mike muttered.

"Where are we?" Lonnie's frightened voice echoed the way voices did in the school gymnasium, giving the impression of a cavernous space.

Doren's chuckle came from a few feet away. "Dreamland, dearies. I suspect we're under Arkham 'where the Words have been spoken and the Rites howled through at their Seasons'. *Iä! Shub-Niggurath!*"

"What now?" Mike muttered.

A worm of cold fear squirmed in Irwin's gut. Irwin Felder, President of the Games Club, intrepid adventurer in virtual dreamland, hadn't the foggiest.

Something slithered in the dark.

The Dreamer's fingers fly over the ivory keys, producing a necromantic music only he can hear. The notes are translated into machine language that transmits the lush imagery of his dreamscape. Seven of the console's multitrack ports are empty. A green RECORD LED glows under the eighth.

Behind closed lids, his eyes jitter the dance of REM. His fingers race, and his creations assemble for the hunt.

A slithering in the dark. A stirring … a scurrying now. It wasn't a single thing, but many. Irwin froze, afraid of stumbling and falling into the mass of fur and claws he suspected surrounded him. Lonnie was whimpering. He looked back to where he thought the others were, and saw a lighter flick on, illuminating Mike's face. Mike's eyes and mouth opened wide, as if he were screaming. It was the face of a man shaking in his boots. Then the scream erupted, echoing and reverberating and multiplying, and underneath it the mass of scurrying, furry bodies excited by the nearness and the reek of red meat and hot blood.

Mike bolted.

"Mike, stop!" Irwin shouted.

"I gotta get out! I gotta get out! There's rats in here!"

He was at the wall now, several yards to Irwin's right, going along it with his lighter, patting the wet brick with his free hand, his eyes flicking back and forth from the wall to the dark corner on his right, which was alive with the noise of a squirming mass of furry, scaly-tailed rodents. Though he knew it was just a dreamie, the rats weren't real, it somehow looked safer over there than over here. Drawn like a moth, Irwin gravitated toward the light. The dark and the noise was unsettling.

Mike's light fell on a door that looked strikingly like the varnished door to his father's library. The flame glowed on a brass knob.

A second lighter flicked on. Doren, with Lonnie and Nora at his heels. The scratching, scraping, rustling sounds of small furry bodies rubbing against each other in the clammy darkness grew frantic in the corners of the chamber. Then a rat ran across Mike's feet, and he yelped and dropped his Bic.

The door flung open—a lozenge of light. Mike passed through, and for a second, before the door slammed shut, Irwin saw a marvelous sight.

Irwin grabbed the knob, yanked open the door and stared in disbelief. He hesitated there on the threshold, taking in the empty seats, the curtained windows, one foot remaining in cold dark stillness, the other planted on a moving surface vibrating to the rhythm of the singing rails. The door at the far end was swinging closed—presumably Mike, too scared to wait for them.

"Ooph!"

Nora shoved him into the car. He made way, remembering the rodents. Lonnie burst through, followed by Doren, who yelped and kicked at the squealing darkness behind as he slammed the door.

A rat clung to Doren's leg, gnawing, its teeth embedded in his thigh.

Doren punched it in the face, grimacing at the pain as the teeth tore free. The rat thudded to the floor. Whiskers bristling, haunches quivering, it was on its feet in a flash and lunging again into the red flow that streaked Doren's designer jeans.

Nora's Doc Marten connected crunchingly with the rat's skull, sending the rodent cartwheeling into the seats.

"Come on." Irwin hurried down the aisle toward the far end of the car and the door through which Mike had disappeared.

Beyond the six or eight seats facing each other in pairs on either side, they passed a series of stateroom doors. Over the door at the end of the car, an oval plaque read Pullman Company. Irwin turned the knob, pushed. The door didn't budge. Nora shoved from behind and he shoved back—the door opened inward. He found himself on a small platform between cars. A desert landscape rolled by under a starry sky. Irwin kept going, not waiting for another prod from Nora.

The next car was like the last and just as empty.

"I'm dreaming," Lonnie said when they were all inside and the door slammed behind them. "That's it. Has to be." She looked at the others for reassurance. Even in the dim light, Irwin could see the fear in her eyes.

"Where's Mike?" Nora demanded of no one in particular, eagle-eyeing the interior of the car.

"Probably hiding in one of the staterooms," Irwin said.

"Looks like a set." Doren gestured at their surroundings. "One of those old train murder movies. Hey! I recognize it!"

"So do I," Irwin said, recognizing the set.

"'The Trail of Cthulhu,'" they said in unison.

"Doesn't make sense," Nora said. "Rats, a deserted train. I expected more from Madison Blake. This is his Halloween extravaganza?"

"Yeah," Doren echoed. "The Trail of Cthulhu?"

They had a point. Cool as the imagery was—and he had to admit the setting was startlingly realistic—the tropes were dated and unoriginal. Yet they'd hacked Blake's CPU and here they were. What to do?

The answer came to him: treat the dream as a game.

He looked around on a sudden inspiration, looking for anything with print on it. There! A small metal plaque over one of the windows, probably brass-colored at one time, but since painted over with the same brown as the rest of the car. He stood on the seat to read what it said.

The single-word message was simply "LISTEN."

A warning. Nora and Doren were arguing. "Shhh!" They fell silent. "Listen!"

At first, all they heard was the rumbling of the train, the sound of steel on steel. They jumped as something massive slammed against the door at the far end, rattling it on its hinges.

The door flew open. They backed away. It was dark out there. Had they had entered a tunnel?

But the darkness wasn't "out there." It filled the doorway, blacker than any night. Irwin strained to make out details. The blackness was alive with an abhorrent, undulant movement that raised the hackles on his neck. Through the rhythmic rumbling of the train, he heard a revolting sound, as if something large and wet were oozing through the doorway, squishing against the jambs … a moist slapping as of heavy appendages flapping down the aisle, and a sinister buzzing. A smell wafted from the blackness: a sea smell, thick and nostril-cloying. The stench of corruption, of rotting seaweed.

By the starlight seeping through the curtained windows, Irwin saw that the bubbling, blob-like thing oozing through the door was not a single entity but a myriad: a boiling hill of flies. So many flies, packed so close together. Not so much flying but crawling over each other. Giant blue-bottle flies, tiny delta-winged sand flies, every type of fly imaginable gathered to create a single monstrous horror that made his skin crawl and turned his bowels to water.

Irwin turned to run—froze. In the seat to his left, empty a moment ago, a familiar figure sat, shoulders hunched, head slumped forward on his chest.

"Mike?"

The others crowded round, the thing oozing through the door momentarily forgotten. Mike seemed to be asleep or …

"He's dead," Nora barked. "Keep moving."

The head began to turn, lambent eyes swinging toward them. Except for the freezing vacuity of his stare, Mike's face seemed all right … and then the far side of his head came into view. It looked chewed to pulp, as if by dozens of tiny, hungry mouths. The blood was still flowing, seeping out of the ravaged flesh, running down his neck and soaking his shirt.

The corpse grinned. Leather soles scraped the floor as it lumbered to its feet.

Irwin stood rooted as if he'd gazed into Medusa's eyes and been turned to stone. Then he realized the others had passed him and he got moving, pounding his way down the aisle. The car had grown impossibly long. The door through which they'd entered receded into the distance past row upon row of seats and stateroom doors.

Lonnie, hurried along by Irwin, ran into someone and yelped. Irwin reached around her and gave the stumbling figure a shove. Doren. "Let's go, dickhead!" Irwin growled.

Ahead, Nora screamed.

"What now?" He pushed Lonnie, who shoved into Doren, who had stopped again. Irwin didn't need an answer. The leather seats on both sides were creaking, as if being relieved of weight. The pre-dawn light illuminated the harrowing scene around them. The seats weren't empty, and the human shapes that occupied them were not alive. The gamesters didn't stop to take in the details; a glance to either side was enough to send them running in panic toward the far end of the car, away from the animated dead, away from the boiling hill of flies that oozed down the aisle blocking their retreat.

A hand, reeking with corruption, touched his arm, left a trail of slime when he yanked it free. One by one, the stateroom doors swung open as they passed. Bringing up the rear, Irwin glimpsed the shambling man-shapes on the thresholds. The stench that bloated out was the reek of the grave. Shuffling leaden footsteps jerked and dragged into the corridor as the living dead fell in behind them.

And back down the corridor, behind the shuffling man shapes, a darker, more sinister sound vibrated through the floor of the car, distinguishable from the rumble of the rails by its regular *thump scrape thump scrape* ... as the ponderous hill of boiling flies forced its mass down the aisle, oozing between the seats.

The buzzing increased, grew frenzied, as the hideous roiling mass advanced, as if the noxious insects had grown angry sensing their presence, the way hornets got when disturbed. Irwin reflected that flies might not have stingers like hornets, but they could bite. He'd encountered biting sand flies vacationing at the Delaware shore when he was little and they'd chewed him up something horrible, so bad his parents had to take him to the doctor to get a shot of Benadryl. Even with the shot, he'd itched all over for days, and the scarlet welts had taken forever to heal. He shuddered at the thought of being surrounded by the mountain of flies advancing toward him. They would literally eat him alive.

Irwin looked away. If he kept staring, rooted to the vibrating boards beneath his feet, he would be consumed by the boiling mass. If this were a game, the very sight of what pursued them would certainly cost him sanity points. He didn't want to think what it might cost him in a Madison Blake dreamie.

He turned and got moving. The door at the end of the car was opening. The others were going through. Then he was out and throwing his back against the door, along with Nora.

They were at the rear of the train, standing on a narrow railed-in platform. The land sloped away on either side of the tracks. On one side in the distance, a range of sharp-peaked mountains jutted against the starry sky. On the other, the desert landscape spread as far as he could see. Irwin watched the sand and cactus roll by. The train wasn't the Silver Streak, but it wasn't exactly crawling either. If they jumped, they risked breaking their necks. On the other hand, how long were he and Nora going to be able to hold the door until the sheer mass of that mountain of flies tore it off its hinges and consumed them?

Doren was on the rail, over it, standing on the other side, hanging on, scanning the slope, his face a frightened grimace, his mouth open, lock-jawed with tension.

"Looks like sand!" Lonnie shouted over the rumble of the rails.

Doren shook his head uncertainly. Irwin started to yell for him not to be a fool, to come back—when the door burst open with an explosive crack, hurling Irwin against the rail.

Doren took one look at the thing in the door and dropped off the train.

Nora ran, jumped high. One foot hit the rail and she launched herself outward, legs pumping as if she were running on air.

Irwin had one leg over the rail when Lonnie screamed. She was being pulled back, away from the rail. Turning, he saw a sight he would remember for the rest of his days. The glistening mass that filled the doorway had sprouted tentacles. Great snaking ropes of swarming, hungry insects waved about in the starlight. One of these encircled Lonnie's ankle. She was on the deck, her leg higher than her back, her foot about to enter the pestilent horde. The horrible buzzing drowned the racket of the tracks, smothered her screams. His stomach heaved as he wrenched Lonnie free and chucked her over the rail.

A tentacle whipped over his head. Irwin ducked and launched himself into the night.

The ground came flying up. Irwin curled into a ball and landed on his shoulder. The teeth-rattling impact was anything but dreamlike. He continued rolling, came to rest face down in the sand. He rose dizzily to all fours, spitting grit, grateful it wasn't rock. His Italian linen jacket was ruined: a sleeve was torn, and his pockets were full of sand.

The *clack-clack* of the train receded into the darkness. By the time Irwin got control of his breath and rose weaving to his feet, it had been swallowed in the distance.

By God! If this was a dreamie, it was more realistic than any he'd ever experienced. His aches and pains were as real as a dentist's drill. He looked around, shivering, and not just from his recent horrific encounter: the night air was cold. Beyond the tracks, the distant mountains stacked up against the Milky Way. On this side, the desert's monotony stretched to the horizon, all but invisible under a sliver of pre-dawn, purple-gray sky.

The others were approaching. Doren was limping. His jeans were soaked with blood where the rat had gnawed him. Irwin couldn't resist taunting, "Hurt yourself, Doren?"

"It's nothing," Doren snapped. His mood was dangerous, but his face was pale.

Dreamie or not, the ache in Irwin's shoulder was painfully authentic. He imagined Doren's pain was a lot worse.

Lonnie put her hand on his arm. "Thank you," she said shakily. The side of her face was scraped. Her eyes were dazed, her hand trembling.

Shock, Irwin thought.

Then why am I not in shock?

Because it's a dream. Because you love it.

Nora appeared unharmed and angrier than he'd ever seen her. She stuck her nose up to his and demanded, "What the fuck is going on?" as if this was all his doing.

"I was hoping, Nora, sweets, that you could enlighten me."

"Come on, we're still in your house, aren't we? You've got that chunky maid of yours throwing switches, putting on a show for us, haven't you?"

"Nothing of the sort, missy," Doren taunted. He was grinning despite his pain. "Michael took the bait. It's a fair bet Blake's on to us."

"We should get out," Lonnie said. "I've seen enough."

Irwin shook his head. "The trap door's closed. I don't think we're going home till Blake lets us. Meanwhile, I vote we enjoy the dreamie."

"Dreamie, my busted ass!" Nora snapped. "This is fucking real!" She stuck out a bloody elbow, scraped raw and gritty with sand.

"Is Mike really dead?" Lonnie's eyes were big.

"Technically no. We're all back in my dad's library, safe and snug. But here ..." He shrugged.

"He's a zombie," Nora said. "What now, *Game Master?*"

Good question. He brightened. So what if Blake was on to them? This was one hell of a dreamie, and he was determined to enjoy it to the fullest. His ticket to Blake's Halloween show had cost him four hundred big ones, and here they were getting a freebie. *Woot!* They'd wake in a few and have Selma's sandwiches. Come to think of it, he thought, rubbing his dry throat, a glass of lemonade would go down pretty good right now.

"Wait for the sun to come up," he said in answer to Nora's question. And, locking his fingers behind his head, he lay back in the sand and closed his eyes.

Waiting for the sun to come up had been a mistake. It had been a scorcher. The land that stretched before them when they started out from the tracks was raw, cracked, red-brown earth, gullied and eroded, varied here and there with scrub grass and gnarled dwarf pines. The sun burning in the white sky roasted them mercilessly. The trek was like walking in an oven and Irwin tossed his ruined jacket before long.

Southwest seemed greener than the rest of the landscape, so they angled off in that direction. The day had seemed like two and Irwin wondered whether the dreamie would ever end. He didn't remember ever having a nightmare last this long.

At noon—or what Irwin took for noon because their shadows were underfoot—they came upon a gray and peeling clapboard hot-dog stand in the middle of nowhere and found a dozen or so beef franks in a microwave rotisserie, just plumping up, and buns and mustard and sauerkraut and onions, and a huge old-fashioned ice chest with its original Coca-Cola logo in red and white across the front. The chest was full of an assortment of pop drinks, floating in a sea of ice water.

Nowhere was there any sign of electrical wires to power the rotisserie or ice chest, but hungry as they were, they didn't dispute the dreamie's minor lapse in verisimilitude but fell to.

"Umm," Doren moaned around a mouthful of dog. "This is fucking delicious."

Irwin didn't disagree. Famished as he was, these dogs were better than the ones from the carts at Times Square. Blake was toying with them. Irwin knew from experience that whenever a game or dreamie offered you a carrot, the stick wasn't far behind.

Sure enough, it was no real surprise when—in the twilight of the day, when they were suffering from sunburn and near dehydration—they encountered another of the Dream Meister's gifts.

"Damn!" Nora stopped in her tracks.

Irwin looked past her. Was it a mirage? Not more than twenty yards away was the shore of the strangest lake he had ever seen.

They had been trudging uphill and only now, with the ground leveling off, were they able to see it. The last of the twilight was fading, and under the hazy starlight, mist coiled like white serpents among the branches that stuck out of the water like bleached skeletal fingers. The setting was eerily silent. No bird, no insect disturbed the stillness, not a ripple touched the pebbled shore. The lake appeared primeval, as if they'd stumbled upon a land that time forgot.

The water, however, looked inviting and smelled … He inhaled: through his parched nostrils came the scent, sweet and wet. Fresh water and not some rank Lovecraftian marsh. Still, Irwin was an experienced gamer: it was a fair bet something monstrous dwelt beneath the lake's dark, unmoving surface.

A flash of fin and glistening scales, a mouth bristling with needle teeth, darted through his mind. Irwin grinned. Blake had implanted that image, and he tipped his metaphorical hat to the Dreamer's attention to detail.

Before he could share his thoughts, Lonnie and Nora broke into a run.

Irwin wanted to run, too; the cool breeze wafting from the lake, carrying the promise of fresh water and relief from the day's agonies, was driving his senses wild, filling his limbs with new-found energy. But it didn't look good for a leader to be the first one into the pool. And if some danger lurked beneath the surface ... well, he thought as Lonnie and Nora splashed into the shallows, it was good to have cannon fodder.

Irwin hung back and fell into step with Doren. The dark-haired boy's limp had worsened. Earlier, he had complained of blisters. After today's trek, Irwin could imagine the condition of his feet inside those narrow, high-heeled ankle boots.

"Care for a drink?" Irwin asked.

"Sure. Drinks're on the house," Doren managed a wincing smile as they approached the lake. "Couple a cold Heinies, please."

"Sounds good." Hot dogs and cold sodas for lunch ... what would be for supper? A fish dinner, perhaps?

Lonnie screamed. It had to be Lonnie; he doubted if Nora was capable of screaming like that—a full-throttle, shrilling, blood-curdling blast that seemed to go on and on, until it ended in a gurgle.

Having frozen for the duration of the scream, Irwin now sprinted down the bank. Doren hobbled after him.

Lonnie was sprawled on her back half in and half out of the water that lapped sullenly at her body like an aqueous beast hungering for flesh. She was convulsing. A hand clutched her throat, the other grasped a clump of sedge. Nearby, Nora was on her hands and knees retching violently.

"What the...?" Doren, coming up behind him expressed his sentiments exactly.

"The water!" Nora gasped between dry heaves, now that her hot dogs were out.

"The water?" Irwin's eyes went big as he turned to the lake. The lake he'd been having fantasies about a moment ago had changed. The water was pellucid, the white-sand bottom undisturbed and pebble-free, clearly seen even by the wan starlight. But something else lit the shallows. The water itself seemed to glow with just enough luminescence to make the sandy bottom look whiter than it should. The lake appeared full of moonlight, though no moon shown overhead. As he watched, the light grew dimmer, and the bottom submerged into shadow.

Irwin knelt beside Lonnie, who had stopped convulsing and lay stiff, one hand clutched to her throat. The way her eyes bulged and her swollen tongue lolled from her mouth, she looked as if she had strangled herself. Irwin assumed the worst. Another of their party dead. Would she rise like Mike and come for them? It occurred to him that the luminescence had subsided when Lonnie's feet stopped thrashing the water. He stood, found a pebble, and sent it skipping across the surface.

Out in the middle, something big burst out of the lake, showering silver droplets into the starlight. Irwin stumbled back, almost tripping over Lonnie's outstretched arm. The thing left a glittering afterimage that looked twenty feet long. The waters closed over it. Lonnie's body rose and fell in the ripples.

Irwin supposed he had been right about there being fish in this lake—but who the hell would want to eat something that lit the night like that? He still saw, out over the water, a humped glowing streak like the afterimage of a camera flash.

Then, as the afterglow disappeared and the turbulence subsided, he saw what Nora had meant when she blurted, "The water!" Where the ripples disturbed the lake, the water was glowing again. He stood at the edge of the shore, leaned closer to see what was causing the phenomenon.

It wasn't the water that glowed. Writhing like maggots, the shallows swarmed, crawled, moiled with tiny, larva-like creatures shining bioluminescently.

He considered scooping up a handful to examine the creatures more closely but thought better of it. Had Nora and Lonnie swallowed these aquatic glowworms? His stomach turned. No longer thirsty, he caught Lonnie under the arms and hauled her out of the water. Doren helped him drag her to higher ground.

They made camp at the crest of a hill overlooking the lake. Or rather, they flopped down, exhausted. Nora made it under her own steam, refusing help. Lying on her side, curled in the fetal position, gasping asthmatically for air, she looked awfully green to Irwin. No one spoke. They were afraid to speak. There was an otherworldliness about the lake that was like nothing Irwin had ever encountered. It wasn't just its primitive appearance; the atmosphere made each of them feel as lonely and as far-removed from humanity as an astronaut might feel stranded on a barren world orbiting a dying sun a billion light years away. It was a world that belonged to fish and insects. From the depths of such a lake, it was easy to imagine Cthulhu rising.

Irwin realized the quality was an effect of Blake's art, and there was nothing begrudging in the appreciation he felt as they sprawled there, watching the fireworks as the larger denizens continued to break the surface, leaving arcs of electric white hanging in the air and ponds of glowworm scintillance in their wake.

Listening for anything that might come for Lonnie's corpse—or one of them—they huddled close for warmth as much as for security. The night grew bitter cold. At length, they slept, and Irwin dreamed fitfully of worms crawling in his belly.

Glowing.

And eating.

Irwin woke huddled against Nora's back, spoon fashion, and Nora was huddled the same way against Doren's. His was the only back exposed to the cold. He sat up shivering and cursed himself for tossing his jacket. It was murk night and mist covered the lake. No longer did behemoths break the surface, yet he heard splashing, a slow rhythmic sound like something emerging from the water.

A patch of mist detached itself and drifted onto the strand. Icy tendrils encoiled Irwin's spine as the man shape stopped at the foot of the hill. Irwin's brain cried, "Run!" but his body was frozen to the earth.

Remembering that he was experiencing a dreamie, that none of this was real, he fought his fear, rose, and, careful not to wake the others, ventured a short way down the slope. His teeth chattered and his knees threatened to buckle as he approached the wraith.

The thing wore tattered jeans and a fur vest. A black hood covered its head. The silken fabric undulated gently in the night air. Its eyes glittered like black stars behind the eye holes.

A blood roar filled Irwin's head. He felt himself drifting, growing weightless. A momentary panic quickly faded into a yielding sense of capitulation, of resignation, as the thing's gaze erased his will and drew him closer. He took an involuntary step forward.

This is wrong! a dim voice somewhere in the back of his brain cried out. Summoning the last of his dwindling will, he tore his eyes from the wraith's mesmeric stare.

His gaze dropped to the corpse face tattooed on the apparition's pale, muscular chest. The ghastly countenance would've stared back at him from behind the crisscross of the vest's rawhide laces—were its eyes and mouth not sewn shut, the stitching coarse, as if done with an upholstery needle and sisal twine.

"What—?" The rest of the sentence didn't get past his parched, fear-choked throat.

The ghostly figure remained silent. The mist floated around it as if it were not some immaterial apparition but a physical presence. Irwin fought the hypnotic pull of its obsidian gaze and kept his eyes focused on the noisome image tattooed on the creature's chest. He tried again: "What do you want?"

The sutures popped. The tattoo's eyes and mouth flung open. Its eyes were a deep blistering red, its mouth bristling with an impossible array of needle teeth that grew longer as the ever-widening maw strained against the rawhide thongs, as if having seen him, the face meant to fly off the chest and launch across the intervening distance. Irwin retreated a step.

"Hey!"

Irwin jerked around, startled by the voice. Nora and Doren had risen. They huddled together at the top of the hill, as if supporting each other.

"What's wrong?" Any other time, Irwin would've enjoyed seeing the fear in Doren's eyes as he searched the lake; under the circumstances, his competitor's expression gave him goosebumps. "Something out there?"

Nora still looked green, her face cheesy in the dim starlight. She, too, searched the lake fearfully. Irwin followed her gaze. The lake was quiet for the moment, as eerily still as when they'd first come upon it. Here and there patches of scintillance rippled through the mist, then went dark. But no monstrous serpent-fish broke its surface.

Irwin looked up and down the shoreline. The wraith was gone. Had he imagined it? Had he risen and sleepwalked down the hill and dreamed the macabre encounter? A dream within a dreamie? Was that Blake's doing or his own?

"Who were you talking to?" Nora demanded.

"Ah, Milady speaks." Irwin affected a cocky tone as he returned to the hilltop. The sarcasm slipped like a well-worn glove over his vulnerability, masking the nausea and fear threatening to unhinge him. "And how are we feeling this lovely evening?"

"Cut the shit, Felder. This ain't no picnic. And it ain't no regular dream either." Nora had reverted to the street-talking tough he'd always suspected lurked beneath the Key Club veneer. "Lonnie's dead. And we're stuck in some madman's idea of a joke."

Irwin looked over to where Lonnie's body lay on the cold ground. She certainly looked dead with her arms folded across her chest, her face collecting dew as her unseeing eyes stared up at the stars of Blake's creation. Again, a chill embraced him. Blake's dreamie was so real; he kept reminding himself they were role-playing and would, eventually, wake in his father's library and share a nervous laugh about their adventure.

"Yeah, and so's Mike. The big question is who's next?" He smiled at each of them as he flopped to the ground. At this point in an RPG, the line would have sounded diabolical; tonight, it seemed ominous and in poor taste.

Nora and Doren didn't respond but sat beside him.

Long after the other two were fast asleep, Irwin watched the edge of the hilltop, wondering if the wraith would reappear. Would he feel its hypnotic gaze upon him, sapping his will? Would it draw him close and let the corpse mouth bulging from its chest devour him? Or lure him into the lake to feed the serpent fish? He wondered if the dawn would ever come, or if the night would be as endless as the day.

And the question *Who's next?* hung in his mind.

Irwin's eyes flicked open.

In the moment of waking, he thought he was dreaming the noise. Then, sitting up, his gaze leaping to the rim of the hill, he thought *The wraith's back!* But that didn't go with the noise; the apparition had been silent.

Dawn was crawling sluggishly over the rim of the world, but except for a thin, gray-silver streak far beyond the lake, night still held sway over the landscape. The electric fish or whatever they were had stopped flashing. The world was silent … except for the noise. Eerie. Like rusty hinges squeaking in the dark. A mechanical sound. There was rhythm to it, a rhythm that made him think of iron birds with hinged wings. Were they coming for him? He shuddered.

Nora was awake now. "What—?"

"Shhh," he cut her off, suddenly afraid that whatever was out there making the noise would zero in on them if they spoke.

Nora poked Doren. He groaned. She clapped her hand over his mouth. He pushed it away and sat up, listening, eyes narrowed, alert, not a trace of wide-eyed sleepiness left.

Irwin touched a finger to his lips. No fool, Doren didn't move.

Other possibilities occurred to Irwin. The sound could be the squeaking of pullies. Or maybe the rhythmic creak of oarlocks—that made more sense—a boat pushing toward them through the mist. His mind's eye pictured a Viking longboat, dragon prow emerging from the mist, the long, low bulwarks slipping through the fog, oars rising and dipping, rising and dipping, powered by moldering, horn-helmed cadavers with murder smoldering in their eyeless sockets. So intensely did he see the image, his eyes squinting into slits, the fear ratcheting up, his heart trip hammering, that, with a jump that startled the others, he thought he saw it.

But what he had taken for helmed men armed with spears were only the branches of dead trees rising spectrally above the mist like the crooked fingers of giants clawing out of their graves, and what he had mistaken for a dragon prow was an exceptionally long bole arcing toward him out of the mist.

"Look," whispered Doren and he jumped again.

Shadowy bat shapes wheeled above Lonnie's body. They looked spooky enough wheeling darkly in the dim light, but their flight was peculiar. They seemed to jerk through the air like bat puppets in a low-budget horror flick. The mechanical, rusty hinge squeaking came from their wings as they flapped through the night.

Nice effect, he thought, despite his unease.

As the creatures weren't attacking, Irwin stood and stretched. "Come on," he said to the others. "Let's get out of here before the sun comes up and it gets hot." Maybe they would find another lunch stand by noontime. Maybe brunch if they started now. He wouldn't mind an Egg McMuffin and a tall, icy Coke, or a mess of IHOP pancakes smothered in blueberry syrup.

Nora grabbed his pants leg. "We've got to bury Lonnie."

His stomach grumbled. He started to remind her they were experiencing a dreamie. Neither Lonnie nor Mike were dead. Nor were Doren's blisters real. This was all make-believe, however real it felt. Sooner or later Blake would tire of toying with them, and they'd wake in his father's library, and they'd feel foolish for having been afraid.

But Nora was right. Not because of human decency or because Lonnie had been a member of their club—not even so much for Lonnie's sake—but so they could sleep come nightfall (if the dreamie lasted that long) without having their heads full of images of Lonnie lying on the hill, her eyes and entrails plucked out by God-knows-what.

"Okay." His shoulders sagged at the thought of the task before them. He had never buried anyone before.

Despite his ragged appearance and his blood-crusted pants, Doren started to quip something off-color or inappropriate. Nora glared at him, daring him to say anything. Looking thirsty and ten years older, the dark-haired boy nodded and lowered his eyes.

The ragged band rose, and Irwin, stomach grumbling, looked about for a rock, a branch, anything he could use to dig a hole deep enough to cover Lonnie's body.

The bat-things still wheeled, squeaking and jerking, overhead when the three tired gravediggers stepped out of the hole and viewed their work.

It wasn't much of a resting place, just barely deep and wide enough to accommodate Lonnie's spare frame. They'd dug the hole in the sand. Irwin had found a piece of driftwood and had set to at one end while Doren and Nora dug out the other end with their hands. It wouldn't last long if something wanted to get at the body, but at least it would keep their consciences clear.

The morning sun was up and the mist steaming off the lake by the time they finished. The sky had turned a hazy blue; soon it would burn white-hot. Irwin saw the bat-things clearly now. His first surmise—that they looked like mechanical bats—turned out to be right. The creatures were indeed mechanical; at least, they appeared so. Dark gray, their vermin torsos resembled the fuselage of a plane. Their wings looked cut from sheet metal, and they flapped through the air like stringless puppets. The effect was comical yet grotesque.

Beyond the lake, marsh grass stretched as far as the eye could see. It was a toss-up between spending another day under the desert sun or finding refuge in the marshes. Either way the day promised to be brutally hot, but at least the marsh land would have water. And Irwin knew from gaming: when one strategy wasn't working, try another.

Doren and Nora seemed loath to touch Lonnie's body. Disgusted and anxious to get moving, Irwin started to grab the corpse by the arms and haul it into the pit.

"Be gentle!" Nora said.

Irwin glared at her. "Then you goddamned do it!" When she didn't snap back, he saw she was genuinely afraid.

Overnight, rigor mortis had set in and Lonnie's body lay as they had left it the previous evening. Nora had folded Lonnie's arms over her small breasts, and they remained folded as he wedged his hands under her arm pits and slid her into the grave. The backs of her exposed arms were purple with lividity. Despite the stiffness of her body, her flesh was soft and unnaturally cool. Irwin shuddered at the touch.

"All right, put her feet in," he growled at Doren.

"Grave's too short." Doren said with conviction.

Crap, Doren was right. Taking the corpse under the arms again, Irwin scooted Lonnie up so that her head and her feet were propped on the sloping ends of the grave, while her back lay flat on the bottom.

They all stood a moment looking down at Lonnie, their sweating bodies cooling in the slight breeze stirring off the lake. Lonnie appeared to have withered overnight. Her cheeks were sunken. Her skin stretched tightly over the bones of her face. Her mouth was ajar, her eyes half-open.

A disturbing thought occurred to Irwin. Since supper hadn't been provided, as lunch had the day before, he wondered, purely in terms of gaming logic, if they, the players, were supposed to turn to cannibalism for sustenance.

On the other hand, perhaps lunch awaited them somewhere out there.... Yeah, imagine eating Lonnie then finding a burger joint giving away free shakes, sandwiches, and fries. More irony. Yep, judging by what the Dream Meister had thrown at them, that would be right up Blake's alley.

Irwin used his piece of driftwood lengthwise to push the sand back in; Doren and Nora knelt and began feverishly filling the hole by hand. The hole was half-filled—Lonnie's midsection covered, her feet and head still unburied—when the body started convulsing.

"Holy sheep shit!" Irwin blurted as he jumped clear of the pit.

Sand flew out of the grave as Lonnie's head and feet pounded the ground as if some invisible hand was shaking her violently. Her arms—no longer constrained by rigor mortis—flopped over the sides of the hole. The violence of the convulsions increased. The sand slipping under the corpse was filling the pit, so that Lonnie seemed to be rising from the grave.

The convulsions stopped, leaving Lonnie more out than in. She had worked her way up in the grave so that her back rested against the shallow slope and her arms and head were sprawled back over the rim of the pit as if she were soaking in a shallow tub.

And still the corpse moved. Irwin watched as the muscles rippled and writhed unnaturally under Lonnie's skin. Every muscle in her body seemed to be knotting and crawling, dancing to an alien and unbearable rhythm. The corpse's midsection arched out of the grave, showering sand.

Its mouth and eyes yawned open as the flesh stretched even tauter; a sound like escaping air rattled past the thing's swollen gray tongue. Then, as the gravediggers stood around the pit frozen in disbelief, light began to glow from Lonnie's mouth and nostrils and from her glazed dead eyes. Dim at first, the glow flickered, then waxed stronger until it became an eerie lambent light. Had it been night, the rictus would have looked like a hideous jack-o'-lantern. Even by day, the effect was unnerving. Lonnie's dead eyes took on a sinister semblance of life as the ghastly light shone behind her dead whites.

The corpse collapsed back into its shallow grave with enough force to kick up puffs of sand. The chest and stomach cavities bulged and rippled. The throat and face swelled as if something was rising in its gullet, about to pour out of the cadaver's straining mouth. The thing had lost all semblance to the Lonnie he knew.

The light intensified.

A fat glowing insect squeezed out of her left nostril. Then bugs were boiling out of her straining mouth. Mosquitos the size of cockroaches, glowing a brilliant electric white as they swarmed into the air.

The trio were under attack. Nora yelped as several of the things lighted on her. Irwin learned why a second later when two lit on his arm and dug in with their glowing stingers. He yelped. They didn't just sting—they gave off an electric shock. He dropped to one knee and slammed the back of his arm into the sand, knocking the things off. Their wings broken, the insects squirmed in the sand. His arm was on fire as if he'd been stung by jellyfish. That had happened to him once on vacation in Florida when he was eight. Splashing in the surf, he had felt something brush against his ankles, and instantly a web of pain had encircled his limbs like hot needles that wouldn't stop stinging. It had hurt so bad he had cried.

Irwin knocked more of the things to the ground as he rose, and he stomped them under his sneaker. Their glow faded and went out. *At least they're killable*, he thought as the three survivors danced around swatting the things.

Then something bigger, much bigger, than the bugs flashed past him, sheet-metal wings nearly grazing his ear. The mechanical bats were swooping into the midst of the swarm, mechanical mouths open, devouring. The bat horde, squeaking, flapping, diving, blackened the sky. Irwin kept his head down and let them do their work.

For a while, the frenzied, high-pitched squeaking, like a hundred rusty swings, filled the air. Then the bats were retreating. He looked up to see a dark thundercloud of bats, their bellies pulsing with thunderless lightning as they flew over the lake and marshes beyond. Except for a few wounded insects struggling in the sand, the mosquito-like swarm was gone, obliterated.

Irwin stood. His back, left arm, and right leg burned as if they'd been ravaged by fire ants.

"They were waiting for the bugs to come out of Lonnie," Doren said, watching the cloud recede as he struggled to his feet.

"You two okay?" he asked when no one asked about him. Unexpectedly, Nora turned on him.

"You've got to be fucking kidding!" she snapped. Defeated, face streaked with tears and sand, she still looked angry enough to eat nails.

Doren was grinning. "What's the matter, cry-baby? Can't take the pressures of the game?"

Nora lunged for him, scratched his face, drew two thin lines of blood from his cheek.

"You bitch!"

Doren slugged her. Irwin felt in his gut the solid smack of the boy's fist against her cheekbone. Nora went down. Without thinking, and totally out of character as he would realize when he had time to think about it, he stepped in and clipped Doren on the chin, dropping the dark-haired boy to his knees.

"What'd you do that for?" Doren rubbing his chin.

"Don't butt in on my fights!" Nora scowled. She was up and pissed and she karate-chopped the air as if to end the matter.

Irwin felt like slapping her. Goddamn, the bitch could tee the shit out of him! But in the interest of conserving energy, he walked past Nora and Doren and started out along the strand, intending to circle the lake and strike out through the marshes.

"Where are you going now?" Nora called after him.

"Away from there." He jerked his thumb toward Lonnie's corpse lying half in and half out of her grave, gaping at the sky, a prey to whatever came along.

"Wait!" Nora yelled. "Aren't we going to finish burying Lonnie?"

"Suit yourself. I'm not stopping you." He stepped up his pace.

Doren started after him.

Nora took one last, hesitant look toward the lake. Except for a few glitters of sun-dazzle on the water, the surface was placid. She turned and followed the living.

Doren was weak. Babbling. Mumbling aloud to himself. But now his voice grew strident. Irwin, who had tuned out the boy's complaining, noted the change in tone and looked back at the straggling teenager.

Doren hobbled along, looking as if he were about to topple onto his face. His blisters had gotten so bad, he'd abandoned his useless ankle boots. The marshes, consisting mainly of mud and soft grasses, hadn't been so bad, but the foothills of the mountains that blocked the horizon had grown slowly out of the distance as the day progressed, and by the time the white ball of the sun waxed red and perched above the rim of the low mountains, the ground had grown drier, the grasses shorter and less verdant, the landscape hillier. Soon they found themselves winding through what seemed like a maze of narrow canyonlike crevasses with steep walls of striated sandstone. Bands of light and dark reds and a darker purplish band lower down, near the rocky floor told a tale of geologic epochs.

Doren's feet, shuffling across the hot stone, were bleeding; it was only a matter of time till he dropped. Seeing that Irwin had stopped, Doren stopped, too.

"Come on," Nora growled. "We can't stop here!"

"Why not?" Irwin said, but began walking anyway, knowing she was right.

Although they had drunk their fill from an algae-covered pond in the marshes, heedless of the consequences because they had no choice, his tongue felt like flaking, dry-rotted leather, and he kept his mouth closed so the heat wouldn't suck up whatever saliva he had left.

Nora had taken the lead. He trailed behind her, Doren stumbling along beside him.

"What's for dinner?" Doren croaked in all seriousness, and Irwin wondered if the guy's brains were fried. They'd encountered no roach coach or hot-dog stand, and they were all weak with hunger. Irwin didn't regret not eating Lonnie—especially after seeing what swarmed out of her—but the thought had crossed his mind more than once during the long hungry trek.

Nora stopped suddenly as they rounded a curve in the crevasse. Irwin almost bumped into her. He saw what she was gaping at.

Ahead, about to turn the next bend, were two figures that looked damned familiar. He saw them only for an instant and Nora was blocking part of the view, but it looked like …

"Lonnie and Mike!" Doren shouted beside him.

"But they're dead," Nora said.

Doren laughed. It was a dry sandpapery sound. "Like Irwin said," he rasped as if afflicted with laryngitis. "You can't really die in a dreamie. Come on." He slapped Irwin on the back hard enough to sting, as he hobbled past, his feverish brain having suddenly awakened at the sight of their missing comrades. "Hey, Mike! Lonnie!" Doren yelled, but they had already turned a bend in the narrowing crevasse. Doren pushed by Nora and darted after their lost companions, seemingly oblivious to his bleeding feet.

Irwin did not question how Mike and Lonnie had gotten ahead of them. There was a logic to dreams and dreamies, but it certainly didn't follow the chronological or syllogistic reasoning of the waking world. He hurried ahead and made the turn in time to see Doren grab Mike by the shoulder.

Mike and Lonnie spun on him. Their eyes had rolled up in their heads exposing bloodless whites. Their flesh was the gray of bad meat. The side of Mike's face still oozed from chewed flesh. His shirt was slick with blood. The bug light still blazed from Lonnie's eyes and mouth, casting a garish glow over the canyon walls, as if she had become a human torch. The two of them snarled like wild dogs, exposing glistening canines, inhumanly long. Doren gasped, backpedaled as their hands fell on him. He screamed.

Irwin started to back away, but Nora ran into him. Seeing what was happening, she shoved him forward and shouted, "Help him!"

But Doren was already dying, the veins in his throat and right wrist exposed, jetting crimson fountains over the sandy rock. Mike chewed at the neck wound; Lonnie slurped noisily at the wrist. Doren's horror-filled eyes glazed and rolled back in his skull even as Irwin watched.

"Oh my God," Nora whimpered.

Irwin shuddered.

Mike and Lonnie looked up now. In the blue dusk that had pooled in the bottom of the crevasse since the sun had passed over the mountain's rim, their eyes, worm-white a moment ago, were red and darkly luminous, the eyes of demons. Blood dripped from their chins as they smiled. The ghouls dropped Doren's body, leapt over it before it hit the ground, and came after them faster than Irwin would have thought possible.

He and Nora nearly knocked each other down getting away, careening off each other as they ran back the way they had come. Laying his sneakers to the sand, flat-out racing as he never had before, he glanced back and saw Mike and Lonnie loping after them. Lonnie's soiled yellow dress and Mike's blood-slick, checkered shirt flapped behind them. They ran hunched over, claw-like hands extended, greedily racing more like rabid, two-legged wolves than the shambling stereotype of the living dead.

Irwin hooked a left. A shadow loomed before him. A cavemouth. Grabbing Nora by the collar and yanking her off her feet, he ducked into the narrow space. Inside, the cave widened. He shoved Nora to one side, flattened himself out against the other as the zombies loped by, mouths dripping blood, murder blazing in their eyes.

His wet footsteps echoing off the slime-covered walls were the only sounds. Irwin listened for other noises, praying he would hear anything he might run into before it jumped out at him as he rounded the next bend or ducked under the next overhang. The thought of running into another of Blake's horrors in these claustrophobic tunnels was especially frightening since he and Nora had parted company. He was on his own now.

The cavern into which they'd fled had turned out to be an antechamber that led onto a subterranean labyrinth, a maze of twisting passages that now widened, now shot up to eight or nine feet, now dropped to three. Branches opened right and left; but no matter which way they turned, the tunnels all seemed to lead downward like some passageway to a Lovecraftian hell where sightless, albino monstrosities mindlessly gibbered and danced to the beating of drums made of human flesh, and white worms whose faces bore a blasphemous resemblance to man's writhed unspeakably amid the niter and slime.

As the path grew steeper and the ceilings lower, the walls had become coated with a gray-glowing phosphorescence that had gradually thickened, growing from a glistening sheen to a thick mucus layer that seemed to ooze from the porous rock, slide down the walls, and collect on the tunnel floor, making traction slippery and dangerous. At first, they were grateful for the light, however dim, but, as the reek of sulfur and excrement cloyed the air, they had come close to vomiting.

At times, the passage had squeezed down to less than three by three and they had taken a bath in the slime, crawling over the stone on their hands and knees while scraping their backs against the greasy ceiling. The last time they'd crawled, they'd encountered spiders. The insects turned out to be harmless, but the way the ghostly scurrying white shadows, almost invisible in the near darkness, crunched beneath their hands and knees, had been unnerving. The ordeal had left them tired and irritable.

They would gladly have returned to the surface—no matter what horrors they might encounter there they would, at least, be out in the open and not crawling through this claustrophobic nightmare terrified of getting stuck or crushed under a gazillion tons of rock—but, as if the Dream Meister was orchestrating their progress, every path they took led inevitably downward. They were hopelessly lost.

So, when they came to a fork and the left-hand tunnel was taller than the right, Nora decided impatiently that they should proceed left, into the larger tunnel.

"I'm sick of crawling!" she said, stamping her foot, splashing muck. Her small dark eyes glittered angrily in the twilight. When he explained that right-footed people—those with dominant right legs—tended to circle to the left because their right legs took longer steps than their left, and that, according to what he'd read in an online survival manual, right-footed people should bear to the right to avoid traveling in circles, she'd rounded on him, arm flexed for a punch, her face radiating disdain. "So what if I go in circles, Irwin? Maybe I'll end up back where we came in."

He knew from the tone of her voice that she was set on taking the left-hand tunnel, alone if necessary.

"Are you prepared to face Lonnie and Mike and probably Doren as well now?"

"I'll take my chances," she growled, her big nose thrust at him.

And so she had. So had they both: she taking the left-hand tunnel because it appeared roomier; he taking the right mostly because of the principle of the matter.

Now he was having second thoughts.

The downward path had steepened considerably. Already, he'd crawled twice since leaving Nora, the last time on his belly: the fear that he would get stuck, that all those tons of rock he felt pressing down on him would, at last, crush the life out of him, was unnerving.

As he slogged along, he toyed with the idea that his subterranean descent symbolized his journeying deeper into the dream world, i.e., traveling farther from the waking world. Did the road to wakefulness lay behind him, back the way they had come? Back across the marshes? Beyond the lake? Back across the desert? He groaned. By that convoluted logic, climbing a mountain would take him home.

But there were no mountains here and every turn he took led deeper into the Blake's VR hell.

Irwin was trembling with exhaustion, about ready to sit down and go to sleep, when he heard the scream. It chilled his bones. Echoing off the dank walls, it sounded far away, yet it was clearly Nora's strident voice.

He ran back the way he had come, dropping to all fours when the ceiling lowered; ran on, crouching, when it rose again. His head more than once scraped rock. Strangely, returning seemed shorter than going, and, for once—as if the Dreamer wanted him to go back—the path led upward. The scream grew loud as he burst into the intersection where he and Nora had parted company. He took the other, larger fork.

The passage got bigger as he ran downhill, the dark gray stone around him glistening with phosphorescent light. Secondary passages branched off to the left and right, but he kept to the straightest track, the one out of which the screams welled. His skull vibrated with the intensity of Nora's shrieks. Apparently, he'd been wrong in his earlier assumption that Nora was incapable of screaming in abject terror.

He rounded a corner and there she was. On her back. Writhing on the tunnel floor. Her attackers looked like slick white eels. Wide circular mouths lined with rows of needle teeth battened on her flesh. He had seen a picture of a similar monstrosity in an encyclopedia: "lamprey" the caption had read. Flicking their tails as they bore in, the creatures attacked, hissing, teeth snapping. Nora's clothes were in bloody tatters. Her face where chunks of meat had been gouged from her cheek and forehead was slick with blood. Two of her fingers were missing. Her eyes bulged out of her head, her mouth opened wide, her shrieks splitting his eardrums.

"*Help me! Oh God! Oh God!*" Her head whipped wildly side to side. While she tried to haul off one attacker, another bit. She flailed her arms in an effort to shake them loose, but the slick, scaleless horrors clung to her by their teeth even as their bodies whipped about in the air.

A ripple ran up her pants leg. She thrashed frantically, her head tattooing a wild beat on the rock, her feet playing a macabre accompaniment.

"*One's inside me!*"

The horror in those words unnerved Irwin. He could only watch as she screamed. "*Oh God! Oh God! Aeeeiiiii!*"

Her scream lopped off abruptly. A red flower bloomed on her chest, and with a sound like a strongman ripping a Philadelphia telephone directory in half, the *vagina dentata* image on her tee shirt exploded in a scarlet geyser, and a loathsome, tooth-filled head reared out of the gory cavity. Her dark eyes glazed over as her body convulsed.

Irwin staggered back, legs rubbery, hand reaching for the wall, seeking support.

And recoiled. Under his touch, the wall had yielded. Though still gray and thickly slimed, the tunnel walls no longer possessed the texture of rough stone but had transformed into what looked like the collective hides of a thousand Elephant Men, crusted with ulcerated lumps and suppurating sores.

His eyes ping-ponged back to Nora. Having fed, the eels were pouring out of the corpse, squirting through the slime toward him. He ran. Sluggishly. Before, the tunnel floor had been hard (as his torn pants' knees and scrapped elbow attested), now the ground beneath his sneakers was soft and squishy as, apparently, the stone had been transformed into rotten meat. The putrescent stench that pervaded the claustrophobic air burned his eyes and choked his airways.

Behind him, the agile bloodsuckers whipped across the rubbery surface. With his one glance back, he saw that Madison Blake had added a further complication to his travails: the tunnel was closing, walls cracking, splitting, spurting blood and pus that whipped in a foaming, gushing tide. Nora's corpse was consumed by the tightening walls. Even the eels, swift as they were, weren't speedy enough to escape the contracting tunnel.

Lungs burning, pain stitching his side, Irwin ran for his life. All thoughts that this was only a dreamie, that you couldn't actually die in a dreamie, were forgotten in his mad dash. The terror of being crushed by the sphincter-like squeeze of those collapsing walls energized his oxygen-deprived limbs. Blind with terror, he sprinted back the way he had come, thankful that this was the bigger tunnel and he wasn't reduced to crawling.

He burst back into the intersection and skidded to a halt.

The wraith that had appeared to him on the lakeshore stood before him. The hood still undulated though there was no draft in the tunnel. Eyes like black starlight blazed from the eyeholes. The corpse face on the apparition's chest appeared glad to see him: it opened its maw and showed him teeth.

Panting, fists clenched at his sides, deep into fight or flight mode, Irwin turned to flee, but the constricting tunnel was closed now, the stone wall rough but showing no sign of a former passage. Gone, too, was the main tunnel through which he and Nora had descended from the surface. The wraith blocked the smaller fork he had taken earlier.

While he weighed his chances of squeezing past the apparition without injury and considered the futility of entering the ever-narrowing tunnel to nowhere he'd traversed before, the wraith reached up and removed its hood.

Transfixed, all thoughts of horror and panic replaced by a sense of wonder, an electric thrill of recognition, Irwin gaped at the apparition's face. Long and thin, blessed with cheekbones women, and some men, cooed over, thin lips curled in a sardonic smile exposing dazzling white teeth, longish dark hair curled over his ears, a vagrant forelock slashed like a raven's wing across a handsome brow, the face before him belonged to none other than the Dream Meister himself, Madison Fucking Blake, Master of Disaster, Duke of Death and Destruction. Blake had inserted himself into the dreamie—or rather his avatar.

Star-struck, all Irwin could say at first was, "Wow!" Then he remembered he'd hacked into the man's dreamatron and the Dreamer had him by the short hairs. Again, his gaze went to the corpse face straining against the leather thongs, then to the small tunnel leading only to despair, and a great weariness fell over him. He was done. No place to run.

"Enough," he said. "We were curious. I'm a huge fan. We all are. Just let us wake up."

The avatar's black eyes made him dizzy. He felt himself falling, as if into a void, a cosmic emptiness where the cells of his body would drift apart until he was only a spreading mist of atoms, and he would be beyond pain beyond sleeping or waking and exist only in a state of nothingness.

Nada y pues nada.

The avatar beckoned, breaking the spell, and Irwin saw he was gesturing with a pale, long-fingered hand with black-painted nails to the mouth of the last remaining passage. But that tunnel, too, was gone. In its place he recognized the door through which they'd escaped from the rat-filled darkness into the zombie train. Again, he was struck by how much it resembled the massive, six-paneled door to his father's library. Was the Dream Meister offering him a way home? An exit from the dreamie's horrors? Or a portal to even worse nightmares?

He felt like the man in "The Lady or the Tiger" story, who, presented with two identical doors, was tasked to choose. Behind one door a beautiful woman, behind the other a hungry beast. Except he was being offered a single door and his choice was stay or go.

Stay, with nowhere to run and that toothsome corpse face straining to get at him? Or take his chances and hope Blake was offering him an exit to the waking world?

His dilemma reminded him of an online article he had read concerning free will in dreamies. According to the author, a psychologist who specialized in the effects of dreamies on live audiences, free will didn't exist in dreamies. Sure, you could role-play some of the characters, experience the dreamie from various viewpoints—which thousands of fans did by attending concerts on multiple nights—even make flight or fight decisions. And there were choices: use chainsaw or flamethrower, enter a building or continue down the street, climb the stairs to the attic or descend to the basement. But these weren't really choices. The dreamer anticipated every contingency and programed the varying plotlines into the dreamie. Making choices resulted in your pursuing predetermined paths. Following this logic, at least while the audience was under the influence so to speak, the dreamer was godlike, determining their fates. And the illusion that one was exercising free will in making choices was just that—an illusion.

But what about chance? His preoccupation with games since childhood had led him to appreciate their construction. Understanding the rules of the game—not just the "rules" printed on the sheet that came in the box but the game's underlying structure—had been instrumental in his success at gaming. True, there were games like chess and checkers that allowed no opportunity for chance to mar their elegant design, the mathematical precision of their movements, but the introduction of dice in other games, as well as spinning wheels and shuffled decks of specialty cards, offered an element of chance to determine outcomes.

He seized on the thought as he would a lifeline if he were adrift at sea, which pretty much summed up his condition. In a fate-determined environment like a chess game or a dreamie, the introduction of chance would be tantamount to chaos. Chance took some of the power of predestination out of the dreamer's hands.

"I have a proposal for you." His voice cracked. (God, what wouldn't he do for a sip of Selma's lemonade!)

The avatar cocked its head ever so slightly. The corpse face stopped straining against the laces and appeared interested.

"You're the Games Master and the Master Dreamer. You control all. I propose we introduce the element of chance into your dreamland." Inspired, he considered another bonbon that might appeal to the Dreamer. "You wouldn't be the world's greatest Dreamer if you didn't have a competitive spirit. As things are, competition in dreamies exists only between audience members and your creations. What if you were challenged?" The corpse face growled, its teeth grew longer and curved over the rawhide laces as if it would snap its bonds. "I don't mean challenge you personally," he quickly added. "But what if we introduced an element of chance? Wouldn't your dreamies be more interesting—to you—if they offered outcomes other than what you programmed?" The corpse face relented; its teeth shortened, slightly. "Just a thought: what if you introduced dice into the game?"

The avatar's black eyes glittered as if it were considering his challenge.

A coin appeared in Irwin's outstretched hand. He understood: as there was only one door and only two choices—go or stay—and no multiple spaces or places to advance to, a flip of a coin logically replaced a roll of the dice.

In the tunnel's dim phosphorescence, the gold coin glowed as if it possessed a light of its own. It wasn't perfectly round but worn away on the edges as if it were very old and had changed hands a thousand times over the centuries. Its obverse or front side featured a Maltese cross with castles and lions in the cross's angles. Latin letters circled the cross on the coin's much-worn edges. The reverse side featured palm trees and more letters and numbers above wavy lines that looked like stylized waves. A Spanish doubloon? Spain had ruled the waves before the Armada.

Irwin ran his thumb over its worn surface. The edges of the letters and images were worn smooth. Like so much in the dreamie, the coin felt as real as anything he'd ever touched in the waking world.

He showed the avatar the coin cross side up. "This is heads." He flipped the coin over showing the palm trees on its reverse. "This is tails. Heads I go through the door; tails you open the tunnel behind me and let me out of here."

Blake's avatar made no commitment.

Irwin flipped the coin. It glittered as it spun, rose till it almost touched the roof of the passage, and fell. It hit the stone floor that had somehow, as happened in dreams, grown smooth. The coin landed on its edge and spun and kept on spinning. It seemed to spin forever as Irwin held his breath. Then it began to wobble and, finally, rattled to a rest.

The cross with the castles and lions gleamed from the floor.

Heads!

His decision was made for him: *Go!*

He looked at the door behind the avatar, licked his lips. What lay behind it? The lady or the tiger? He'd let chance make the decision for him. But with a sinking feeling he remembered whose coin he had tossed. Had he really opened the door to random outcomes? Or was he still playing by house rules?

Blake's avatar waited. Corpse face watched him from behind its leather restraints.

Tired of thinking, hoping the Dreamer was finished with him and the portal would lead him home, he squared his shoulders, looked the avatar in the eye, and said, "Screw it. Let's do this."

The avatar stepped aside. The door swung open. The corpse mouth hissed as he passed, and the reek of offal billowed out. Irwin quickened his step.

The door closed behind him. He turned and it was gone. The moist brick walls and dirty cement floor told him he was back in the rat-filled basement room into which he and the others had fallen at the beginning of their journey. The rats were gone now, the room lighted.

He turned back to the room and saw he was not alone.

The others were there: Lonnie and Nora and Doren and Mike. His companions were as dirty and travel worn as he, but they appeared far worse for their injuries. The side of Mike's face was a pulpy mess, his checkered shirt, even his cargo shorts, a bloody ruin. A dazzling electric glow shown from Lonnie's eyes and mouth. Doren's black designer jeans were ripped and bloody from the rat bite and severed veins protruded from the raw wounds in his neck and wrist. Nora looked worst of all: with her exploded chest it was a wonder she was standing.

But worse than their wounds—far worse—their eyes were dead, vacuous, as if their souls or minds or whatever made them the individuals they had been had vacated their bodies.

All part of the dreamie, he told himself.

The thought reminded him that nothing had changed, that he was still stuck in Blake's nightmare. The game had been fixed all along. The Dreamer dispensed fate. Chance had no place in the dreamie's universe, and he'd left free will in his father's library the moment he and his friends put on headsets and hacked Blake's dreamland.

He had no time to further consider the philosophical implications of dreamies or to lament his choices. His fellow gamers were coming in low, crouching like stalking animals, hands extended claw-like before them. They closed around him. Lonnie and Doren circling to his left, Nora to his right, Mike straight ahead like an NFL linebacker hell bent on sacking the quarterback. With the brick wall at his back, they had him cornered. Irwin scanned the big room beyond. There was no door, only brick walls. The place was a prison, a trap. There was nowhere to run. Even if he broke through their ranks, they would get him eventually. Blake was ending the custom dreamie he'd fashioned just for them, and Irwin's demise at the hands of his fellow hackers was to be the climax. Maybe he should feel honored, but he felt only terror and a bottomless hopelessness.

"Come on guys. Attacking me isn't going to get us home."

Pleading wasn't going to work. Mike, no longer the easygoing teddy bear, looked as big and dangerous as a grizzly as he lumbered toward him, a growl rumbling from his chest. Doren and Nora looked nastier than they ever had in life, with their bloodied clothes and snarling sneers. Even sweet, polite Lonnie, who never had a bad word to say about anyone and a smile for everyone, looked as dangerous as any wilderness beast with her bared teeth and blazing eyes.

Mike took a swipe at him. Irwin ducked. The open hand barely missed taking his head off. Irwin tried to dodge under the big guy's arm, but Mike shoved him back with his other hand. Irwin slammed against the bricks.

The wall knocked the breath out of him. Bright lights swam before his vision. He shook it off, raised his arm to ward off further attack. Lonnie grabbed his arm and bit into his wrist. He screamed as her teeth sank through meat and grated on bone. Calling on reserves he didn't know he had, he punched her in the face, sending her sprawling on the gritty floor.

But Doren and Nora were on him. Nora came in low under his arm and sank her teeth into his side just below his ribs. One of her arms wrapped around his back, the other held onto his belt. Doren grabbed his face and bit his ear. Doren's thumb jabbed into his mouth and wrenched his cheek back. Irwin bit the intruding digit as hard as he could. He tasted blood and felt his teeth grind on bone, but if Doren felt pain, he didn't relent but kept biting until Irwin felt the top of his ear rip free and saw Doren shake his head like a dog with a piece of steak, splattering Irwin's eyes with his own blood.

Irwin spat Doren's blood out of his mouth. "Stop it!" He hammered Nora's back and head but didn't dislodge her. She snarled as she shook her head like a pit bull with a cat in its teeth, as if trying to rip his side open to get at the organs inside. Lonnie was back, coming in fast, nails reaching for his eyes. Her open mouth was a floodgate of brilliant light, as if dragon fire were pouring past her snarling lips. Mike's fist slammed into his chest over his heart, knocking the wind out of him and driving him into the bricks again. He swung his own fist to ward off Lonnie's attack … and slashed her across the eyes.

Lonnie staggered back, hand covering her left eye. Half her nose hung from a strip of exposed cartilage. She removed her hand and snarled at him, head jutting forward, snapping her teeth. A deep bleeding wound stretched diagonally from her eyebrow, across her nose and opposite cheek. Her left eyeball was ruptured, blood and fluid running down her face.

Irwin's ears roared. Nausea swelled up his throat at the sight of Lonnie's ruined eye. He gazed in wonder at the object that had appeared in his hand. A hunting knife, its newly christened blade at least seven inches long. Blake was making sport of them. Irwin didn't have time to contemplate the image of the Dreamer comfortably seated at his dreamatron enjoying his deadly puppet show. The pain in his side was unbearable. He drove the knife into Nora's back. Oblivious to the damage the blade surely caused, she continued to grind her teeth into his side. With an effort, he pulled the blade free and drove it into the back of her neck, severing her spine. That did it. She fell to the concrete spasming.

Doren grabbed for his other ear. Irwin ducked and plunged the blade into the boy's heart. Doren's nails gouged furrows into his cheek, but the knife did the job and the once cocky gamester staggered back flailing his arms as he toppled to the floor.

Mike's fist whistled past, an inch from his nose, and Lonnie, her remaining eye still blazing like a Roman Candle, leapt onto his back. Her legs wrapped around his body, her hands grasped his hair and shirtfront. She sank her teeth into his damaged ear. He threw himself back against the wall to dislodge her, but Lonnie only bit deeper. Mike grabbed for his face, and he slashed a long red swath down the big guy's forearm. Hot blood sprayed him from the severed veins.

With his free hand, Irwin grabbed Lonnie's hair and tried to throw her over his shoulder to the floor. When that didn't work, he stabbed behind his head three times in rapid succession hoping the blade would get her and not his own neck. He must have hit something vital; she stopped mauling him and slid off his back. That left only Mike. Irwin had never seen the big guy move so fast. Again, Irwin ducked as Mike's meaty fist whistled over his head. He came up inside the bigger boy's defense and stabbed upward, driving the blade through the flesh under the boy's chin. The blade punched through Mike's throat and into his brain. Irwin wrenched the knife out and tried to jump aside, but the big guy grabbed him as he toppled. Mike's throat gushed a red geyser into Irwin's face as his momentum drove them both into the wall. Irwin cracked his head against the bricks and his lights went out.

Irwin came to in his father's library. An overwhelming joy brought tears to his eyes. He was home! They'd escaped Blake's never-ending nightmare!

It took him a moment to realize he was lying on the floor looking up at the coffered ceiling. Then the pain registered. His head throbbed and his side was in agony. He put a hand to his head. It came away bloody.

His other hand was bloody, too. He stared at them, stunned. They were crimson, fingertips to elbows. He rolled onto his side.

Under the table, he made out the legs of his seated companions. Mike's thick, hairy ones, Lonnie's slim ones, Doren's bloody jeans.

That startled him.

He rose to one elbow. A sea of crimson spread beneath and around the table. His Dad's terribly expensive Persian carpet was ruined. He gagged on the blood reek. So much blood.

Dad's going to kill me.

He remembered. He brought his hand to his head and nearly swooned from the rush of adrenaline that roared through his vagus nerve. The top of his left ear was missing. He pressed his hand against his side, felt the teeth marks through the hole in his shirt. Nora had tried to take a chunk out of him.

He groaned. He grabbed the edge of the table for leverage and tried to pull himself up. It took two tries: his bloody hand slipped on the polished oak the first time and he nearly clipped his chin going down. What he glimpsed during the fleeting second his eyes were above the table brought him back up fast.

His fellow gamers were seated where they'd sat when they entered Blake's domain. They still wore their VR headsets. They were all slumped over the table like a bunch of kindergarteners with their heads on their desks during naptime. But this was no kindergarten scene, nor were they napping. He stared at their still, seemingly lifeless bodies. Took in the litany of wounds that ravaged their flesh.

A length of blood-streaked bone peeped out of the long gash in Mike's forearm. Blood spread across the table and dripped down into his lap from the wound rupturing his throat.

Lonnie's nose was half off her face. He knew if he removed her headset only one eye would stare across the table.

Nora's neck wound had stopped pumping, but a great puddle haloed her head.

Doren's head and neck were intact, but Irwin remembered the impact of the knife hilt slamming into the boy's ribs as the blade pierced his heart.

Irwin collapsed into his chair. Again, he examined his bloody hands.

My God! What have I done?

The library door opened.

"Ir—"

His father, dressed in his golf clothes, stopped just inside the room, mouth open, sentence forgotten. His eyes grew wide under his bushy brows as he surveyed the chaos. When his gaze finally settled on Irwin, he echoed his son's thoughts.

"My God, what have you done?"

⁂

The lights came on automatically as the Dreamer rose from alpha into beta, the wave form of the waking mind. Seated at his dreamatron, its gleaming control panel curving around him, Madison Blake experienced a moment of vertigo; then the room came into focus.

He checked his Apple watch. Three hours had passed while he was under. He stretched his arms, rolled his neck. He was thirsty. He would get a Perrier from the fridge in a minute. First, he wanted to check out tonight's work.

He fast-forwarded and sampled some of the more hellacious scenes. After a while, he removed the headset, powered off his machine. For an impromptu piece, he found the results quite chilling. The scene where the albino lampreys burst out of the one called Nora's chest brought a smile to his lips. And the look on Irwin's face when he found his friends on the other side of the door was priceless. His mind set to work how he could use the material in his Halloween concert. Maybe he should downgrade his security protocols, let more curious visitors in. His dreamwork had never come so easily or felicitously.

He pushed back, rose, and went to get that drink. Screw the mineral water; this called for bubbly.

⁂

The following day

"This morning police arrested a Philadelphia teen suspected

in the slaying of four local teenagers with a knife. The youths were reported to have been playing an online virtual reality role playing game. According to the coroner's initial report, all the victims died from stab wounds. One of the victims bore what appears to be a defensive wound on his arm, indicating a struggle, although the victims are alleged to have been found seated at a table. No motive has been given for the murders. No knife was found at the scene.

"In other news, popular dreamie artist, Madison Blake's much-anticipated Halloween show at the Wells Fargo Center has sold out and, due to popular demand, Ticketmaster has announced additional tickets will go on sale at midnight tonight. Franklyn, you're a dreamie fan. Are you excited?"

"Absolutely. I'll be there opening night. Taking the wife. Can't wait. Word on the net is the Dream Meister has something special in store for his legions of fans."

"I'm sure it'll be a Halloween to remember."

—Marcy Graham, Co-Anchor 6abc *Action News*

GRANNY

Bobby woke when he left his body. There was a feeling of separation, like a rubber band stretching, then popping. He floated up and bobbed against the ceiling like a cork on a lake. He thought he must be dreaming, but the suspicion that something new, something miraculously unordinary was happening both thrilled him and left him disoriented and uneasy.

The crack in the ceiling above his bed had been there as long as he could remember. He had seen it so often he no longer noticed it. Now it was inches from his nose. He ran a finger over the narrow flaking crevice. It felt so real, so ruggedly alive. He reached out and pressed his hand against the nearby light fixture. The darkened glass was cool against his palm. The air conditioner clicked on, and a draft flowed over his fingers.

He looked over his shoulder. Below, his body sprawled on his twin bed, comforter tossed aside, sheet tangled about his legs. He pushed off from the ceiling and tried to swim down. As if gravity had reversed, he didn't get far before floating up.

Panic squeezed his heart. What if he couldn't return? Would his body wither and die? Would his parents send it to the funeral home and bury him not knowing he wasn't really dead? He looked at his hand. Was this his spirit? His soul? His hand looked as normal as it ever did, neither transparent nor formed of white mist like some ghostly appendage.

He hung there for a while, chewing his phantom lip, his back against the cold ceiling, staring down at his sleeping body, his heart throbbing to return to it and terrified he could not.

But wait. His body would wake eventually. Wouldn't it? And if it did not, either his mother or Granny would come to see why he wasn't up getting ready for school.

The thought calmed him, and he took stock of his surroundings. The room was dark with only the faintest bit of light shining around his window shade, but he saw things quite clearly in the gloom, as if he had developed night vision. There was the scarred maple desk where he did his homework and worked on his models. A brush and bottle of Testors red paint sat ready to bloody the Gill-Man's outstretched paws. On his wall was the map of Middle Earth he had used to follow the Fellowship of the Ring on their journey.

He had always wanted to fly, and while bobbing against the ceiling wasn't exactly flight, this new experience had possibilities. He decided to explore.

Scuttling across the ceiling on his fingers and toes, he made his way to the door, kicked off with his feet, and dove for the knob. It took a couple tries—he kept floating up before he could turn the knob—but he finally wrenched it open. He grabbed the top of the door frame and pulled himself under. His sister's bedroom door at the other end of the short hall was closed. The stairs beckoned.

How to get down them?

He licked his lips, decided to use the same strategy that had gotten him across his threshold. Planting his feet firmly against the ceiling, he shoved off as hard as he could and dove down the stairwell. He missed the first time, but on the second try grabbed the handrail and hauled himself to the middle floor.

Passing his parents' bedroom, he heard his father's rumbling snore. He repeated the dive at the end of the hall and pulled himself down to the kitchen. Again, he marveled at how real the dream was: despite the dim light, he made out the table and the worn green-and-white tiles.

Movement caught his eye. At the sink, a plump gray rat gnawed the bar of Lava soap his dad used to wash up when he came in from work.

You're in for it, Mr. Rat. Tomorrow Dad would be on a mission.

He dove under the archway and came up in the living room. The blinds were closed. The TV was dark. His grandmother snored softly on the fold-out sofa. He was extra quiet as he passed over her. He loved his Granny. She was his best friend. She made him hamburgers and French fries and had bowls of Spanish rice and SpaghettiOs ready when he came home from school.

At the door, he pulled himself down and looked out the fanlight. A car passed; otherwise, the street was silent. He thought about going outside and sailing above the roofs, but a sudden fear gripped him. He had had a hard time descending the stairs. The only thing that kept him from floating into space was the ceiling. Out there …

His eyes drifted to the power lines atop the telephone poles and a chill crept over him. No, he would not be going out.

Granny stirred. Her head rolled back and forth on her pillow as if she were having a nightmare. She mumbled something. She talked in her sleep sometimes. He listened, caught the word, "No."

She opened her mouth and screamed.

Bobby jolted awake, heart pounding, pajamas soaked with sweat.

Granny's scream welled up the stairs. Its intensity raised the hair on his arms. He wanted to go to her, to race down and wake her, but his mother had told him not to. She was better left asleep. She would stop in a minute and not remember having screamed when she woke. Mom said Granny suffered from night terrors, had off and on for years. She had screamed her head off, thrash about. Sometimes, she sleepwalked. The first time he had seen her sleepwalk, he had been five and it had scared the bejesus out of him. Mom had told him never to wake her when she was sleepwalking. It wouldn't do any good, and it might do her harm.

The next morning, Granny didn't remember screaming. She sipped her coffee while he ate his Frosted Flakes before sending him off to school with a PBJ in a paper bag. Bobby didn't tell Granny about his dream, which he remembered more vividly than any he had ever had. He wondered if he would have the dream again. All day he couldn't take his mind off the novelty of floating and was impatient for the day to be done, to climb into bed, and take flight.

He spent much of the day contemplating the problem of how to fly over houses without drifting into space, but he couldn't come up with anything and kept doodling in his notebook instead of taking notes. His math teacher caught him daydreaming and had to call on him twice, to the delight and titters of his classmates. Back home, Mom had to call him twice to dinner because he was out front gazing at the sky. Maybe if he got a long enough rope … but did the rope have to be real or would he need dream rope?

Finally, he got to bed, pulled the covers around his neck, and closed his eyes.

And couldn't sleep. And couldn't sleep.

Until he did.

The sudden pop. The thrill of floating. This time he was ready and extended his hands and toes as the ceiling neared.

Wasting no time, he hauled himself down the stairwell to gaze out the fanlight in the hope that his phantom self might solve his flight problem. Halfway across the kitchen ceiling, he froze.

Granny was sleepwalking.

Ghostlike in her white gown, she stepped beneath the arch onto the checkered tiles. Her porcelain skin glowed in the eerie dream light. Her white hair, fixed in a tight bun at the back of her head during the day, fell about her shoulders to her waist. He loved her hair. Sometimes she let him brush it. It was fine and silky. Her eyes, a lighter blue than his own, were open. If he didn't know better, he would think she was awake, but her mouth was slack, her gaze unfocused.

What was that above her head?

It appeared to be a cloud. A boiling mist that hadn't been there a moment ago. Though he saw the details of the room clearly, the cloud seemed to shift in and out of focus. Now it was thin as wood smoke, now thick as river fog.

A buzzing caught his ear. It came from the cloud. His flesh crawled as the mist grew denser, the buzzing louder. The darkening cloud radiated fear and dread, and a hungry evil, as if it harbored a beast that yearned to devour him body and soul. He fought the urge to flee.

Voices rose within the cloud. Angry voices. Bobby strained to make out what they were saying, but Granny screamed. Her night terror shriek went on and on, surely loud enough to wake the dead.

He woke, heart flailing against the cage of his ribs. He stared at his open door, expecting to hear the trailing end of Granny's scream, but the house was silent.

He flung off his comforter and sped down the stairs.

In the living room, Granny was curled like a baby atop her bedding.

Shadows encircled Granny's eyes the next morning. Her smile was forced. At school he forgot all about flying over rooftops and worried about Granny. Whose voices had he heard coming from the cloud over her head? One of them was male, he was sure. Angry, threatening. A source of terror. The other sounded like Granny. Frightened but also angry.

That night he found her sleepwalking again. The cloud was darker than the night before. The voices clearer.

"Stay away! I'll kill you, you bastard!" Granny's voice, defiant, terrified.

A man's rumbling laugh. "Like hell you will. Put the knife down and take your medicine."

A loud smack as of fist meeting flesh.

Granny's shriek spurred him on. He launched into the cloud.

He was in a kitchen, floating with his back against the ceiling. An old-timey avocado refrigerator hummed in a corner. A fluorescent fixture cast a bluish dream light on the scene below.

A woman was on her knees, blood on her mouth. The woman was Granny, but she was younger, her hair red, and no longer frail but looking at once tired, angry, and sad.

Her lip curled as she tasted blood. "I'll kill you, you bastard."

The dark-haired man would have been tall if he had been standing erect, but he was bent over Granny, a big hand raised to strike.

She flinched but the slap connected with her cheek, drove her to the ancient linoleum.

"Not today." The man laughed, then hauled Granny by the hair to the next room.

Bobby followed, arrived in time to see the man grab Granny's house dress and rip it down the front, exposing her bra.

He looked away.

And woke.

This time he ignored Mom's warning and raced down the stairs.

Granny lay across her bed, one bare foot on the floor, hands fumbling at the neck of her gown. He gently shook her. She was slow to wake, and when she did, she blinked and muttered, "What?"

"You were dreaming," he said.

Her smile was weak. She mussed his hair. "You get back to bed now. You've got school in the morning."

The next night was the same. Only, when the man tore Granny's dress, Bobby didn't wake but retreated to the dream kitchen where he covered his ears to shut out the brutal sounds coming from the bedroom.

After a while, the man came through the kitchen. He stopped to take a long drink from a bottle he pulled from a cabinet before going out the door.

Granny came out later, her face bloody, her torn dress hanging from her shoulders. Her bra was missing, and her breasts were exposed, but Bobby did not look away. He needed to see what she would do, learn how he could help her. The dream was showing him Granny's past. He was sure of it. The horrible thing that caused her night terrors.

Granny got the man's bottle from the cabinet, set it on the counter. Then she took a small can from under the sink with a laughing horned devil on the label. The label read "RED DEVIL LYE." She took a glass from the dish rack beside the sink, poured some water from the tap, and mixed in some white powder from the can. The resulting liquid looked like watered-down milk. She poured some of the contents of the man's bottle down the drain.

She stood there for a bit, staring at the bottle and the glass, her fists curled on the scarred green Formica. At length, she sighed. Her shoulders slumped. She poured the lye solution down the drain, capped the bottle, returned it to the cabinet.

The next day was Saturday. That afternoon he asked Granny if his granddaddy drank.

Granny was at the sink finishing up the lunch dishes. She stiffened.

"Why do you ask, child?"

Though, according to snatches of conversation he had overheard, his granddad had died long before he was born, drunk driving on his way home from a bar, the man still haunted Granny's dreams.

"Just wondering. Lou Albanese's father drinks."

She gave him a shrewd look. When he waited and didn't look away, she said, "Yes, your granddaddy drank. He was a mean drunk."

That night when he entered her dream, Bobby found himself in the bedroom instead of the kitchen. Granny tried to hold off his granddaddy with a pair of scissors, but he slapped them away, then backhanded her and threw her halfway across the room. Bobby recognized a smell this time. His daddy didn't drink, but he recognized the sharp odor from the breath of a dentist he had gone to once.

Whiskey.

The man reeked of it.

Granddad didn't tear Granny's clothes this time but left without saying where he was going.

After a bit, Granny went to the kitchen and got the whiskey bottle and lye out again. He had researched "lye." It was used to clean households, to unclog drains, and to dissolve roadkill. Again, Granny mixed her elixir, stared at it, and ended up pouring it down the drain.

He had to do something. Every night, Granny sleepwalked and screamed. The circles under her eyes darkened. Even Mom, who left early for her job as a receptionist in a doctor's office and came home late, noticed the change and asked Granny if anything was wrong. Granny said she was fine and went about fixing dinner, and Mom, too tired to argue, went upstairs to shower. But Bobby knew what ailed Granny and was determined to help.

But how? He was a dream within a dream. Granny couldn't see him, couldn't hear him. But he saw clearly the power of dreams to hurt.

Back in the dream, after the beating and the mixing of the elixir, he gazed down, the kitchen ceiling cold against his back. Below, Granny stood with her fists curled on the green Formica, staring at the lye solution and the whiskey bottle. Finally, as she had every night, he had visited her nightmare, she reached for the lye glass to pour it out.

"Don't!" he shouted. He startled himself at the loudness of his voice.

Her hand hesitated inches from the glass. Had she heard him? Or was she merely thinking?

"Do it, Granny!"

He tried to dive down to her, to put his hand over hers and help her pour the elixir into her tormentor's bottle. Her terror was his terror now. He had witnessed the cause of her nightmare and it cut him to the core to think that she had to relive it over and over for the rest of her life. But the ceiling was high, and he floated back up, frustrated, powerless.

"Please, Granny. You have to."

Her shoulders straightened. She lifted the glass and poured the milky liquid into the bottle.

A soft hand shook him gently. He came groggily awake.

Granny sat on his bed, hand on his shoulder. She was in her night gown. She must have come upstairs to check on him.

Granny smiled. "You were dreaming." She wiped his damp brow. "Having a nightmare. Want to talk about it?"

He shook his head. No, he didn't want to talk about it. More than anything, he wanted to forget the horrors he had witnessed in the dream cloud.

"I had a nightmare too," she said. Her smile was weary, but her eyes were clearer, her back straighter. "I don't remember, but I feel better now. Can I get you anything?"

Tears welled in his eyes. His granddad had deserved to die. And though the man had passed long ago, he couldn't shake the wormy feeling that he was somehow guilty of murder—even if it was only in a dream. If he had helped free Granny from the terrors that haunted her, it was worth it, but he feared the nightmares that would come.

He buried his face in Granny's neck and let the tears flow.

"I love you, Granny."

She stroked his hair and whispered in his ear, "I love you, too."

MAD ART

"Manhattan Psychiatric has a number of therapy programs," Dr. Laurel said.

Detective Lt. Mercedes Cruiz, Second Whip of the Twenty-fourth Precinct, had half-expected an officious administrator type. Lab coat, graying hair in a bun. Instead, Laurel was young, stylishly dressed in a navy suit, white blouse, and paisley scarf, with lustrous brown hair bobbed at the collar.

"We try to tailor the therapy to the patient's needs," the psychiatrist continued. "They all start with individual counseling. Some require drug therapy. But we find that outlets can help. So we offer support groups, drama therapy where patients act out their anxieties. And, of course, my program."

"Art therapy."

With its track lighting and white walls, the room attempted a gallery atmosphere, but the squeaky rubber-tiled floor gave it away as part of the institution.

"Yes. Please understand we don't use painting and sculpting as a substitute for basket weaving. The activity is not just to calm them, take their mind off what's bothering them. We want them to focus on what's bothering them, paint it, make a visual representation of their anger, frustrations, resentments, fears. Doing so forces them to face their reality. And if they face it enough, hopefully, to overcome it. Or at least lead more organized, fruitful lives."

Watercolors of flowers, cats, dogs, a birdfeeder with two sparrows in a scuffle, shared wall space with more disturbing artwork that begged interpretation. Like the picture that showed a bright red ball in the grassy sunlit foreground while two indistinct childlike figures stood in the background under the shadows of trees.

"The woman who painted this lost her sister last month."

Cruiz stopped before a narrow shadowy painting depicting dozens of chalk-white hands thrusting inward from the sides of the frame. Only the backs of the hands showed, fingers curled as if pulling something (the artist?) into the picture. A huge erect penis, slug-white with ropy gray veins, thrust up the center of the picture behind the hands. Menacing chrome-irised eyes stared between some of the fingers.

"The woman who painted this was kidnapped by three men, beaten, and raped repeatedly for four days. This is her memory of the experience. She was literally out of her mind. She wouldn't talk to therapists. But we managed to coax her into venting her emotions on canvas."

Cruiz' jaw clenched instinctively with the desire to clap handcuffs on the perpetrators.

Still, nothing here was as disturbing as what she had walked into that morning. The images of the pulverized body (some lunatic had caved her head in with an air fryer), the blood-splattered kitchen, and the art the killer had left on the wall in the victim's blood. She had stared at it long and studied the photos afterward. As she had with the previous homicide two days prior. The woman attacked while walking her dog. The sidewalk art done in her and the dog's blood. The images stuck in her head. She would dream about them. No avoiding the dreams. That was okay. Every detail mattered; it was too easy to miss something if you didn't memorize every detail of a case.

Five homicides. Five brutal violations of human flesh. All that blood and no footprints, handprints, nothing. How did the killer transfer the blood to their canvas?

The homicides had the brass at the Puzzle Palace chasing their shadows. The victims appeared to have been chosen at random; at least no connection had yet been found between any of them. The victims ranged from an affluent banker residing in an Upper East Side apartment overlooking the East River to a waitress in Spanish Harlem to a middle-aged homeless man who had taken up residence in the basement of a Hell's Kitchen tenement. The methods of murder differed. The killer apparently didn't bring a weapon to the scene but used whatever was at hand to rip, hack, and bludgeon their victims.

Capt. Leo Sciacca of the Criminal Assessment and Profiling Unit at police HQ had sent her to Manhattan Psychiatric Center to see if Dr. Laurel could provide any insight. Cruiz had shown Laurel photos of the artwork. She had to hand it to the doctor. Most citizens would upchuck at what the photos depicted. Except for a tightening of her lips and a slight flaring of her nostrils, Laurel had maintained professional aplomb. After studying the photographs for several minutes, Laurel spoke. "Such rage." She passed a hand over the photos as if they gave off heat and might blister her skin. Her nails were trimmed short and clear-polished. Her office walls were pastel pink. Cruiz recalled reading pink had a calming effect on violent psychotics. Personally, the walls made her think of Pepto Bismol. "You say the drawings mimic the crime scenes?"

"In an abstract way. Almost as if someone dashed off a caricature of the victim."

"To say the artist is psychopathic isn't telling you anything you don't already know. But the artist is talented. With a minimal and precise use of line, the artwork captures both the subject and the killer's emotional state." She tapped a finger on the glass-topped desk. "But the style ..."

"What about the style?"

"It reminds me of the paintings of one of our patients."

Cruiz had perked at this.

"One of your patients?"

"Yes, Mr. Morgan's been with us over a decade. A sweet man, well-liked by patients and staff. Keeps to himself mostly, as schizophrenics do."

Desperate for a lead, Cruiz had requested Laurel show her the man's art.

"Here we are," Dr. Laurel said, stopping before a particularly gruesome painting.

The canvas stopped Cruiz cold. She shuffled through the crime scene photographs, held one before the painting. While the killer's art was a rapid sketch dashed off in blood and Morgan's was a more complete portraiture, there was no mistaking they both depicted the same scene. Cruiz tried to make out more of the face, but it was too badly damaged to distinguish features. She examined the one hand that was visible. The nails were black and there was a ring on her finger with a small red stone. The ring was done with a couple strokes of the brush so the representation was more impressionism than realism.

This morning's victim had black nails and wore a garnet ring.

"Oh my," Dr. Laurel said. "I didn't realize."

"Does Mr. Morgan go out? Supervised or unsupervised?"

"No." Laurel was staring at the painting, seeing what she saw.

"You're sure?"

"Manhattan Psychiatric's security is state of the art. In addition, Nurse Hargrove works nights on that ward. Nothing gets by her."

"CCTV?"

"Yes."

"I will need to see those."

"Certainly."

"You said the artwork in the photos were the work of a psychopath, yet Morgan is schizophrenic."

"If you're thinking Mr. Morgan could have anything to do with your murders, you're mistaken. A schizophrenic could never commit such violence. Schizophrenics are among the most docile people you'll ever meet. They are a third less likely than the general population to perpetrate a crime."

"But the violence in the painting."

"There's a difference. A psychopath's violence is organized. They are clever and use deception to reduce their victims. A schizophrenic's mind is too disorganized to plan, let alone carry out, an act of violence. In the rare instance they do commit violence, it is because they are following a strong command hallucination."

"Someone or something telling them to commit violence."

"Actually, they'll be acting under a delusion or hallucination that someone is making them commit violence. Visual and auditory hallucinations are particularly common among schizophrenics. I would say the paintings your killer leaves are a message. Psychopaths have no moral concept and are incapable of empathy; however, they do have high-self-esteem. Your killer is probably enjoying shocking the authorities."

Cruiz studied the painting before her, noting the similarities between Mr. Morgan's and the killer's subjects. "Then how do you explain this?"

"I can't. I'm as shocked as you."

"I need to see Mr. Morgan."

Mr. Morgan was in the Day Room. While other patients watched television or worked a jigsaw puzzle or stared out the window at Ward Island Park, Morgan had an easel set up at the far end of the room and was so involved in painting that he was oblivious to their approach.

"Good afternoon, Mr. Morgan. You have a visitor."

Morgan paused the tip of his brush millimeters from the canvas and turned wide eyes toward Cruiz.

"Mr. Morgan, I—" was as far as Cruiz got before Morgan interrupted.

"No portraits. I am quite busy, as you can see."

"Oh no, Mr. Morgan. I don't want my portrait painted. I just wanted to ask you a few questions. Would that be all right?"

A slight nod of his head as he resumed painting was his answer.

"Where do you get your ideas for your paintings?"

He gave his temple a single tap with the handle of the brush.

"I think what Detective Cruiz means," Dr. Laurel said, "is why those particular subjects. I'm speaking of your recent departure from landscapes."

At the mention of "Detective," Morgan turned and observed Cruiz more carefully. "I paint what I see," he said.

A chill washed over Cruiz' back. "And what do you see?"

He smiled. And for some reason, she thought the smile wasn't as innocent as the sweet, well-liked man other's saw.

"May I see what you're painting?" she asked.

A slight shrug of his shoulder. He'd already returned to his work.

Cruiz came around the table. The painting was perhaps half done. The foundation colors had been applied, the composition sketched in, and part of the finished detail work completed. The woman on the campus was slumped against a wall. Blood slapped on with a frenzy of brush strokes flowed from her many wounds. On the wall above her head, Morgan had sketched in a caricature of the victim. An unfinished figure on the right of the canvas stood in shadow. He (she got the distinct impression it was a masculine figure) was thin almost to emaciation but exuded a sense of lethal power. The figure appeared to be wearing a black cloak pulled tight about himself. His hands were not visible. His eyes were the only thing with any luminosity. Morgan had captured in their gaze a sense of dark brooding malice.

To the left of the victim, the wall gave way to a hazy image of a city street. There was a sign on one of the façades. The name had been painted with deliberate clarity: "Conception."

The painting was not a portrait of any previous crime scene. "Who is that, Mr. Morgan?" She pointed to the stealthy figure glaring from the shadows.

"His name is too hard to pronounce. He said I could call him Victor."

"When do you talk to Victor?"

"In my dreams."

"They used to call it 'Mad Art.' Back in the early twentieth century. That's probably politically incorrect now. Still …" Cruiz sat facing Capt. Leo Sciacca across his big desk on the thirteenth floor of One Police Plaza. She was filling the captain in on her visit to Manhattan Psychiatric. Lean, white-haired, and square-jawed, Sciacca looked as distinguished as the citations and degrees in criminology and psychology mounted on his wall. He was also a deft infighter when it came to HQ politics and was a formidable contender in the Puzzle Palace's struggle to the top.

"I've seen madness," Sciacca said, looking up from the photos she had taken of Morgan's art and the crime-scene photos he had laid out on his desk for comparison, "and this qualifies. But this last one …" He tapped the photo of what Morgan had been painting when she interviewed him. "Assuming there is a connection between Morgan's paintings and the crime scene art—and from what I see, we can rule out coincidence—this last one represents either a murder we haven't discovered or …"

"Or one that hasn't happened yet."

"A more likely scenario is the killer has been in contact with Mr. Morgan. Perhaps an employee at Manhattan Psychiatric. Psychopaths can appear completely unassuming. He could be the janitor or an IT guy. They're also narcissistic. Goading Morgan into replicating their art work is consistent with pathological behavior."

Sciacca nudged a folder toward Cruiz' side of the desk. "This came in while you were at Manhattan Psychiatric. According to forensics, all the murders happened around 4 a.m."

Cruiz scanned the folder's contents, handed it back. "That coincides with something Laurel told me."

"What's that?"

"Laurel said a typical night's sleep consists of four to five sleep cycles. A person's dream or REM stage follows periods of deeper sleep that last about an hour and a half, the first REM stage lasting about ten minutes, the final lasting up to an hour." Cruiz did some mental calculations. "Four a.m. would coincide with the fourth dream stage."

Sciacca cocked an eyebrow. "You're suggesting Morgan's dreams are connected to the homicides?"

Cruiz grinned. "That would be delusional, wouldn't it? And I'm not ready to go on psychiatric leave. I'm just pointing out an interesting correlation."

Sciacca leaned back and tented his fingers. "Don't see where it helps. What else did you learn?"

"The name of the shop in Morgan's painting: 'Conception.' Turned out there's a Chelsea art gallery by that name. I went there after leaving Manhattan Psychiatric. Asked if any of their employees were missing, hadn't called in. The proprietor told me no. Everyone was accounted for. I did the same at every shop on the block. Same answer."

Sciacca nodded. "It was worth a try. The CCTV files are being examined. In the morning I'll order a background check on every employee at Manhattan Psychiatric. It's been a long day. Get some sleep, Lieutenant."

Cruiz stood and scooped the photos into her document bag. "With all due respect, Captain, I think I'll stake out the Chelsea gallery."

"You still thinking Morgan's painting is foretelling the future?"

"Just following the leads, Captain."

Sciacca nodded. "Gotta respect that."

At 3 a.m. Cruiz and her driver, Sgt. McNalty, were sitting in an unmarked down the block from the gallery. Unlike Morgan's painting, the name Conception Gallery was not blazoned over the entrance but tastefully displayed on a placard in the window beside the six steps leading up to the door. During her visit the previous day, Cruiz had seen a mixture of the avant-garde and the traditional. A sculpture made of wheelchairs and crutches stood near a series of realistic paintings by a Montauk artist depicting fishermen unloading their catch and a shark being butchered. The Conception was on Twenty-Second Street in the heart of the Chelsea Art District.

Cruiz had filled McNalty in on what she'd learned at the psychiatric center. McNalty, a fifteen-year veteran of the NYPD, was as skeptical as Sciacca. Cruiz knew they were playing a long shot, but she didn't want to wake up tomorrow and find that insistent tickling in her brain had been right and she had squandered the chance to catch the killer.

"I'm skeptical too, Oscar. But we're here. Enjoy the overtime."

A grin split McNalty's beefy face. "You won't hear me complaining, Lou."

With the windows halfway down, the cool air and the relative quiet of the hour were a relief. Despite feeling she was being absurd, Cruiz kept watching for a slim dark figure to come walking up the block. She knew her preoccupation with Victor was groundless, a product of Morgan's psychosis, but the image of its menacing eyes persisted, as if they projected a subliminal message she wasn't getting.

"Hey, did you hear about the head the Transit cops found in the Forty-Second Street Shuttle tunnel?"

She'd heard the story but let McNalty tell the tale his way. He would embellish it with gruesome humor, but the night was long and his rumbling voice and occasional laugh were welcome companions.

Four a.m. passed. Four-thirty. She was about to tell McNalty to head back to the station when they heard sirens approaching and a call came in.

At 3:58 a.m. Broderick Morgan entered his fourth REM stage of the night. As he sweated and writhed, tangling his legs in his sheets, Victor—he whose real name Morgan could not pronounce and sounded something like *vekrashanataranckna*—rose above the roof of Manhattan Psychiatric Center and, spreading black membranous wings, flew across the Harlem River heading for Manhattan.

So many beating hearts. Their combined drumming was thunderous. He chose one and began his descent.

The woman woke. Had she heard a noise? A scratching sound? She slept with the door open and the night light she kept in the hall spilled a soft lozenge of light onto her carpet.

There it was again! Like a dog's claws scraping against her hardwood floor. Then silence.

Gooseflesh rippled over her back. She sat up and strained her ear toward the door. Fully awake now, she found she was sweating. She told herself her fear was irrational. She had imagined the noise.

Or she had a mouse in the kitchen!

The thought brought a breath of relief. A mouse made better sense than an intruder in her sixth-floor apartment in a high-security building. Still … Her hands were trembling and the gooseflesh had spread to her neck and arms.

She rose from the bed, opened the drawer of her night stand, and removed her stun gun. Her building might be safe, but New York was a dangerous place, and she never left home without it.

She rose, slipped into her robe, and went into the hall. The night light gleamed along the hardwood floor. Another in an island outlet vaguely illuminated the space between the kitchen and living room. She tried treading softly, but the old boards creaked under her slippers. She stepped out of the hall, stopped, and scanned her surroundings. The big TV mirrored the living room. She saw nothing out of place. She went into the kitchen, flicking on the overhead lights as she rounded the breakfast bar. She blinked until she could see again. The kitchen was empty. The only sound was the soft hum of the refrigerator. She stepped through the arch into the dining room, turned on the lights, glanced under the table and around the baseboards.

"Silly goose," she chided herself. "Getting all worked up because of a mouse." She would have the super put out mouse traps in the morning.

She turned to go back to bed. A black shape rose in the kitchen. Under the bright halogens, every aspect of the creature was starkly lit. It was taller than her and utterly naked. Its skin glistened like wet leather. It was wolf-faced, and its scaly fingers terminated in black talons. Most soul-shocking of all were the great bat wings that rose above its head.

She dropped the stun gun, turned to flee. The demon-thing waved its hand, and the knives flew out of the rack on the kitchen counter, sliced across the island, and punched deep into the woman's body.

The crime scene was on West Twenty-Fourth, two blocks over from where she and McNalty had kept vigil for the past two and a half hours. The similarities between the crime scene and Morgan's painting were shocking. Slumped against the wall, the dark-haired, middle-aged woman sat in a pool of blood, her hands splayed at her sides, her chin resting on her breast. Her body was a pincushion of kitchen knives. There was no sign of forced entry. Cruiz was certain there would be no prints on the knives, nor would tell-tale footprints show under the footprint lamp. The killer was a phantom.

"This what you saw in the patient's painting?" Oscar had asked.

Cruiz could only nod. More shocking than the homicide was the fact that she had seen the aftermath of the crime *before* it was perpetrated.

What was Morgan?

She received a further shock when she learned the victim's name. Rosemarie Concetta. Concetta being a form of Concepción, both referring to the Immaculate Conception.

The gallery had been a red herring, meant to send her on a goose chase while the killer did his work. Someone—Morgan? Someone manipulating Morgan? Victor?—was playing with her.

By the time she arrived at Manhattan Psychiatric, the patients had breakfasted, and Morgan was in the dayroom painting. He seemed excited. He looked up when she approached. "Be with you in a minute, Detective. I'm almost finished."

She and Laurel sat in plastic chairs on the opposite side of the table. She had shared no details of the latest crime scene with the doctor, but from Laurel's pallor it was obvious she suspected the worst. Cruiz resisted the urge to sneak a peek at the painting, but she was tired and not yet ready to look upon the killer's next victim. She was sure now … however unlikely a psychiatric patient could gain entrance to a locked apartment and commit homicide while he was sleeping miles away, she was as certain as night follows day the seemingly innocuous-looking man seated opposite her was connected. Even if someone was influencing him, how did that account for either Morgan or the killer predicting with such precision the location of the body, the method of murder, and the appearance of the crime scene? Was Morgan clairvoyant? She was a pragmatic policewoman who believed cause preceded effect—not the other way around.

She decided to press. "Does Victor tell you what to paint?"

Morgan nodded without interrupting his work.

"Mr. Morgan," she said more firmly. "Who is Victor?"

Morgan did not respond but continued furiously applying paint to canvas.

"Is Victor someone who works here? Has someone in the hospital been telling you what to paint?"

The brush slowed but Morgan did not return her gaze.

"Are you Victor?" She ignored Laurel's warning hand on her forearm. "You are, aren't you?"

Morgan lowered the brush and turned to face her. Gone was the expression of benign euphoria, the sweet half smile. A shadow passed over his face. A narrowing of the eyes accompanied by a malevolent frown. He did not answer her but turned the easel so she could gaze upon his subject.

Her jaw dropped.

The face on the canvas was her own. The look of abject terror on her portrait's face mirrored the chill that sluiced through her gut.

※

"No chance of multiple personalities?"

"Dissociative identity disorder is what we call it now," Laurel said. "No, his score on the Dissociative Identity Disorder Test was 15. His score on the Schizophrenic Screening Test was much higher. Mr. Morgan is more than capable of painting from memory. And you did talk to him yesterday."

They were back in Laurel's pink office. Cruiz had a headache. Though Morgan had painted her portrait from memory with photographic accuracy that was all he had painted. Unlike the subjects of Morgan's other portraits, she wasn't a corpse and there was no sign of blood or trauma. She remembered the gallery. How helpless and angry she had felt knowing she was just blocks away when the killer did his wet work. Her portrait was more bait, meant to manipulate her emotions, throw her off her game.

"No, for me to declare Mr. Morgan suffered from DID would be tantamount to a mathematician accepting that two plus two equaled some arbitrary number other than four."

"But that look he gave me."

"Well, he is human."

※

That night in her apartment, Cruiz prepared for an encounter with the unknown. Before leaving Manhattan Psychiatric, she had made Laurel swear to keep watch over Morgan in the pre-dawn hours and be prepared, if her phone rang, to wake him instantly. Laurel was skeptical but acquiesced. Everything in the doctor's extensive learning might be telling her what Cruiz suggested was impossible, yet Cruiz saw the niggle of doubt that had crept into her eyes.

Cruiz had every light in her apartment on. Too wired to sit, she paced. It was a small apartment, and she circled the living room and kitchen, scanning for movement and remembering to breathe. In one hand she clutched her service weapon, safety off; in the other, her phone, thumb ready to press Laurel's number.

Sgt. McNalty was positioned downstairs in the foyer. The big cop's vigilance should have made her feel better but didn't.

An hour passed. The refrigerator hummed. Sirens occasionally cut through background noise of the city that never sleeps. She was rounding the sofa for the hundredth time when a cold draft stirred the hairs on her neck. She shivered, sensing a presence. She spun, the short-barreled automatic close to her body so an assailant couldn't knock it from her hand.

Victor towered over her in all his satanic glory. While his features had been indistinct in the painting, they were hideously vivid now. Wolfish eyes glared down at her. Black lips stretched exposing fangs. Talons clicked, and black wings rustled. The horror of what stood before her drove all rational thought from her brain.

In a spasm of terror, she pressed Laurel's number.

In Manhattan Psychiatric Center, Dr. Laurel stood beside Morgan's bed, an ammonia ampule in her hand. Her cell, set to ring and vibrate, lay on Morgan's night stand. Despite the hour, she was wide awake.

On the bed Morgan tossed and turned in the throes of dreaming. He appeared to be engaged in a struggle. With what night terror she could only ponder. She was tempted to wake him, free him from whatever battle he was waging. But Lt. Cruiz' instructions had been clear. Though the detective had stressed her assistance was only cautionary and unlikely to be needed, Laurel shared the woman's anxiety. There was a mystery here. A Pandora's box you opened at your peril.

She jumped when the phone rang and began clattering on the table top.

She shoved the ampule under Morgan's nose and popped it. Morgan bolted upright, blinking and shaking his head.

※

The apparition's eyes flew wide. Its snarling maw turned to gape-mouthed surprise. The thing swept toward the living room window ... and vanished.

Cruiz rushed to the window, drew the blinds. Over the rooftops, backlit by the gibbous moonlight filtering through the fleecy clouds, Victor flapped his great wings as he sailed out over the Harlem River toward Wards Island.

※

The following day, Cruiz visited Morgan. He wasn't painting but staring out one of the dayroom windows at Manhattan across the glittering river.

"Hello, Detective," he said, returning her greeting. He bounced on the balls of his feet. "I feel good today. I think I'll have ice cream." He mused for a moment, then brightened as if he'd made an important decision. "Chocolate."

"That sounds like a plan. Did you sleep well?"

His smile wilted. "No, I don't think I did. I had a bad dream. Dr. Laurel woke me."

"Do you remember your dream?"

He shook his head. A flock of birds flew past the window drawing his attention. He leaned his face close to the glass so he could follow their flight upriver.

Before leaving, she met with Dr. Laurel and thanked her for possibly saving her life. Laurel didn't know what to make of that but said, "You're welcome. Oh, and Mr. Morgan said to give you this." The doctor handed her a cardboard poster tube. A canvas, presumably one of Morgan's paintings, was rolled inside.

Cruiz accepted the gift as if it were a snake.

In her car, she removed the artwork from the tube.

"Whadda ya got there, Lou?"

"Not sure, Oscar."

She unrolled the canvas. A chill swept through her.

"What the…?" McNally said.

A photorealistic portrait of Victor stared from the canvas. The creature's glistening leathern wings arched over its head. Its lupine muzzle was stretched in a snarl. Its black, demonic eyes bore into her soul.

A Private Affair

"Y ou want me to enter your dreams?"

"That's what you do, isn't it?"

"That's what the sign says."

The sign I referred to was on the door of my reception room, the one with my name, Aloysius Griffith, and my calling, Private Dream Investigator, stenciled on the pebbled glass. If you've never heard of a P.D.I., don't get your shorts in a twist; there aren't many of us around. It's interesting work though. I could tell you stories…. But then I can't, can I? I mean, that ethics clause. You know, the one that guarantees client-dreamer confidentiality.

The big man seated on the other side of my desk didn't tumble to my snarky sense of humor. He waited me out with an impatient stare. He looked tired. I don't mean as if he'd had a rough day and his dogs needed a rest. He looked as if he hadn't slept in a week. The name he'd given me was Eugene Belasco. It even said so on his card, along with "Importer of Fine Goods," an address, and a phone number. It was a nice card, glossy raised black letters on glossy white cardstock. Eugene had the well-fed face of a gourmand who liked rich food and plenty of it and a wallet that could support the habit. I don't mean he was fat; just portly with plenty of broad-shouldered muscle beneath his brown serge suit. He wore a gold and green tie with the suit. Its fat Windsor knot was loosened, and his top button was open, as was my own. It had been a hot day and looked to be a warm evening.

The air conditioning was broken—again—and the smells from the Chinese restaurant downstairs drifted in the open window along with the sound of the saxophone panhandler on the corner. It was a Friday afternoon, quarter to five. I had been about to lock up, go home and grab a shower before heading over to Enrico's for a steak, preceded and followed by several gimlets to satisfy my sweet tooth when the chime alerted me I had a visitor. I don't have a secretary, can't afford one, so the reception room just has a desk, a couple of easy chairs, and a sign on the inner door that says ENTER. The arrangement suits me fine. It's not like I get a lot of traffic.

The thought of gimlets made me remember the bottle I kept in my desk drawer, but if I pulled it out, I'd have to offer the big man a drink, and it was Friday closing time. I had a bottle in my kitchen cabinet, and I figured I could hold out till I got home.

"Why?" I asked.

"Huh?"

"Why do you want me to poke around in your dreams? I always tell potential clients dreaming is a private affair. There may be things you don't want seen." This was true. The subconscious has a habit of airing dirty laundry in dream time.

"But I'm covered under client-dreamer confidentiality, right?"

"That's what it says in the contract. Also why I have clients sign a disclaimer. I don't want anyone coming after me because I saw something they didn't want me to see. And believe me, brother, you dream it, I'll see it. So again, I ask you, why?"

"To find something I've lost."

"What have you lost?"

"That's just it. I know I have it in my dreams, but when I wake up, I can't remember what it was." Belasco's broad forehead bunched in a frown as if he were trying to remember. His face was ashen, and he could have carried groceries in the bags under his bloodshot eyes.

"Well, sounds like a pretty straightforward job. Unless your mind has set up blocks."

"'Blocks'?"

"To remembering."

"That possible?"

"Sure, the mind's more twisty than a nest of serpents. Any number of things could erect a barrier: a traumatic event is the usual culprit. Could be as simple as an embarrassment. The brain's way of protecting you."

"How do you do it?" Belasco asked. "I mean, do I have to do anything to let you into my dreams?"

"You already did."

He looked puzzled. I enlightened him. "You have to invite me in. Like the vampire. In our case the contract serves as consent"

"But you could go into someone's dream without being invited?"

"That wouldn't be ethical. And I'm not a voyeur. Poking around in other people's dreams is messy and exhausting." I was being evasive. When I'm not on the job, when I'm sleeping normally, I pick up snippets from the neighbors in my apartment building and for blocks around. That's why, when I really need to get away, I go up to the lake house where there's nothing but me and the fishes.

"Take a check?" Belasco pulled out a nice-looking leather checkbook.

"Sure. But I gotta warn you, it doesn't pay to bounce a check with someone who has access to your dreams."

Belasco, pen poised above the check, stared at me over the desk.

I felt sorry for the guy. His brain wasn't firing on all cylinders.

"Just kidding," I said.

After passing me the check, he told me more or less what time he and his wife, Eyde, went to bed. I figured I'd wait about an hour or so after that before I got to work. I sure as hell didn't want to drop in on him and his wife doing the tango. I'd enjoyed those peep shows when I was a teenager; they were entirely too exhausting and sordid now.

There's nothing especially peculiar or difficult about entering another's dream. Well, some of us have a knack for it while others don't. I can't carry a tune or solve equations in my head, others can. Slipping in and out of others' dreams is my forte and my curse. Whether it's biological or psychological I don't know, but I'm a natural. The government tried to round us up. Thanks to a class action lawsuit, I got a bit of change out of that and didn't end up in an NSA institution with electrodes stuck to my scalp.

Anyways, after taking a doze to sleep off the gimlets, I woke to my phone alarm about 2 a.m., peed, got a sip of water, and went back to bed. Before I go on, it's important to understand how the sleep/dream cycle works. Everybody dreams. Some people say they don't; they just don't remember them. After about an hour and a half of deep sleep, we enter REM. sleep. You're just skimming under the surface of wakefulness, your eyeballs are boogying about under your lids, and you're dreaming. The first REM stage lasts a few minutes. The later ones can last an hour. Those are the ones people remember, the longer ones that come closer to your rising for that cup of morning joe. I hit Belasco's second REM. Not surprisingly, he was dreaming about me. Not about watching for my dream body to show up but about his visit to my office. I say not surprising because most dreams simply rehash in realistic or symbolic form the day's events. Some experts say this is the brain's way of clearing house. I say bull scat to that. It's remembering, that's all. The cerebral cortex sifting through the day's short-term memories.

An hour and a half later, Belasco dreamed he was alone inside a stuck elevator and needed to pee. After checking for cameras, he turned to a corner, whipped it out, and let 'er rip. He woke, did his business, and went back to sleep.

Toward morning, he started struggling. He was hot. In his dream, he kicked off his covers. He rubbed his chest. He felt pressure there, something weighing him down. I'm sure you've experienced being both an actor in a dream and an observer watching the dream. When that happens, it never feels weird but seems perfectly natural. What happens to me is pretty similar, only, when I'm investigating someone's dream, I'm an observer but my client is the actor.

Anyway, Belasco was struggling and experiencing a mixture of emotions I found truly interesting, stimulating even, as his conflicting emotions were so strong I experienced them sympathetically. He was violently repelled by something that terrified him. At the same time, he was excited, squirming with anticipation. While erections are common in REM, Belasco pitched one hell of a tent. I ached sympathetically. The uncomfortable part for me in a sex dream is I sense what the dreamer senses, think their thoughts, feel their pleasure or pain. It takes an act of will to remain aloof and just observe. So here I was, horny as a teenager with a box of porn, experiencing terror and desire, when I sensed another presence in the bed. She was blond, gorgeous, and as sinuously attractive as a serpent.

I felt her mouth on me.… I mean, on Belasco. He writhed, I writhed. It was really quite erotic, yet all the while I wanted to shove her off but was helpless, paralyzed, to deny her. Then she was on me … on Belasco. I shuddered. It was all so real. Gazing up at her in the dreamlight as I rose to meet her, I admired her perfect symmetry, her gorgeous breasts, the curve of her waist. Her face had a Nordic beauty. Her blue eyes were widely spaced, her pink lips full. Yet—and this jolted me even as I was lost in the throes of passion—as I gazed at her I sensed a presence within the wife. I couldn't get a clear look at this other woman, just caught a glimpse of dark eyes and raven hair. If Eyde Belasco's sex appeal was a ten, this second persona's was a fifty. I found myself mad to see her clearly.

And then she was there. As if Mrs. Belasco had become a ghost, her flesh as transparent as wavering mist, I saw the scorching lynx riding Belasco. I stared in feverish awe. I've never wanted anything or anyone more in my life. I felt lust and jealousy and madness, and I knew why my client had looked so sleep-deprived in my office. The desire she stimulated was exhausting. I could barely imagine how her nightly visits must take their toll on the dreamer. Yet I was enthralled. I ached to bite her shoulder while I came. As if responding to my thought, Belasco bit her shoulder as he came.

A strange thing happened then. She, whoever or whatever she was— and I had no illusion she was merely a dream phantom—smiled at me. Perfect white teeth showed between scarlet lips as dark, knowing eyes held my gaze. She was seeing me. *This erotic vixen was seeing me.*

Her lips spread wider. She clenched her teeth. Her nostrils flared. Her eyes closed. And I saw, like heat waves rippling off blacktop on a sweltering day, waves of energy lift off Belasco's sweating body and pour into hers.

I woke, drenched, heart pounding as if I'd sprinted a mile. Uphill. Wearing a thirty-pound weighted vest.

I now knew what Belasco had lost. It wasn't an object, an heirloom, the combination to a safe, the keys to his car. It was a memory. A memory that compelled and repelled, that made of a strong man a quivering puddle of jelly. His wife was not what she appeared to be.

The notion that Mrs. Belasco suffered from dissociative identity disorder, what they used to call multiple personalities, flit through my brain, but I pushed it aside. As I did the thought of demonic possession. We're talking events that transpire in a dream. I would have to know more about the woman to ascertain if there was any evidence of duality in her waking life.

Another worrying thought needled me: She'd looked right at me and smiled. Was it possible that she'd seen me? I'd never had a client claim to be aware of my presence. And she wasn't the dreamer but the dream.

I sat up on the side of my bed with my feet on the carpet and followed that thought while I got my breathing under control. What if the lynx hadn't been a fixture of the dream? What if she was a visitor from the outside? Like me.

I woke, drenched, heart pounding as if I'd sprinted a mile. Uphill. Wearing

The following morning after a black coffee braced with Scotch, I called the number on Belasco's card. Unlike me, he had a secretary. A smooth voice. A swell voice. Possibly a dog, but I imagined long legs and a red-lipped smirk that wasn't off-putting at all. Mr. B. was busy. Clients. Could I stop by at eleven? I could. I hung up. I figured it would be worth stopping by if only to see if the body lived up to that voice. I shook my head and grinned at my train of thought. I wasn't usually like this. I liked to admire a swell figure as much as the next guy, usually from the rear as she walked away from me (says a lot about my relationships, or lack thereof), but after watching Mrs. Belasco or whatever possessed her in action last night, I was as randy as a sailor who hadn't had a woman in months. Just listening to that honeyed voice on the phone had made me half hard. What the hell was wrong with me?

※

The secretary didn't match the voice. Her square jaw, short-cropped hair, and plus-size business suit made her look mannish. Which was a good thing. I didn't need more stimulation.

The warehouse was in Long Beach, near the Port. Belasco's office was on the second floor at one end of the building with a view of a truckyard. The truckyard was a nice touch, made Belasco look like a blue-collar everyman just humping through the week like the rest of us lugs. He looked worse. Last night had done him in. His cheeks were hollow, his complexation gray as a chain smoker. He appeared to have lost weight since I'd seen him. I couldn't be sure, but his hair seemed grayer than I recalled.

There was a framed photo of Mrs. Belasco on his desk. It was the women I'd seen in his dream. She was a looker. And not just a trophy wife. Some of the accomplishments listed on her LinkedIn page included a B.A. in Marketing, fashion fundraisers for the ASPCA (using dogs and cats as models apparently), and membership on the Culver City Cultural Affairs Commission.

Belasco offered me a Scotch. I said that sounded swell. He joined me. As we sat facing each other across a coffee table, our eyes looked everywhere but into each other's. It was funny really. He knew I'd been peeking in on his dreams and had no idea what embarrassing detail I might have seen. While I had seen the man at his most intimate.

I sipped my Scotch. It was good Scotch. Single malt. Smooth as a silk stocking.

I told him what I'd witnessed. It's best to get these things out in as straightforward and plain English as possible. I told him what he was forgetting were the sex dreams he was having with his wife and how there was another presence in the bed with them. He seemed confused then amused when I mentioned another women as if he thought I meant he was participating in a *ménage à trois*. I corrected him. "I don't mean two separate women. The second woman appeared to be inhabiting your wife."

"'Inhabiting.' You mean like demonic possession?"

I spread my hands. "I'm just telling you what I saw. I don't mind telling you this is the strangest case I've ever had. It's not like helping you find your keys."

He pursed his lips, making his tired face look peevish. "Absurd. Absolutely absurd. You don't really believe in demonic possession, do you?"

"Of course not. I'm sure there's a rational explanation for what I saw."

"Enlighten me."

"One, you dreamed the second woman." I wanted to ask how his sex life with his wife was going but didn't. If he wasn't getting any, maybe the subconscious was compensating by providing a little dream entertainment. "But if it were just a puerile sex dream, I doubt your mind would have created a barrier to hide the dream from your waking mind. Is there another woman you'd rather your wife didn't know about?" I watched Belasco's reaction. Having a mistress and experiencing some measure of guilt at keeping the secret from his wife made more sense than possession.

"No, no mistress," Belasco said, taking no more offense than if I had asked him what he'd had for breakfast this morning. "I'm very happy with my wife. Besides, I'm much too busy. And tired." He gave an exaggerated sigh.

"Okay. Two, a dreamer like me is infiltrating your dreams. I'm leaning toward this one for the moment because she looked at me."

"Looked at you."

"Yes. And smiled, as if to let me know she was being invasive and didn't care if I knew."

"Sounds melodramatic."

"Perhaps. But your health seems to be deteriorating."

"I'm a busy man. I admit I might need a vacation." He took a slug of his Scotch.

"It's more than that. Do you have an enemy? Someone who might hire a dreamer to wear you down?"

He set his glass on his coaster. "I'm in import-export. I have competitors, not enemies. Besides, I thought dreamers were bound by an ethics clause to observe and not interact with a client's dreams."

"If they're licensed and want to keep their license, yes. But not all dreamers are licensed."

"I've heard rumors. Yes, it would make sense for a criminal to hire someone like that. To get the combination to a safe or to learn the hiding place for a witness."

"Or to dig up dirt for blackmail." I paused a moment to let that sink in. "But," I added, "in those scenarios, it would make more sense to plant some autosuggestion but otherwise remain a hidden observer. That still doesn't explain why the dreamer is resorting to sex, or why your health is deteriorating."

He waved me off. "Never mind my health. So, we're back to demonic possession. Or maybe witchcraft." Belasco looked disgusted with the whole conversation.

I wasn't too pleased with it myself. The more I thought about it, given the sex angle and the visible alteration of my client's appearance, the more possession or witchcraft fit the bill, even if all that mumbo jumbo was the stuff of fairy tales.

"So, do you want me to drop in on you tonight? See if I can get a better handle on your interloper?"

"Good God, no. You've done your job. You learned what I couldn't remember. I'll take it from here."

On my way out, I couldn't help feeling I'd left the job unfinished and that my client's life was in danger. Whatever was happening to him in his dreams was draining the life out of him.

In my car, I took out my cell and placed a call to UCLA's anthropology department.

"A female sexual demon, one that drains a man of his semen, i.e., literally drains the life out of him, is called a succubus."

"I've heard of them. Old legends."

"Maybe. There's a lot of truth in old legends."

Dr. Parisa had pretty eyes over a schnoz that would make Cyrano proud. Dressed in a print dress and navy slacks, she sat cattycorner to me in one of the unmatched armchairs. Nothing in the office matched. Her desk was vintage oak. Instead of a credenza, a federal blue media cabinet with chipped paint stood against one wall. Her books lined a corner book case. A large ficus stood in a pot below her south-facing window. Nothing matched, but the effect was eclectically pleasant.

"The male equivalent of a succubus is an incubus. In folklore studies they're not classified as demons per se. They don't appear among the demons listed in any grimoire. The succubus and incubus have more in common with the vampire. Only instead of drinking blood, they maintain their eternal life by draining the lifeforce from their victims." As if anticipating what I was about to ask, she added: "I'm not saying your client's dream visitor is a succubus, only that, from a folkloric viewpoint, a succubus fits the bill."

"There's no evidence of their existence?"

"Just anecdotal accounts going back centuries. Some say succubae and incubi are the children of Lilith, Adam's first wife. Others say they are fallen angels. Still others claim the succubus and incubus are the same creature or, as some would have it, two forms of the same creature, and can assume either male or female form, whichever is convenient. Some argue that they are corporeal. Others that they are astral visitors." Parisa rose and selected an old leather-bound volume from her book case. Returning to her seat, she opened the yellow pages. "Here's what Sinistrari of Ameno has to say on the matter: 'The Catholic Church is really of opinion that they are intelligences, but not entirely bodiless and senseless' and 'ascribes to them a subtle body, aerial or igneous, according to what is written: He makes the spirits His Angels, and the burning fire His Minister.' Further on Sinistrari writes: 'Although not corporeal in the same way as ourselves, made of the four elements, yet it is impossible to say that Angels, Demons and Souls are incorporeal; for they have been seen many a time, invested with their own body, by those whose eyes the Lord had opened.'"

She closed the book.

"So how would you get rid of one—assuming they exist? Would you perform an exorcism?"

"Ah, there lies the problem: 'assuming they exist'. A strong faith is needed to expel them—and the intercession of a bishop or a priest to perform the Rite of Major Exorcism."

"Do you believe in demons and succubae?"

She sighed. "Personally, I believe in human psychology, in the forms of dementia, both psychological and physiological, and of course human gullibility. As much as I like to romanticize the folklore and mythology that is my bread and butter, I am a pragmatist. Until I witness their existence with my own eyes, I guess I'll have to count myself among the faithless." She looked at me. Her gaze was wistful. "You haven't found anything that might substantiate their existence, have you?"

The following morning, I was in my office looking down on South Broadway—the air conditioning was still broken, my window open; a teenager was window shopping the XXX shop across the street; down the block, a wheel-chaired vet was setting up shop under the marquee of the old Palace Theatre—when the door to my reception room opened.

"Read the sign," I called over my shoulder. Though ENTER was stenciled on my office door, invariably my visitors knocked. A knuckled double rap sounded and in walked two detectives; one in gray, one in blue. Both had their top shirt button open, their ties loosened. The cop in gray was taller, older. He flashed me his tin. The gold and enamel winked at me in the morning light.

"You Griffith?"

"The last time I looked."

"Detective Engels." He jerked a thumb at the blue suit. "My partner, Loomis." The tin disappeared.

"How can I help you boys?" I didn't offer them a seat. I didn't mean to be uncordial, but for some reason I hadn't slept well and couldn't remember my dreams.

Blue suit was a bruiser. You could tell he spent time in the gym the way his suit bulged in all the right places. He walked around checking for dust with his finger.

Engels, whose hair was as gray as his suit, took out a notepad and a cheap pen, the type you can get at a realtor's office with the advertising on it. "I understand you know a Eugene Belasco."

"That's a statement, not a question."

"Don't get wise," Loomis said, too intent on inspecting the dust on my desk to look at me.

"Can't help it. My mother was a fortune teller."

Engels looked annoyed. "Do you know him or not? For the record. We know you do."

"He was a client."

"'Was'?"

I nodded. "He fired me yesterday."

The detective fraternity exchanged glances. "'Fired'?" Engels said.

I'd gotten a sick feeling the second Engels mentioned Belasco. They don't send detectives around to deliver good news.

"Look fellas, I can be a lot more helpful if you'd get to the point. Do me a favor, Detective Loomis. Leave some of the dust on the filing cabinet. I'll have to fire my cleaning lady if you do her job for her."

"Funny guy," Loomis half growled.

"As a crutch," I said.

Engels wasn't amused. "What was the nature of your business with Mr. Belasco?"

"You both look like bright boys," I said. "I know you know what I do for a living. So you also know I can't discuss my client's business. It wouldn't be ethical."

"*Riiighht.*" Loomis drew the word out. He was inspecting the frame of my diploma that hung on the wall.

"Mr. Belasco died in his sleep last night," Engels said in a deadpan voice, as if he was quoting the time of day. He consulted his notepad. "Around four in the morning."

A chill crept over my back. I felt the need to sit. I remained standing, but stepped away from the window, feeling the draw of that four-story drop. Engels had delivered the psychological equivalent of a sucker punch. He was watching my reaction. It took me a second to remember to put on my wise guy face. (My poker face was a sure giveaway that I was hiding something.)

"So this is the first you've heard?"

I nodded, cleared my throat to ready myself for the next question, got the bright idea to toss in one of my own.

"How'd he die?"

"Ticker stopped."

Loomis had quit checking for dust and was fingering one of my cards. I assumed it was the one I'd given Belasco. "So, Dreamwalker, what's it like poking around in other people's dreams."

Before I could remind him of what he already knew—that I don't "poke around," Engels continued. "Belasco looked shrunken. I understand he was a big man. An avid golfer. Wife said he'd been 'under the weather' lately. Her words."

Grinning, Loomis interjected. "You wouldn't want to poke around in my dreams."

"Sexual or excretory?"

"'Ex—?" His brow clouded as if I'd said something unpleasant about his mother.

Engels sighed. "He's kidding, Mike. Don't get heated. Day's hot enough already."

Mike unclenched his ham fist but continued to roast me with a side-eyed glare.

Engels continued. "The body was deflated, shrunken, the flesh gray. His face shrink-wrapped to his skull as if all moisture had been drawn out. Mrs. Belasco showed me a recent photo. Looked nothing like the corpse."

Loomis snapped his fingers. "How do we know you didn't pay the deceased a visit last night?" he said.

"You implying I shut the lights off before I left?"

"Naw, I'm just speculating. No harm in speculating, is there?"

I ignored the question.

"I thought he fired you," Engels said. "Did you enter his dreams last night?"

I told myself never to play poker with this guy. He had small eyes. His pupils bored right through me. "I did not." I wasn't about to mention I didn't recall my dreams. It happens, but it might have sounded convenient if I'd mentioned it.

"You guys ought to take your show on the road. You'd draw a crowd in Poughkeepsie."

"Fun-ny," Loomis cracked.

"Come back tomorrow. I'll have some new material."

❦

Not five minutes after the detectives left, I was about to pour myself a short one when my outer door opened and heavy footsteps crossed my waiting room. I set the bottle and glass back in the drawer and was about to say, "Come in," when the door opened without an accompanying knock. By dang, the boy could read!

My visitor was tall, maybe 6'3". Broad shoulders, narrow waist in a tailored black chauffeur's uniform. Wavy blond hair over a triangular face. His nose and his chin were a little too pointy for drop-dead handsome, but he could pass in a muster. His thin lips and blue eyes wore a practiced indifference. Another guy I wouldn't be playing cards with.

"Help you?" I asked. I was tired, and I hoped he wasn't here to play tiddlywinks like the previous mugs.

He didn't tap dance. "Name's Trevor. Car's downstairs. Mrs. Belasco wants to see you."

"She does, does she?" I hadn't slept well and wasn't my witty self.

He didn't say anything, just cracked his knuckles, as if that was supposed to intimidate me. It did, actually, but I wasn't going to show it.

"I'd like to see her too," I said, grabbing my jacket. "I understand she's quite a looker."

I watched his reaction. The eyes narrowed, the corners of his mouth tightened. I wondered if Trevor was another of the succubus's conquests. I found myself sizing the man up as if he was competition. I was amazed at where my mind was going. This was my chance to look into those lovely eyes and see if anyone other than Mrs. B. looked back.

"Come on," I said passing the chauffeur. "You drive. I'll nap in the back."

❦

Trevor led me through the Belasco's modest six-thousand-square-foot Mediterranean home, through a foyer as big as my one-bedroom apartment, up a few steps, and down a long hall to one side of a curved staircase. He knocked lightly at a white-enameled double door with polished brass starbursts radiating from crescent handles. A sultry voice that made Belasco's secretary's sound like a wheezing smoker's lilted, "Come in."

Mrs. Belasco didn't rise from one of the two white leather sofas facing each other across a glass-topped coffee table that, were it ice, could substitute for the LA Kings hockey rink.

"The peeper, Ma'am," Trevor announced.

"Thank you, Trevor. You may leave Mr. Graham with me."

Trevor shot me a warm glare as he went out, suggesting he wasn't as detached as he'd like you to think.

Mrs. B. waved a slim hand at the opposite sofa. I took a seat.

For a woman whose husband had just hitched a ride in the meat wagon, she didn't seem too concerned. At present she seemed more interested in me. Which should have raised an alarm but didn't. The woman was breathtaking. Her physical attributes matched her social accomplishments. She was tall, blond, and svelte. Tanned skin, flawless breasts lifting the front of a lavender blouse, pink lips like spring roses, and green eyes that could tickle your fancy or cut your heart out. Her sending for me meant she knew what I did for a living. Question was, was she alone in there, or was there another woman (succubus?) sharing that pretty skull? And, if so, had she joined me in her husband's dream and caught me peeping? My flesh crawled at the thought.

Her gaze made me uncomfortable, and it takes a lot to make me uncomfortable. I glanced around for a drink cart but didn't see one. She didn't offer me a drink. It occurred to me she wanted me to squirm. Then again, maybe I was reading too much into the situation.

When my wandering gaze found hers, I said: "Sorry for your loss, Mrs. Belasco."

"Eyde, please."

Okay, so we were going to be on a first-name basis. I was ambiguous about that. As I was about her cool demeanor that both amused and scared the hell out of me. While I was gazing into those emerald greens, I watched for any sign of the dark-eyed lynx. I didn't search just out of caution. The sexual pull was magnetic. I figured if that other did make a show, I'd be too enthralled to run for my life. To simmer myself down, I reminded myself how Belasco had died, of Detective Engel's description of my client's corpse.

"In that case, Aloysius. Please."

The silent air conditioning brought me a whiff of her perfume: something musky, mysterious, maddening.

"I don't suppose you'll tell me why Eugene hired you … Aloysius."

I gave her the line about client-dreamer confidentiality. I was hoarse. Both the cops and Trevor had interrupted my morning snort and I was dry.

"My husband is dead," she said, as if I was ignorant of the fact. "I am his widow. I have power of attorney in the case of my husband's incapacitation. I would think death counts as incapacitation, wouldn't you … Aloysius?"

Trick question. I compromised. "Death has its disadvantages. I'm still not discussing your husband's business."

There was a flash of heat in those baby greens, like summer lightning. Then they were cool again.

She buzzed for Trevor and dismissed me. On my way back to the limo, I remembered the way she watched me in her husband's dream, as if she was a speed reader and I was an open book.

That night I dreamed.

Eyde crawled into bed with me. She was naked. Her long, athletic body was hot and cool at once. Her breasts, heavier than they looked, lay against me as if that more voluptuous dark-eyed lynx was there as well. Two babes in one delicious bod. The thought made me delirious. Then her mouth was on mine and our tongues intertwined. Again, there was that sensation of three tongues doing a snake dance and I was rock hard in an instant. She mounted me. I closed my eyes out of sheer terror at what

I might see. I reached up and caressed firm heaving breasts much fuller than Eyde's. I didn't kick her off and run screaming for the elevator. I filled my hands and met her thrust with thrust. Then her mouth was on mine again, and that curious sensation that I was making love to two insanely desirable women at once steamrollered me into the asphalt.

The next morning, I was exhausted. I felt like death warmed over, like a brown stain on skivvies. You get the drift. I stumped into the bathroom and made a bungling attempt at shaving. Splashed too much aftershave on because it helped clear some of the fog.

Unlike Belasco, I remembered my dream. I wiped steam off the mirror. My face looked feverish, the flesh at once sallow and flushed. I thought I might be running a fever. A shyster could carry his brief to court in the purple-gray pouches under my eyes.

"Succubus."

Once I said it, I believed it. A year ago, two days ago, I would have scoffed at anyone believing in such superstitious crockery. (Not to their face; I'm a considerate guy.) I gave up believing in the boogeyman before I learned the truth about Santa. Werewolves and vampires were the stuff of fiction, right? But suddenly I knew beyond a shadow of a doubt this was the case with Mrs. Belasco. No mortal woman could be that overpoweringly sensual. She was a force of nature. Or un-nature. I don't know. I was losing my perspective. And she could enter my dreams and leave me treading Belasco's footsteps.

Two black coffees laced with Scotch was all I could get down for breakfast. They helped get me dressed and out the door. I drove to Mrs. Belasco's. Eyde of the high tits and long, clamping legs. Eyde the dark-eyed lynx. Not Eyde—the lynx was a mystery. I had to see her, had to find out if the succubus was real or if I was losing my mind.

Or both.

When I pulled into the drive, Trevor was dusting the Mercedes on the landing pad in front of the four-car garage. He stopped dusting and scowled at me for a moment, then went back to dusting more aggressively than before.

Touchy. I didn't think much got under his epidermis. Maybe Eyde did.

The front door was open. Down the hall, through the double doors I went, clueless as to what to say, my head in a fog.

She smiled when I entered, as if yesterday's curt dismissal never happened. Her white blouse showed plenty of cleavage. She was standing by a table arranging flowers in a vase. She put down her scissors, came to me, and gave me a kiss on the cheek. That left me more confused than ever. I stammered something. I had no idea what I said. Being this close to Eyde Belasco crossed my wires something terrible. I might have short-circuited and blown my transistors if she hadn't stepped back and laughed. It was a sweet laugh, like a young girl's, innocent and carefree. I imagined she had another laugh she reserved for more intimate occasions.

"You came back. I thought you would." She gestured toward the sofa. "Won't you have a seat … Aloysius." It wasn't a question, and I took a step toward the sofa before I knew what I was doing. Had she just manipulated me? Or was my tired brain imagining it?

"No thanks. I'll stand. This isn't a social call. I can't divulge your husband's business with me, but I want to ask you a question."

"Certainly, Aloysius. You can ask me anything." Before I could speak, she said, "You want to know what I am." She stepped closer, rubbed a forefinger over my lips. I parted my lips. The finger entered my mouth. I sucked it. The temperature rose. The room grew foggy. No, it wasn't fog and it wasn't the room. As in my dream, Eyde Belasco grew ghostly. The blond vision faded. A sultry, raven-haired beauty emerged. I was looking at the lynx of my dream. I felt the electric tendrils of her thought in my brain, and I caught a name.

Lilit.

I was sweating profusely, but I couldn't lift my hand to loosen my tie.

Lilit looked over my shoulder and smiled. Before I could turn, I heard the swoosh, felt a crack that drove a bolt from the back of my skull to the front.

The next thing I knew I was waking up in the desert. Sun was in my eyes.

I tasted sand. Trevor was nearby. Digging. He saw me and came after me with the shovel raised. I tossed a handful of sand into his eyes and rolled. The blade of the shovel came down inches from my head. Adrenaline helped me to my feet, helped me lean in low while the shovel whooshed over my head and I planted a fist into his solar plexus. I put my hip into it and knocked him back, all six foot three of him. I didn't have time to congratulate myself on my handiwork. Trevor had ditched the shovel. He was coming in low, arms spread wide like he was planning on taking me down. I'm a boxer, not a wrestler. Someone gets me on the ground, I'd better be packing, and I don't carry. I couldn't evade him, could never outrun him: he was a decade younger and had legs. And I'd been sapped in more ways than one.

I met him halfway. I'd taken some judo at the Y back in my early twenties and had learned some of the basics. I remember my sensei paraphrasing the immortal Bruce: "Don't fear the man who has practiced ten thousand kicks once; fear the man who has practiced one kick ten thousand times." I had learned only a handful of moves well. If you're not packing, there's only two ways to stop a guy with a reach like Trevor's coming in low: both involve him going over you. One, you pivot, slam your hip into his gut, grab an arm and a handful of shirt and flip him over your hip; two, you drop to the floor and kick him up and over as high and as far as his momentum will carry him. I stepped in, pivoted, and tossed. Trevor's head came down on a rock. Hard. He didn't get up.

I didn't bother burying Trevor. He'd only finished half the hole and I was in no shape to complete the job. Besides, the cops would really be pissed with me once they learned where the body was. And they would learn. I'm a sucker for telling the truth. In fact, I planned to go right down to Central and report the accident as soon as I finished with Mrs. Belasco.

Eyde.

Lilit.

I didn't know yet if I would have more to confess. I didn't have a plan. I was playing it by ear.

Mrs. Belasco was where I'd left her. She was wearing a white bathrobe. Her hair wrapped in a towel. This time she had a drink cart ready. Her left eyebrow lifted when she saw it was me and not Trevor who walked in. She smiled.

"I see the better man won," she said and dropped ice cubes in two thick-bottomed, cut-crystal whiskey glasses. She poured two drinks.

I was covered in dust. I brushed my pants. Dust drifted toward the sofas. "Sorry," I said.

She gave a little shrug of her pretty chin as she drifted toward me, one cool glass outstretched. I took it, gulped it down. "Thanks," I said around an ice cube. Gad, I hadn't been that thirsty since I went hiking in the Boy Scouts and refused to drink out of my canteen after Ron Hurley with food stuck in his braces drank out of it.

I set the glass on the coffee table, stepped close to her. She smelled floral and herbal and of clean skin fresh from the shower. Getting near a succubus is a tricky business. She was like a black hole in the sense that, if you got too close, her gravity would suck you in. She would suck me in no matter what I said or did. I was already spiraling down the rabbit hole. I conjured images of Belasco's withered corpse to dampen my ardor.

The back of her hand stroked my cheek. "Sweet boy," she cooed. A manicured, pink-nailed finger traced down the front of my shirt. On its way to my belt, the nail seemed to lengthen and turned a dark glossy red. I looked up and Lilit stood before me. Raven-haired, ruby-lipped, eyes so dark they were nearly black. She wore a sexy negligee, black silk, the material barely thick enough to leave some mystery. I understood I was seeing what she wanted me to see. Someone else might see a tall, shapely blonde, while I saw a voluptuous dark-eyed vixen. I peered into her eyes. Her irises were almost as black as her pupils.

Her gravity seized me, dragged me closer. I unconsciously stretched my mouth wide, then clenched my teeth in an involuntary reaction as I was seized with the desire to bite her shoulder while I clasped her back and took her there on the floor.

Instead, I grabbed her throat and squeezed. I wasn't going to go out like Belasco, and there was no way I was ever going to escape a creature that could pursue me in my dreams.

I squeezed. Lilit faded and I was looking into Eyde Belasco's purpling face. Fear flashed in her eyes. Only a flash. Then I felt the press of hard steel and she smiled as she pumped two slugs into my gut.

☼

Lilit and Eyde were in bed with me. I was in one. The other pressed against my back, sucking and licking my neck. The one I was in kept sticking her finger in my mouth and I kept sucking it. Which was which kept changing. Lilit was before me, then Eyde, then Lilit.

I was in heaven and I was in hell. I could feel more than my bodily fluids drawn out of me, and the desire to run was a small voice whispering far off beneath the roar of my carnal desire to rut and bite and yield myself to the goddess who swallowed me whole.

I woke. I was lying on my back in a hospital bed. I hurt all over. My stomach was trussed up with a layer of bandages thick as a bulletproof vest. Which—as I remembered why I was in the hospital and not buried in the desert beside my chauffeur buddy—I could have used back at the ranch.

How long had I been here?

Two familiar faces strolled into the room. It was a private room. A single bed.

"How's my favorite comedy team?" I said to Engels and Loomis. My voice came out as a croak. I was as thirsty as when I'd come off the desert.

"Not so funny when you hear what we got for you," Loomis said.

"Chocolates?"

"Ha."

Engels took over: "You're under arrest, Griffith. I gotta read you your rights." He read me my rights: "You have the right to remain silent. Anything you say can and will be used against you in a court of law. You have a right to an attorney. If you cannot afford an attorney, one will be appointed for you."

I fluttered my right hand, *comme-ci, comme-ça.* "Not bad. Keep practicing. What's Wonder Boy got for me?"

Loomis sauntered over. "How'd you like me to tickle your stitches, wise guy? What a sap."

"Mike," Engels said.

Mike sauntered back to the window, took a toothpick out of his pocket, and started chewing.

"Who'd I murder?"

"Glad to see you're taking it seriously. Thought for a second the meds were making you loopy and we were going to have to come back and read you your rights again. You did understand your rights?"

"Yeah, got it. Who'd I kill?" I knew there was at least one choice, maybe two. Had they found Trevor?

"You're under arrest for the murder of Mrs. Eyde Belasco," Engels said. I was about to tell him that one came off better, but he hadn't finished. "The department is looking into any misconduct in your involvement with Mr. Belasco."

I smiled. I would have to recuperate some before I tried laughter. I figured a murder rap trumped misconduct, but I didn't want to hurt his feelings. "Good luck with that," I said.

Engels wasn't fazed.

When Abbott and Costello left, a nurse popped in. A curvy bit of eye candy that took the starch out of me. Her face was too long, her eyes too far apart, to be beautiful, but she packed a sensual wallop that pinned me to the wall like a bug. I smelled her perfume: musky, mysterious, maddening.

Alarms went off in my head.

She smiled. I would know that smile anywhere. Even in my dreams. *Lilit.*

HOMECOMING

Jacob Rawling never meant to visit his childhood home again, but when he received word that he'd inherited his father's house, he made the trip from New Jersey to Iowa to see what needed to be done to get the best price for the property.

The rambling dwelling was once a farm house, back before the farm crisis of the 1980s. By the time Ralph Rawling bought the place, two years before Jacob was born, the acreage had been sold off. Never an attractive dwelling, the house looked significantly worse for wear when Jacob drove up the dirt drive.

After settling himself in his old room (the sour old-man smell of his father's room made the decision for him), he gave the house a cursory inspection. Jacob did not consider himself a nostalgic man, at least not when it came to his depressing childhood home, but as he passed from room to room, noting the creaking floors and peeling wallpaper, memories of bleak Christmases and birthdays uncelebrated kept poking their unwanted noses into his thoughts.

Besides the house, the property consisted of a detached garage and a pole barn in the rear. The sagging front porch looked across a weedy lawn to power lines and a two-lane blacktop, along which an occasional pickup blatted past. The roof was weathered, but he saw no signs of leaks in the attic. Thank God for that. Summer was the rainy season with intense thunderstorms and frequent tornadoes, and he did not want to get caught on the roof in a sudden storm. Some of the gutters were sagging, and water had rotted the fascia behind them. He would paint the kitchen cabinets, replace a cracked toilet and some boards on the porch and under the eaves, mow the lawn, and maybe rent a sprayer and paint the house white.

He sighed. He couldn't afford to hire someone to help him. Luckily, his father had left his tools in the pole barn, and since going it on his own at seventeen, he'd had plenty of experience fixing places to make them livable.

Back upstairs, he paused before the door to his mother's room. His parents had kept separate bedrooms as far back as he could remember. Her door had been kept locked after she abandoned him and his father. His hand shook as he tried the knob and found it still locked. Telling himself he was going to have to unlock the door anyway if he was going to sell the house, he went down to the kitchen and rooted in his father's junk drawer. He supposed every house had one, a drawer where homeowners kept odd keys and screws, coupons, business cards, maybe a box of matches, a screwdriver or razor knife. He found a few keys, took them up, and tried them one by one until her door lock clicked open. The musty smell of abandonment hit him when he stepped inside. He had forgotten how hot and humid Iowa summers were. After sundown, the upstairs bedrooms would stay uncomfortably hot until the sun rose to bake them again. He parted the dusty curtains and opened a window. The light and air helped. He was feeling a little nauseous and he knew it was from being in this room after all these years. It hadn't changed. His father had thrown out her clothes but hadn't touched the furniture. He'd simply locked the room and told Jacob never to go in there. Her bed with the burled walnut headboard stood against one wall, her matching dresser with its clouded mirror against another. There was the industrial-looking metal wardrobe cabinet in which she'd kept her clothes. He opened the door. The few hangers were empty, but on the floor of the wardrobe were items that stirred memories. He reached down, picked up the pair of pink ballerina slippers. A chill ran up his arm as he remembered his mother in her manic "happy" moods putting them on and trying to pirouette on her toes. A framed photograph that used to sit on the living room mantel before his father got rid of all her pictures showed a lovely young brunette with soulful brown eyes. That was taken before he was born. His memory of her was of a woman who had cut her hair mannishly short and whose figure had declined as inactivity and the tide of years bore her farther from youth. She never mastered pirouetting and retired the slippers after a while.

Her old snare drum also lay at the bottom of the wardrobe. It was an inexpensive beginner's model. She'd take it out, set it up on its stand and, using her wire brushes, would shuffle along with one of her jazz CDs. The drum was another of her transient interests.

He mounted the drum on the stand, pulled up a chair, twirled the sticks, and fired off a drum roll. He tightened the snares and ran through a series of fast and slow percussion patterns, ending in a sustained six-stroke roll that concluded with a clack on the rim. Maybe her desire to master the drums had inspired him. He'd taken up drums and bass guitar in his early twenties. He wasn't particularly good with either and didn't have the drum kit anymore, but he enjoyed taking out the bass on occasion and laying down some bottom.

The thought of his mother's many artistic frustrations—drums, ballet, water coloring, poetry—was sobering. Ruth Rawling had been a restless spirit, yearning to fulfill, he supposed, some fretful desire to be a musician, a dancer, a poet. He hadn't known the word back then, but she was at heart a bohemian. Or maybe her creative impulses were her feeble attempts at escaping her small-town Iowa existence. Maybe she'd imagined a more interesting life, but she'd married, had him, and her manic depression had grown worse.

He remembered her mood swings. One day she would be as sweet as pie, all smiles, flushed face, and animated eyes. Talking up a storm between exaggerated puffs on her cigarette about what they would do next weekend, next summer, next Christmas. Hers was an exhaustive energy that drained everyone around her and left her, by evening, wilted and morose.

The next day she would burn him with her cigarette if he got too close.

He rubbed his arm, remembering the sudden shock of the heat of her lit cigarettes on his flesh. Never enough to burn him, just sting him. A little flick of her wrist, never seeming intentional. Maybe it was his fault, an accident; he hadn't watched for the cigarette. Only it happened often. And she never apologized. Just passed an expressionless gaze over him, put the cigarette back in her mouth, and continued whatever she was doing.

She had been kinder to him when he was little. He remembered the first day of kindergarten. Her racing him down the driveway and up to the crossroad where children waited for the school bus. Him running beside her in his short pants and new shoes. Both of them laughing. He'd cried for her when the bus pulled away and he saw her out the window waving.

By the time he was in the second grade, he learned to pour himself a bowl of cereal because mother was up all hours and slept late, and on weekends and days when there was no school, he had to keep quiet and watch his cartoons with the volume turned down low not to disturb her. Waking her resulted in being sent to his room or, worse, made to stand in a dark hall closet until she let him out.

In the end, she stayed in her room most of the time. His father took over the cooking—hamburgers, franks and beans, breakfast for dinner, and occasionally a big pot of spaghetti or chili—and she remained upstairs, coming down to eat leftovers in the early hours of her sleepless nights. He remembered listening to the sound of her small television through his wall late at night as he lay in bed. The sound was comforting, a substitute for her company and a reminder of when they'd been closer.

He set the sticks on the dresser, went over to her night stand, and opened the drawer. It was her medicine drawer. Here she'd kept her prescription meds: Valium and sleeping pills that barely affected her, uppers to get her going in the morning. So many little bottles. The meds were gone. She probably took her stash with her. He stared at the three small notebooks lying in the bottom of the drawer. He'd forgotten about those. They were her medicine journals. He opened one. The pages were covered in orderly columns of tiny chicken scratch that recorded every dose of every medicine she'd taken during the twelve years before she left them. Just up and grabbed a Greyhound bus and disappeared into the Great Unknown. His father claimed he had learned she'd taken the bus to Osceola. He'd followed her there but whether she'd taken the Zephyr east to Chicago or west to San Francisco or somewhere between, he couldn't learn. He'd filed a missing person report. Cops didn't pursue it. Chalked it up to her leaving his father.

Jacob replaced the notebook, closed the drawer, went downstairs, and put on a pot of coffee.

Any house that's been lived in long enough is haunted. Standing on the dirty green-and-white tiles looking around at the ancient stove and avocado fridge, at the sad yellowing country curtains, he could still hear their voices, strident, not disagreeing about any one thing but expressing their mutual dissatisfaction with life, with each other. Mother railing against his father for never taking her anywhere. Father arguing that she never wanted to go anywhere. Her shouting that she was sick and tired of the local café, the drive-in, the prime-rib dinners at the Elks Club. She wanted to go to a Caribbean isle, to New York to see a play, to Paris for the ballet.

He ran his finger over the dust on the pale-green Formica table where he and his father had eaten in silence in the years between her leaving and his own departure. The kitchen hadn't always been such a gloomy place. She had baked Christmas cookies when he was little, and he'd mixed and spread icing on Santas and Christmas trees and stars. Come Easter, they'd color eggs together. He remembered Easter Sunday when he was nine, one of her bad days. They'd planned to go to the church picnic. There would be baskets for all the kids and an Easter egg hunt. She'd promised to take him. They'd colored eggs the night before as they did every year. He didn't like eating the cold hardboiled eggs over the next few days, but he loved coloring them with the special Easter egg coloring kit. The following day she said she had a headache and couldn't go. She'd make it up to him next year.

Next year!

Next year came, and *he* didn't want to go. Nor did they ever color eggs again.

Two ten-hour days of driving and the anxiety of facing his boyhood ghosts had worn him out. After a dinner of sweet tea and a turkey sandwich, he went up to bed. He stopped before her room. He had left the door open to air it out. Following an impulse that both drew and repelled him, he stepped inside. The moon cast a soft trapezoid upon the ancient planks. He crossed to her bed, tossed the dusty bedspread aside, and lay down. He laced his fingers behind his head. When he was young—five, six, seven— she would make him lie next to her on the bed while she napped. If he moved, she would wake and make him go stand in the hall closet in the dark until she let him out. Invariably she would be in a bad mood when she released him, complaining that he'd ruined her nap and she couldn't go back to sleep.

The air cooled, slightly, and he dozed and dreamed. His sixth birthday was the only time he'd had a birthday party. Some of the kids from his first-grade class and a couple friends from Sunday school had come. Most of them had brought him presents: a cup-and-ball game, a cardboard kaleidoscope, a yo-yo, a plastic boat. The party was held outdoors. They'd played Pin the Tail on the Donkey. Father had grilled hamburgers and hotdogs. Mother brought out a chocolate cake. The shadows grew longer as the afternoon waned and the day grew cooler (his birthday was in September), and the kids left. Mother grew tired and went inside to sit in the living room and smoke. He'd come with his arms full, excited to show her his presents. Sure enough, he got too close, and the glowing end of her cigarette found him. He dropped his treasures and ran upstairs crying.

The dream changed. He stood in the kitchen doorway. Behind him the living-room TV was on. He'd been watching an afternoon cartoon but got up when he heard his mother's voice raised. She stood by the sink, backlit by the sunlight falling through the kitchen window. His father sat at the table, trying to enjoy his coffee. In the dream he was eight. It was an old dream, one he'd had often as a boy. It was based on a real event, and he knew what happened next. So, standing in the kitchen doorway, covering his ears and hyperventilating and wishing they'd stop, he was torn between running upstairs or staying and watching the inevitable unfold. He stood and watched, wide-eyed and trembling because that's what he had done the day it happened. His mother's voice rose, strident. She was accusing his father of sleeping with Mrs. Mills from church. At eight, the image of the pretty blond pianist sleeping with his father made him squirm for unknown reasons. Now, being an adult dreaming he was eight, he knew what his mother had meant by "sleeping" and his eight-year-old dream self cringed. Father continued to ignore her.

Suddenly, a white ceramic plate appeared in her hand. She hurled it across the kitchen. As if in slow motion, he watched his father fling up his arm to protect his face … the ceramic disk shattering…the spray of bright blood across the table cloth … Father wrapping a towel around his arm and running out. The pickup started, tore out of the drive. An hour passed, another. Then the cars coming up the drive. Two policemen accompanying his father. His father's forearm bandaged, his sleeve cut off. One of the policemen told his mother if she ever did anything like that again, he would arrest her. Lock her up. Did she understand?

His mother's eyes narrowed as if she would spit in the officer's face, but she nodded she understood.

The dream changed. His mother was sitting on the porch. It was late afternoon. The sun was behind the house, so she sat in shade. He brought her a glass of iced tea. She thanked him, took a sip, and set the glass on the table between the rocking chairs. She continued staring across the yard at the two-lane blacktop. She had only recently cut her hair in a short masculine crop, maybe something she had seen on TV or in a magazine; certainly no one else in town wore the like. He wanted to ask her how she was feeling, but she lit a cigarette, a warning for him to keep his distance. He stared out at the highway, wondering what was going on in her mind. He stole a sidelong glance at her. Her skin had turned corpse-gray. He held his breath. A black spot appeared on her cheek. Similar spots blossomed as if seeping from her pores. Her skin peeled. Now black mold dappled her face.

He started awake. For a disoriented moment he was a boy. Fearing he had awakened his mother, he glanced right. Expecting her to be lying beside him, he cringed in anticipation of her disapproval. He was alone.

Did the dream mean his mother was dead? Not knowing where she'd gone and given her bohemian proclivities, he'd imagined she'd headed for California or maybe Manhattan. Lying there sweating, catching his breath, he decided he did not believe in prophetic dreams, or any kind of divination for that matter.

He unclenched his fists, took a deep breath. It was a bad idea coming back here. Too many ghosts.

⚜

The next day Jacob went down to the hardware store to pick up supplies.

The town had prospered marginally better than the house. The pickup trucks parked nose-in along Main Street were newer than those he remembered but not in much better shape. A lot of young people, himself included, had left Iowa for better prospects, and the average age of the townsfolk appeared older than when he was a boy. Hanley's Hardware and Building Supplies hadn't changed much. The lawnmowers lined up out front were new models, but inside, the tin ceiling, worn plank floor, and zinc counter were the same as he remembered. The proprietor was new—not young, just not old man Hanley.

"Can I help you?" the burly man in a John Deere T-shirt asked when he approached the counter.

"I believe you can," he said, returning the man's smile.

Before going over the list, he explained about inheriting the house, and wondered if the man knew his father. Growing up here, he remembered everyone knew just about everyone else.

"Sorry for your loss," the man said. "Place needs a bit of work, does it?"

"A bit."

"Yes, I knew your father." The man wagged a finger, recollecting. "Remember your mom, too. She was the first local woman to cut her hair short as a man's back then. Of course, you see it more often now: young women and some of the blue-haired crowd. But back then, she was the only one. Your dad really loved her, didn't he?"

That took Jacob by surprise. "Why do you say that?"

The gentleman drew back, as if sensing he might have offended Jacob. "I mean he kept coming in here, and about every other store on Main Street, asking if anyone had news of your mom."

⚜

Back home, he went up to his father's room. The sour stink of unwashed flesh and unchanged sheets was heavy and he opened the windows. He found what he was looking for on the closet shelf. It was an old boot box. When he opened it, he was surprised to find two bundles of greeting cards secured by rubber bands that crumbled when he tried to remove them. One stack was from his father to his mother, the other from her to him. They consisted of birthday, Christmas, and Valentine's Day cards. His father's bundle was twice as thick as his mother's.

He sat on the old olive-drab Army trunk at the foot of his father's bed and read through them. He started with his father's cards to his mother. They were dated so he began with the earliest ones which predated the year of their marriage. The first couple were brief: Wishing you a merry or happy and closing with "Your friend." The next year's Valentine's Day card advanced to "Love." A folded sheet of stationary fell out of her next birthday card.

"Dear Ruth," he read. "I really enjoyed going to the movie last weekend. You know I'm not the most talkative person and this isn't easy for me to put into words, so I'll just write it as if you were standing in front of me and I was brave enough to tell you how I feel about you. You know I've found you special since the junior dance last year. What I mean to say is I've loved you since dancing with you that night. There, I've said it! I'm going to hurry and get this in the mail before I lose my nerve. I hope, the next time I see you, I'll learn you feel the same about me."

He put that one down and shook his head. He saw what Hanley's new owner meant now. Now that he thought of it, he remembered his father holding his mother's hand when he was little. He read a few more. They grew more intimate following engagement and marriage.

Curious, he scanned through the cards his mother had given his father. There were no letters tucked inside, and they were considerably cooler, the early ones making an attempt at sincerity and inserting a carefully printed "Love" above the signature, the later ones simply a Best Wishes and a signature. They ended some years before her disappearance. His father's ended a couple of years later, as if he'd given up trying. Still, the fact that he'd kept their cards was a testament to his father's feelings for his mother.

A surge of anger washed through Jacob. Manic depression, what they now called bipolar disorder, was partially to blame for Ruth Rawling's inability to return her husband's affection, but she had hurt him more than Jacob had realized. Before she left, Jacob would see him with an occasional beer flipping burgers on the grill or watching a game—"Go Hawks!"—but he'd embraced the bottle only after his wife left. Jacob had always resented her for that. Bad enough she abandoned them, but even in her absence she'd continued to hurt his father. Never the most affectionate man—Ralph Rawling had grown distant and morose, and spent his evenings and weekends watching TV, not for any interest in what was on but to kill time while sipping his highball.

He'd thought it hot in Camden, where he stocked and repaired vending machines. His T-shirt was soaked by the time he got the ladder propped against the side of the house and the tools he would need set out on the grass. He intended to replace the rotted fascia behind the rain gutter. He had fresh lumber and a circular saw set up outside the pole barn. He was taking a drink of Gatorade when a car pulled into his driveway and honked.

Walking over, he saw it was Bobby Fray, a friend from high school.

"Hey!" Bobby said, getting out of the late model Lexus. "I heard in town Ralph Rawling's son was fixing up the old place to sell it."

They shook hands. Bobby hadn't changed much. His waist was a little thicker, his double chin more prominent. He was wearing navy dress slacks, black brogans, and a white shirt with a red and blue club tie. Jacob thought, with some bemusement, that he was going to regret getting out of his air conditioning. "Bobby Fray. What have you been up to?"

Bobby flicked out a black-and-gold, raised-letter business card. "I just happen to know a realtor," he said. His teeth were blindingly white.

"So you got your license."

"Yep. You should stay in touch. I don't hear from you in a decade …" He nudged his nose toward the house. "How is it? I mean coming back?"

"Honestly? Depressing."

Bobby nodded, returned his gaze to the house. "You've got your work cut out for you." Jacob noted he didn't offer to help. "Condolences about your dad."

Jacob thanked him.

"I remember how sweet your mom was," Bobby said. Sweat stains were starting to appear under his arms. "I guess at that age, I mean when your mom left … adults do stuff, and if it isn't something bad that they're doing to you, you don't pay it much mind. Looking back, I guess I should have been shocked that Mrs. R. left."

"I was shocked enough for both of us. But I know what you mean. Kids are selfish. Not in a bad way. Just they're not mature enough to be altruistic and worry about anything that doesn't affect them personally."

"Adults worry about others; kids worry about themselves."

"Yeah, that's it. But about my mom. You saw her on her good days. The days you didn't see her, she was in her room, smoking, watching TV, sneaking miniature peanut butter cups."

"Didn't know that," Bobby said.

They talked for another couple of minutes, Jacob asking about this or that mutual acquaintance and Bobby filling him in. Then Bobby made a show of checking his wrist, even though he wasn't wearing a watch. "Listen, I've got to meet a client. Give me a call when you're done, and we'll get this baby sold." He opened the car door. "And don't work too hard," he called over his shoulder as he sank into the cool interior. "Don't want you getting heat stroke before I get my commission."

Replacing the fascia turned out to be more work than he'd bargained for. He would have to hire someone to help him do the other side. He almost fell twice getting the rain gutter off. He finally lowered it to the ground by securing one end with a rope looped around the chimney. He worked his way down the gutter's length, loosening the fasteners and hangers and walking the far end down the ladder, then going to the secured end and lowering it by the rope. After guzzling half a bottle of Gatorade, he went back up to remove the old fascia board. He was about halfway down the first section, when he heard the buzzing.

A swarm of wasps erupted from the rafters. He tossed the pry bar, but before he could slide down the ladder, they were stinging him on the face, arms, and back. He tried to wave them off and fell. The impact knocked him out.

He dreamed.

He was six and he had the chicken pox. His fever was raging. He felt sick. His head swam and he itched all over. His mother was reading *James and the Giant Peach* to him. Her voice was soothing, and he closed his eyes to picture James hiding from his wicked aunts and crying into his hands behind the laurel bushes.

When he opened his eyes, he was in the upstairs hallway. He wasn't a boy but himself, full-grown. His mother stood beside him. She looked as he remembered her, with her close-cropped hair, print blouse, and violet slacks. Only she looked insubstantial. He could see the wallpaper through her body.

She took his arm. Her touch was cold. The hairs on the back of his neck rippled like seaweed. She didn't speak but led him to her room. They stood in the open door. In the room were his mother and father. They were arguing. He couldn't make out what they were saying, but his father held one of the bottles from her medicine drawer. His face was red, but he appeared more upset than angry. Shouting something incoherent, his mother rushed his father. She had her nails out to rake his face. They were polished violet to match her slacks. His father sidestepped and shoved her. She fell and struck her head on the cast-iron radiator. She didn't get up. There was no blood. She lay there silent and unbreathing.

His father dropped to his knees, rolled her over, and cradled her head in his lap. Her forehead was dented, the flesh surrounding the dent a purple bruise.

He looked from his mother's corpse to the ghost beside him. She returned his gaze. Her face was sad beyond measure. She vanished.

Then he was lying in a dark place. Bound head to foot. He couldn't move, couldn't breathe. A hot, fetid smell gagged him.

He woke with the sun beating down on his face. He ached all over, and his flesh burned where the wasps had stung him, but he pushed himself to his feet and hurried into the house and up the stairs. He had left his father's door open. The smell had spread to the hall. No longer musty and sour, it had become a living pestilence, something poisonous, cloying and clinging.

His guts went cold as he walked toward the bed. The smell was coming from the mattress. No, not the bed—from the wall behind the bed. Shoving the frame from side to side, he walked the bed away from the wall. Low on the wall, there was a square door, maybe three by three. An access door to the attic. The door was nailed shut. He ran out of the room, returned with a pry bar.

Hot, fetid air billowed into his face when he opened the door. Inside, was a narrow space between the wall and the sloping roof. It wasn't completely dark. The daylight seeping up under the eaves showed a long, plastic-wrapped bundle to the left of the door. He shined his cell's flashlight into the space, and now he made out the vague impression of a desiccated face beneath the yellowed plastic.

His father had loved his mother. That knowledge alone made him glad he had made the journey. Jacob did not want to trash his father's memory by calling in the police and have his father called a murderer on the news, so he buried her in the back at one end of the pole barn and planted roses over her grave.

When the work was completed and the rooms were aired and a fresh coat of paint replaced the sweet-sour scent of death, he called Bobby, put the house on the market, and returned to Camden and stocking and repairing vending machines.

When he left, the only things he took with him were his parents' cards and his mother's snare drum.

THE HUNGRY STARS

I dreamed the dream again. This time something new was added. I didn't turn to see what was breathing its rancid breath down my neck. I sensed something feral and dangerous that made my hackles rise and resorted to my adopted escape plan. I willed my sleeping self to kick violently, thereby propelling myself awake. The trick always works. It is a good thing I sleep alone; otherwise, I would surely launch my partner onto the floor.

A note on free will. While the older, more superstitious dream philosophers assign an external cause to nightmares—the Oneiros of the Greeks, the demons and witches of medieval pedagogues—and while the current associationist-sensationist dogma of the psychologists ascribe an interior etiology—i.e., some physical morbidity such as illness, pain, or irritation of the digestive tract, or the emotional and mental residue of trauma experienced during the day's events—all of these preclude the agency of volition, of free will. In other words, our subconscious minds, whether by indigestion or morbidity of mind, project a magic-lantern stream of dissociated imagery and sensory impressions upon the screen of our consciousness. I beg to differ. While I *believe*, as an experienced and creative explorer in Dreamland, that I have some degree of volition in choosing the path of my dreams, I *know*—upon the profounder evidence of my reaction (I kick, therefore I wake) that I exert a degree of free will in my sojourns there.

Still ... if I am in control of my dream, why is something I had not engineered appearing in it? No matter how much concerted reason may shape the dream logic, the subconscious finds a way to assert its influence.

"What have you found?"

Charlotte started. She had been so engrossed in the book she'd picked up she didn't notice Florence approach. The visit to the bookseller was always one of her favorite excursions. Florence, who had gone off on her own exploring the book shop's brimming stacks and bins, cradled three books to her breast. Some fourteen years her senior, Florence had been her governess when she was a child and had stayed on as her companion following the railway accident that claimed the lives of her parents. Charlotte had survived the ill-fated excursion to Scotland but remained wheelchair-bound from her injuries. Truth was, Florence was her best friend (to be honest, her only friend). They went to the opera together and the galleries and the Christmas concerts at the Royal Albert Hall, and they read to each other from their bookshop finds—well, Florence hadn't always been totally forthcoming: some of her reading material was somewhat racy and had to wait till Charlotte's majority for sharing. Some of the passages in Marie Corelli's *The Sorrows of Satan* and George Egerton's *Rosa Amorosa* had, to Florence's amusement, made her blush.

"It's a private journal." Marking her place with her finger, Charlotte held the book up for Florence's inspection. The handwritten journal was leather-bound. The sewn pages were a little loose, attesting that the book had been opened and closed often. Most entries were dated, others not, as if the author had been in a rush to get the essentials of his dreams on paper. Knowing well the frustration of trying to recall the details of a dream upon awakening, she could empathize with the author's haste. "Appears to be the dream journal of a Harold Maudsley."

"Interesting?"

"I think so. It will be amusing to read of his dreams. He calls himself an 'explorer in Dreamland.' Elsewhere, he talks of using his dreams as the inspiration for his stories. I wonder if he's published?"

"When is the last entry dated?"

Charlotte turned to the final entries. These were about two thirds of the way into the volume; the remaining pages were blank. "1906," she said. The last entry was decidedly more hastily written than those earlier.

"Two years ago. I wonder why the journal would be at the booksellers. I would think the recording of one's dreams would be a private affair. He hasn't written anything to make you blush, has he?" Florence's dimples were showing; she was being devilish.

"Not yet," Charlotte said, meeting Florence's smile with her own.

Seated in her wheelchair, Charlotte watched the proprietor, a little man with a large mustache, wrap their purchases. When he came to the journal, she said, "Wait."

"Yes, miss?"

"That book you're holding. Can you tell me anything about it? I mean, who the author is and if he's published anything?"

He pulled the book closer to his face. The cover bore no inscription. He opened to the bookplate where Charlotte had learned the author's name.

"Ah, yes indeed." His eyes were merry with the self-satisfaction of one who knows the answer. "To both your questions; Harold Maudsley was a moderately popular author of ghost stories. Well, not ghost … weird tales, strange stories."

"'Was.'"

"Yes, miss." He brushed his mustache with the back of a finger. "That's why I have his journal and his library. Bought the lot from his heirs, two nieces. I understand he never married and had no children."

"You have his books?"

"I do."

She flashed Florence a smile. "I'll take those too."

That night after dinner, Charlotte retired early. Sitting on her featherbed, her quilt drawn over her lap, she read from her morning purchases. The night was warm. Her bedroom window was open. It was quiet out, the only noise intruding on her revelry the rare rumble of a passing car. She began by examining Maudsley's two collections of short stories. The contents pages listed intriguing titles: "The Somnambulist," "The Crystal Grotto," "Invitation to a Drowning," "Mirror Shards." She picked one from the second volume. It turned out to be a pirate story about a pirate ship that was blown off course to a mysterious island with a great central mountain rearing its head above the jungle. Within a minute the story had captivated her totally. She chewed her lip absently as she turned the pages.

Guards died, each death marked by a thin discordant piping. The piping led the captain and a group of armed sailors to a great cavern deep within the mountain where they found the statue of a tall man carven of black stone.

The idol—for in this place and standing upon the dais, it could be only some relic of a long-forgotten pagan cult—was naked and marvelously wrought so that its powerful muscles stood out in sharp relief. So lifelike was the statue that it seemed at any moment it might step off the dais and approach us.

But as marvelous as the sculptor's art was, what commanded our attention was its face. Or I should say its lack of face, for where its features should be, a black void, scintillating as with black stars, gazed down upon us. And, as we stared transfixed into that monstrous gulf, bewitched as it were so that no man might wrench his gaze away, it was like falling into a sea of darkness that seemed to expand so that you were engulfed, as if the idol's face had depth that transcended the stone surface and plumbed fathomless deeps so that I felt as though I stood on the shore of eternal night, into which—God help me—terrified as I was, I longed to plunge.

Mesmerized by the idol, the captain ordered his officers to fire upon the crewmen. A sacrifice to the faceless god. Back in camp, the remaining crewmen were slaughtered by the ghosts of all the sacrificial victims ever stranded on that abominable isle.

As I ran the gauntlet, slashing my way to the lifeboat tied up on the shore, I saw Jim Wilkins take down two attackers, his blade severing them shoulder to sternum, before three of the animated dead hacked him to pieces. And all the while, drowning the screams of dying men, the maddening piping fell about my ears out of the vast eternity of night.

"Whew. I may not sleep tonight," Charlotte said to herself. Now she understood what the bookseller had meant when he said Maudsley was a writer of "weird" stories. She set the book aside and opened Maudsley's journal at random.

I dreamed again of the strange city with its star-reaching turrets and airy bridges arching over glittering canals. This time I saw my dream city slumbering under black stars and illuminated by twin black moons that should have given no light but did. My heart ached for the city as one might, in a nostalgic moment, long for a favorite childhood place recalled by a scent of pine or dew-damp grass or a whiff of wood smoke, sharp and comforting.

What sort of person are you, Harold Maudsley? she wondered, closing the book. She yawned, thought *Maybe I will sleep after all,* set the book aside, pulled the linens about her neck, and slept.

And dreamed of walking by a canal whose ebony waters reflected a sky scintillating with black stars that shouldn't have given off light but did. In the near distance, black towers stretched their spires toward the eternal gulf. The night was neither hot nor cold but caressed her like the lover she'd never had.

She was walking, as often happened in her dreams, her thin, useless legs grown supple and strong. She felt the click of each heel upon the pavement, rejoiced in the flex of muscle, the spring of each forward-moving step. She wore her green walking skirt, its fluted hem terminating at the tops of her boots rather than falling to her feet. A thought came to her, as if she'd suddenly remembered something she'd forgotten. She looked up: twin black moons bathed the ethereal city in dusky twilight.

It occurred to her that she had a destination, and she turned from the canal onto a broad avenue that led her past the ornate entrances of colossal towers. There were no street lamps, and the buildings were windowless. She was alone in the dark-light, a single beating heart treading a Plutonian necropolis.

Or was she alone? The thought gave her pause. Gazing into the gulf, she felt a predatory stare as if the stars were hungry eyes following her progress. A shiver rippled her flesh. There was something prescient about the night, as if the runes had long been cast and read and waited only for her to fulfil her part in the cosmic cycle. Looking up into the dizzying gulf, she felt infinitely small, vulnerable, and afraid.

She rounded a corner, as if her feet had a clearer understanding of where she was going than her brain. She saw him before he saw her. Her heart leapt with the shock of coming upon a living person in this chthonic nightscape. Her startlement was immediately replaced by a joy of recognition. Though she had no idea how she knew, she understood with overwhelming conviction this was the man she'd been subconsciously seeking.

Harold Maudsley.

She stopped, a dozen paces from his back. As if sensing her presence, he turned, and her heart leapt again. He was handsome. Lush side whiskers framed a youthful face that might once have been ruddy but had grown pale in this lightless city. Maudsley waited for her to speak, as if she might be a product of his imagination and would vanish in a moment.

"Mr. Maudsley," she said, having no idea what else to say.

He took a step toward her, stopped as if afraid he might scare her off. He searched her eyes, as if to learn if she were real. "You appear out of nowhere, and you know my name." He looked beyond her down the spectral avenue. His eyes flicked from doorway to arching doorway.

She followed his gaze. "What are you looking for?"

"It's you, isn't it?" he said, his gaze returning to her. "Your being here is keeping it away."

She smiled. He was scaring her, but she was intrigued. Here was a dream more realistic than any in her memory. And faced with a living ghost of a man who was mystery incarnate.

"Whatever do you mean?"

"Never mind." He appeared to relax, as if a weight had been lifted from his shoulders. "Whatever the reason for your visit—" He spread his hands and glanced about at the cyclopean architecture. "—welcome to Carcosa."

"Carcosa?"

"My version of it anyway. I think every dreamer, consciously or unconsciously, makes their own."

"You haven't answered my question: what were you looking for?"

"The beast," he said flatly and watched to see her reaction.

She remembered the passage from his journal—*I didn't turn to see what was breathing its rancid breath down my neck ... something feral and dangerous*—and shivered.

"I get the impression it is toying with me and has eternity to play."

She looked around. The place was intimidating enough, but to imagine a predator stalking them ...

"I don't feel its presence tonight," he continued. "Ha! Listen to me—in this place there is only night."

"Why don't you use your practiced kick to wake yourself?"

He looked at her as if she had picked his pocket. "You've read my journal?"

"I purchased it."

"'Purchased'? How can that be?"

"Mr. Maudsley …"

"Harold, please. And you?"

"Charlotte. Mr.—Harold, when do you last remember going to sleep?"

"Why, I don't know. Some nights ago, I suppose. That doesn't make sense, but it seems as if I've been dreaming a while." He snapped his fingers. "I remember. Yesterday—it must have been yesterday—Wednesday, March 17."

"And the year?"

"The year? Why this one!"

"The year?" She waited.

"1906."

"Nearly two years ago."

His wonderstruck look broke her heart. "Then…?"

She nodded. "You died that night or the next. Your cleaning lady found you."

"Dead … I've been dreaming I'm awake and going about the business of the day and then dreaming of going to bed and awakening here." His consternation turned into a smile. "Perhaps I'm dreaming you, and since I'm dreaming, I must be alive and soon I'll wake and record this dream. Yes—" He smacked his forehead. "—of course. That's how you can quote my journal: I'm dreaming you, so you know what I know." He laughed, a hearty baritone she found immensely attractive.

"Or I'm dreaming you," she said. "Remember, I'm keeping the beast away."

His smile faded. "You shouldn't be here."

As if to underscore his admonishment, the thin, monotonous whine of an ill-played flute rose out of the twilight. He searched the sky from which the piping seemed to come. She gazed up, then quickly looked down: the stars appeared hungrier still; she felt a myriad malicious intelligences tugging at her brain.

"I haven't heard this for ages," he said, a look of wonder widening his eyes.

She remembered the hideous piping in his pirate story but said nothing. She would search his dream journal for the passage that inspired the story when she got the chance.

"Where do you ... Do you have a place to stay?" she asked. The night was growing cold. She no longer felt caressed but threatened, as if the dark was alive, probing for an entry into her mind.

He shoved his hands in his pockets, shrugged. "All the doors are locked and there are no windows."

They walked, he with his hands in his pockets, his shoulders hunched; she clutching her shawl more tightly about her neck. They turned into a broad plaza, its four sides lined with sky-reaching towers. Windowless, locked, the buildings themselves now felt threatening, ominous. On a low pedestal in the center of the plaza stood a statue of a tall man at least eight feet tall. They had approached it from behind. The figure was naked, its muscles thickly corded. The black stone from which it was carved glistened dully in the starlight.

"I remember dreaming this," he said, his wonder barely suppressed. "Only it was in a jungle. I wrote a story about it."

"I read it."

"Then you know the danger of looking into its face."

She shuddered, remembering the black void, scintillating as with black stars, where its face should be. "But this is just a dream, right?"

"Dreams can be dangerous. Take my continued sojourn here as evidence."

She started forward, intending to go around the idol anyway, determined to overcome her fear and look into its face, to prove this was just a dream.

He caught her arm. His grip was firm but gentle. She felt a warm flush go through her at his touch. She stopped and gazed into his haunted face, his soulful dark eyes. In that fleeting second, she wished that he would put his hand on her cheek and draw her to him and kiss her. But then, as if immobile, rigid stone had become flesh, the idol began to turn.

Maudsley—Harold—threw an arm around her and started back the way they came. She couldn't resist looking over her shoulder as the monstrous visage swung around and she felt its will compelling her to gaze into the infinity of its face. She tripped and fell, her withered legs suddenly failing her.

She woke into darkness. After minutes of alternately gazing upon the memory of Harold's face and the idol's imagined unholy visage, she lit a candle and retrieved Harold's journal and searched for the dream that had inspired his pirate story. She found it and read: "Pirate story. Bay of Bengal. Buccaneers attack a Mogul sloop, then flee an East India man-o'-war. Blown off course by a gale, landfall on a seemingly deserted island." The rest pretty much summarized the plot of the story she had read.

Could it really have been only a dream? A dream shaped by the entries she'd read from his journal and the details of his story?

On impulse, she turned to his final entry. The date took her breath away: March 17, 1906.

The next day they took a cab to Paternoster Row where they met with Maudsley's publisher. Florence had called ahead for an appointment. They arrived after lunch and the girl in the anteroom ushered them into the publisher's office. Mr. Anthony was a prosperous-looking gentleman of middle age sporting bushy side whiskers and Harris tweed. His smile was affable and appeared unaffected. He offered Florence a seat in front of his desk and removed the other chair so that Charlotte could park her wheelchair next to Florence. After offering them coffee, which they declined, he asked, "How do you know my former client? I do not mean to pry if there is a personal connection—" This he addressed to Florence, which Charlotte thought curious. "—but the man was always something of a mystery and it was my curiosity that agreed to an interview."

Charlotte showed him the journal. He spent a few minutes perusing its pages. "Why, this is marvelous," he said, returning it. "How did you come by it?"

Charlotte started to answer, but Florence beat her to it. "We found it in a lot containing the author's disposed library." Florence was smiling, a little too broadly. Was she flirting with the publisher?

"I'd like to know more about the author," Charlotte said. "He keeps a dream journal, refers to himself as an "explorer in Dreamland," and suggests he is—*was*—able to influence his dreams. How did he die?"

Mr. Anthony puffed his cheeks and let the air out slowly. "To the best of my knowledge, he died in bed. Although his body wasn't found till two days later by his cleaning lady. The autopsy established the time of death but not the cause. It really is a mystery. He appeared to be in fine health." He spread his hands. "Sad, really. He showed great promise."

"How so?"

"Have you read his stories?"

"Just one."

"Harold Maudsley's imagination was boundless. Most of his characters were, in one way or another, autobiographical. But his style has a dreamlike, lyrical quality that makes you wonder what he might have achieved had he lived to write in the coming decades." He rattled off a few more details: A University of London graduate. Taught English courses at a prep school for five years prior to publishing. Took on editorial work on the side. Never married.

"Do you have a photograph?" Florence asked.

"I do." Mr. Anthony pulled an envelope from his desk, passed it to Florence.

Florence withdrew the sepia-toned photograph, glanced at it, passed it to Charlotte. Charlotte gazed on it for what seemed like minutes. It was a professional photograph, probably a publicity portrait. The likeness left no doubt it was the man she had visited in Dreamland. She replaced the picture in the envelope. She wanted to ask if she could keep it but didn't dare. She laid the envelope on the desk.

"Did Harold—I mean, Mr. Maudsley—ever talk to you about Dreamland?" she asked.

"Hmm." Anthony pulled his chin. "He might have. I don't remember. We had lunch a couple times and he'd talk about what he was working on. At my prompting, I should add. He wasn't a man to go on about himself, so mostly the conversation steered to people we knew in common, writers and editors mostly, or to the German problem."

"I want to read you something."

Anthony clasped his hands and sat back in his chair. "By all means."

Charlotte opened the journal. "This is his final entry, dated the day of his death."

> I am exhausted. I have slept little these past two weeks. Tired as I am, I fight to stay awake. And when I sleep, I return to the accursed canyons of those dream-haunted streets.
>
> The beast torments me. It hasn't shown itself, but I feel its presence, smell its feral stink. Sometimes I almost feel its furry paw brush my cheek and I thrust myself back into the waking world. For weeks now, I've tried to dream other dreams set in other locales, but it is as if I am a prisoner in Dreamland fated to return to Carcosa and the beast. I've had enough. Since childhood I have always been the master of my dreams, steering them in whatever direction I saw fit, plunging into the thick of danger or tacking clear of the storm into calm waters. I refuse to be bullied by my own dreams. Tonight, I will face the beast—or rather I will face its master; for I feel some vast malign intelligence whose attention my adventures have attracted is behind my tormenting. Tonight, I will find my way out of the maze.

Anthony steepled his fingers when she finished and gazed across his desk at her. Horse and motor traffic and the combined voices of a hundred pedestrians came up from the busy Strand through his open window. "I had no idea," he said when he'd had time to collect his thoughts. "By dating that entry, he signed ..."

"His death certificate," Florence finished for him.

"Yes, I should say so." Placing his hands flat on his ink blotter, he shook his head. "It's true what they say."

"What's that?" Florence asked.

"Truth is stranger than fiction."

"You're back," he said when she found him seated on a bench beside the canal that night. "Don't get me wrong—" He stood as she approached, her back straight, her legs strong. "—to be honest, I've never been so glad to see someone in my life." He grinned and shook his head. "Or since my death. The jury's still out on that."

Her heart ached at the agony of his plight. She felt pity for herself as well, having finally met someone who made her feel things she'd only imagined vicariously through reading and find him, what? a tormented ghost? Gazing into his lovely brown eyes, she saw an active, intelligent mind at work. How he was able to smile considering his circumstances, she couldn't imagine, but it spoke of an impressive resiliency. If Harold couldn't return to the waking world, she would spend as much time in Dreamland as she could.

She sat beside him. She longed to lean against him, to put her head on his shoulder, but she was timid, so she sat with her hands folded in her lap. Still, it was her dream, wasn't it? She should be able to do whatever she wanted in her own dream. As if reading her thoughts—or perhaps because she subconsciously willed it—he placed an arm about her shoulders. She leaned into him.

He chuckled. It was a pleasant sound, almost cheerful enough to compensate for the greasy slop of canal water against the piling. "You know, Charlotte," he said, "I do not remember you. I mean from my waking life. You might be an amalgam of women I have met. The subconscious mind is capable of that."

"Or I might be someone you haven't yet met."

"Ah, a prophetic dream." She felt his smile. "I like that better. If I ever wake up, I'll keep an eye out for you."

"And I for you," she said, glad he could not see the tear roll down her cheek.

She thought of the story she had read before retiring. This one involved twin sisters. Neither could determine which was alive and which a ghost. However, if one was dead, it fell upon the living to join her sister. Most author's works were autobiographical to some degree. She wondered if he had lost a sibling. Or a lover.

A solitary wave rolled down the canal, splashing water over the curb as it passed, soaking their feet. Harold jumped up, offered Charlotte his hand. "That was unusual. Let's find dryer ground."

They walked. They stayed on the broad avenue. Passing the tenantless façades, she hoped they would not encounter the faceless idol. Or the beast. She fought the urge to cling tighter to his arm. She did not want him to think her afraid.

No sooner did she think the thought than the piping began. The reedy unmelodious fluting set her teeth on edge. Harold's arm tensed and he quickened his pace, hurrying them along. The night and the city, eerily still, had grown expectant as if watching their progress.

She started. Harold, who had been examining doorways as if expecting something awful to be lurking in the shadows, turned to her. "What's wrong?"

She rubbed her cheek with the back of her hand. "Something touched me. Something furry."

Harold looked up and down the street, searching. She followed his gaze. She saw nothing, yet before she could turn to Harold and tell him she must have imagined it, she felt again the brush of stiff fur against her face and smelled the carrion breath of a predatory beast. She panicked, ran, her legs remembering in Dreamland the long-denied activity.

"Wait," Harold shouted after her. She heard his footfalls on the pavement behind her but couldn't stop. He grabbed her shoulder, pulled her into his arms.

"It's all right, it's all right." He rubbed her back as if to soothe her terror. Pressing her face into his shirt, she smelled him, a clean linen scent combined with a masculine aftershave: she caught hints of bergamot and juniper berry. She concentrated on the smell and her panic subsided.

She felt him tense. She followed his gaze.

Ahead in the gloom of the next intersection stood the black eidolon. Before she could look into its face, Harold was retreating back the way they had come, pulling her along. He stopped again; ahead at the next intersection, the idol blocked their way.

Charlotte spied an alley and tugged Harold's arm. They hadn't run more than twenty paces before they encountered a smooth obsidian wall.

"You'd think I would know my way around by now," Harold said, "But the city keeps changing, as if it's toying with me."

The idol stood in the alley's entrance, tall and glistening in the twilight. It did not enter but barred their exit. The piping grew strident, a shrill, earsplitting frenzy that raked needles across her nerves.

Harold staggered away from her, put his hand against the wall. Charlotte saw terror in his wide-eyed stare. His mouth opened. His lips moved. He shook his head.

"What's wrong?" she asked, but she saw it now: his face, his body, was growing faint, like a dissolve at the cinema. "Harold!" She reached for him, then pulled her hand away, afraid it would go through him.

"You need to wake!" he shouted. His voice seemed to come from a distance.

"What's happening to you?" she shouted back.

The apparition glanced skyward. His smile was a grimace; he was fighting his terror. "I'll be another hungry star, watching and waiting for some prideful imbecile to stumble into Carcosa. Please Charlotte, you've got to wake! Will your sleeping self to kick!"

"I can't," she said, realizing the irony of her situation. "I'm paralyzed." She wouldn't have thought how much it hurt to admit that to him, but it did. She had forgotten her waking self, hobbled to a chair, an invalid, bound to the earth by chains of paralysis.

And now, as if the memory had made it so, she was in her chair, her hands gripping the hand rims, powerless to help Harold or herself.

"Come back!" she shouted. But he faded. The last she saw of him his teeth were bared, his eyes gazing in horror and defiance at the black stars burning in the gulf. Then he was gone.

Angry tears scalded her face. She wiped them away. She looked to the mouth of the alley expecting the faceless idol, but it, too, had vanished. She was alone in the dream city. She wheeled herself out of the alley into the middle of the broad avenue. Florence would find her in the morning. Dead. She prayed Florence would destroy the journal and not read it and follow her into Dreamland. She looked up at the cold stars.

The beast was cosmic. The paw, the eidolon, the city were manifestations of something vast, eternal, and ravening. She closed her eyes and willed herself asleep, hoping to escape by dreaming a dream within a dream. After a time, she felt the brush of the paw and smelled the feral reek of the beast. It would toy with her, as it had with Harold, for a while, till it tired of play. Then she would join Harold in whatever hell awaited, she thought as she wheeled her way through the twilit city under the watchful gaze of the hungry stars.

THE PALIMPSEST

Dobson Halsworth, Chief Linguist, Doctor of Philology, and Professor of Paleography paced the floor of the Orne Library's Rare Book Room. For weeks, he had sat at his computer trying to make headway on the articles he owed *Le Journal International de Paléographie* and *Manuscripta*, only to grow restless anticipating the conclusion of Dr. Lewellen's efforts to conserve the leaves of the manuscript and the Rochester Institute of Technology to complete its multispectral photography.

Unable to concentrate, he would retire to the Rare Book Room and pace between the tables and the stacks, occasionally gazing out at the President's House and the Quad's reddening October foliage. Then back to pacing. His nights fared no better. He had not felt such eagerness, such ambition, for a project since he had joined Miskatonic's faculty as a young linguist with a hunger to wrest secrets from the leaves of ancient manuscripts.

The object of his obsession was a decidedly ordinary black-letter breviary once used by monks for observing the canonical hours. The Liturgy contained psalms, hymns, and prayers to be recited at fixed times of the day. The drab, much-thumbed quarto volume displayed none of the colorful miniatures or ornamental initials found in ecclesiastical books destined for the princes of the Church. Nor was it clad in stamped leather stretched over wooden boards but possessed a "limp" binding made of parchment, making it a sort of sixteenth-century precursor of the paperback. The tome's only distinguishing feature was the parchment it was printed on, paper being more commonly used at the time of its printing. That in itself was unremarkable, unusual but by no means rare.

Brought to the University in 1933 by a young Randolph Trilling, Halsworth's predecessor, dead now twenty years, as part of a lot acquired from a Budapest bookseller, the book had languished for decades between handsomer examples in the stacks' Religion section. It might have stood so for decades more, were it not that, one night some six months ago, Dr. Halsworth had dreamed.

In his youth, Halsworth had been a frequent sojourner in the darker regions of dreamland and had, from necessity and a morbid joy, discovered that he could influence his dreams. He had learned early that he was both the dreamer and the dreamed, and that, as the dreamer, he could observe from without and direct the actions of his dream self. Serving as both director and actor, he had taught himself to rise above the maze when he could find no exit and to summon a door when needed. His dreams stayed with him upon waking, and in his younger years he had kept dream journals recording his adventures. But he had aged, and just as his pace had slowed and deep slumber had given way to bouts of insomnia, his sojourns in dreamland became less frequent and his memory less facile.

This particular dream had been singularly vivid and fraught with a sense of wonder he had not felt since he had learned to fly in his prepubescent dreams. The dream had haunted him on his walk to work—his West Saltonstall residence was four blocks from the campus—and, sitting at his desk trying to get his day started and tapping his finger on his mousepad, he had decided to follow the dream's instruction.

In the dream, a gaunt-faced, gray-bearded man with soul-chilling pale-gray eyes, wearing a skull cap such as John Dee wore in his portrait, appeared before him and, unspeaking, pointed a bony finger at a manuscript that lay open on one of the Rare Book Room's oak tables. As keeper of the keys, Dobson Halsworth had spent much time imbibing the forbidden lore inscribed in the necromantic tomes stored in locked iron boxes in Orne Library's Vault—the obscene *Cultes des Goules*, the forbidden *Unaussprechlichen Kulten* of von Junzt, the diabolical *Pnakotic Manuscripts*, the loathsome *Book of Eibon*, the blasphemous *De Vermis*

Mysteriis, and the dreaded *Necronomicon*—and he thrilled at the prospect of his dream visitor showing him another, perhaps as yet undiscovered, such tome. Leaning close to view the pages, he brushed the man's ragged cloak and smelled ashes and something ghastlier—the reek of singed hair and burnt flesh. With the scent, he caught a vision of this same man bound to a crucifix, glaring defiantly as flames climbed his naked flesh. He shuddered as a wave of horror washed over him, but his visitor continued to point to the manuscript.

The room was dark in the dream, but his oneiric vision saw the text clearly. The parchment glowed as if with an inner light, making each letter stand out with such clarity the words seemed to float above the leaves.

Trying to ignore the apparition's unnerving stare and the hellish stench worming into his skull, Halsworth identified the black-letter Latin as a psalm—Eighteenth in the Vulgate, Nineteenth in the King James. "*Caeli enarrant gloriam Dei, et opera manuum ejus annuntiat firmamentum.* The heavens declare the glory of God, and his handiwork is shown in the firmament." David's commentary on the glories of nature manifesting the handiwork of God. Why was his dream guide showing him this? For that matter, who was this stranger whom he felt he should know and whose supermundane presence made it abundantly clear this was no ordinary dream?

He looked to the stranger for answer. The apparition pointed again to the text. Still it did not speak, but Halsworth thought he heard in his head a stern voice bidding him, "Observe."

Peering closer, he discerned tell-tale evidence of an undertext beneath the printed Latin. The pale, almost invisible cursive was scrawled at right angles to the printed text, as was common when overwriting palimpsests. Having spent the better part of a lifetime poring over classical and medieval manuscripts, he was intimate with the process by which older codices were recycled for the use of later scribes and, still later, for the printer. One medieval recipe advised the scribe to soak the parchment leaves in milk, followed by covering them in oat bran or flour to absorb the moisture, followed by stretching and drying under pressure. Other methods called for flour and egg whites, followed by rubbing with milk. The purpose of erasure was not to remove the former writing completely but to clear the surface adequately to accept new script. With the advent of the printing press, the more expeditious practice of scouring with pumice powder destroyed the underwriting irretrievably. The gentler medieval methods allowed modern scholars to reclaim ancient works that would otherwise have been lost.

Many early parchments—erased and overwritten either because the Church deemed the text heretical or because of the unavailability of fresh materials—had been recovered over the centuries. The most famous was the Archimedes Palimpsest, in which three lost works of the Greek mathematician were discovered lurking for centuries beneath the text of a medieval Greek prayer book. Unfortunately, finds of complete works were rare, as scribes mixed cleaned and trimmed parchment sheets indiscriminately for reuse so that most lost works were recovered only in fragmentary form and the discovery of additional pages left to the whims of chance.

With a wave of its hand, his phantom guide spun the book ninety degrees, making it easier for Halsworth to decipher the undertext. His long acquaintance with archaic hands helped. Still, the cursive was new to him, and he experienced a flutter of panic least he wake before he could grasp what his visitor meant him to see.

His pulse quickened as the printed text faded and the undertext, the *scriptio inferior*, emerged. The hand was clearly no calligrapher's. There was no grace to the cursive; rather the Latin was inscribed in a hurried, spidery script, as if dashed off to outpace a ticking clock. Despite his eerie conviction that this was a premonitory dream and his compulsion to grasp its import before he woke, the scholar in him took over and he lost himself in a close analysis of the luminous text, his visitor nearly forgotten.

The script contained few capitalizations and no punctuation other than an occasional *punctus*, or end stop. The extended, angular ascenders and descenders marked the writing as a type of ProtoGothic, a transitional script in use around the twelfth to thirteenth centuries as intercession between Carolingian minuscule and Gothic *textura*. The script was used in Germany, the Low Countries, and England around the time of the later Crusades.

Halsworth began to get a sense of the wording. In addition to the crabbed handwriting, there were numerous abbreviations, as was common in medieval writing. *Omnibus hominibus*, for example, might be rendered *omib hoib*. Because such abbreviations were conventional and saved ink and parchment, the intended readers would have understood. After decades of poring over manuscripts, Halsworth considered himself such a reader.

A phrase caught his eye: "*og sototh porta est.*"

"Yog-Sothoth is the gate."

Gooseflesh rippled across his shoulders.

Halsworth woke suspecting his visitor's identity. The dream remained vivid. Looking in the mirror as he hastened to dress, he saw the stranger's face superimposed over his. Unlike his own well-fed and relatively unlined physiognomy, the stranger's visage was cadaverous. The cheekbones were razor sharp, the mouth cutting a thin slash through the gray beard, the eyes burning with the fiery gaze of the far-traveled adventurer who might have conversed with efreet in the Arabian desert and beheld from the prow of a Byzantine galley the minarets of Alexandria rise above the horizon.

At his office computer, he called up Zierick Verhaegen's *Lives of the Magi*, a controversial and fabulous analogue to the hagiographies, or lives of the saints, popular in the Middle Ages. Verhaegen had included, in his section pertaining to the trial and subsequent public immolation of the sorcerer Ludvig Prinn by the secular arm of the Inquisition, a page from the journal of one Sibold Bossaerd, a Dominican priest, reputedly present at Prinn's Brussels trial. Halsworth, who prided himself on his recall, scanned the lines until he found what he was looking for. Yes, here it was. The text was in sixteenth-century Flemish, with which Halsworth was not as fluent as he was with Latin, French, or German, but he mentally translated.

"The necromancer remained unrepentant. Nay, he remained close-mouthed until the end, never once offering the least sign of contrition; thereby refusing the mercy of the garrote before being committed to the flames. Already lean when arrested—which condition some attributed to the meager fare of his hermitage, others to the fasting required by his sorcerous rituals, while yet others argued his emaciation was a product of extreme longevity, which, if one credited his assertion that he accompanied Edward's crusade to the Holy Land in 1271, would make him over two centuries old—his months-long imprisonment had left him cadaverous. However, his constitution, like his will, had proven unbreakable. If anything, the torture which he had endured at the hands of his questioners had toughened him, as fire will temper steel, so that at his trial, as sentence was passed upon him, committing his body to the cleansing flames and his soul to the nethermost regions of Hell, he stood straight as a spear, his baleful glare fixed on the tribunal, particularly on the magistrate, the Honorable Piers De Bruyn. His lips, silent to this point, remained so throughout his sentencing, his eyes radiating a cold fire as if his gaze might freeze or burn his accusers. In truth, though the trial occurred on an exceptionally warm June day, as I may attest, it felt as if Prinn, by his very presence, radiated a sepulchral cold that, as many of those present later confessed, chilled them to the marrow."

Halsworth closed the window. "… radiating a cold fire." Yes, that captured the essence of the man who had appeared in his dream. Having weathered fifty-four frigid New England winters, he knew well how cold could burn.

"Ludvig Prinn …" The hairs on his head bristled as Halsworth spoke the name in a hushed tone, as if the speaking might summon the man, dead now five-hundred years, to stand before him. Author of the ghoulish *De Vermis Mysteriis, The Mystery of the Worm*. Legend had it that Prinn had written that execrable text in his cell just before his execution and, somehow, managed to have the manuscript smuggled to Cologne, where it was printed. The Church soon banned it, and most copies met the fiery fate of their author. A few copies survived over the centuries, most incomplete or expurgated and, therefore, unreliable. The Orne's Vault possessed one of the rare reliable Latin copies. Halsworth, who had scoured the volume cover to cover more than once, shuddered at the memory of the book's necromantic revelations, the most sinister of which were contained in the chapter titled the Saracenic Rituals, which instructed the intrepid practitioner how to call down from the very stars invisible monsters to do one's bidding and inflict horrible retribution on one's enemies. Though Prinn, according to contemporary accounts, had chosen to live his later years in a pre-Roman cave on the outskirts of Brussels, attended by invisible servants, Halsworth noted with skepticism that they did not save him from the Inquisition's embrace.

If asked, he would have said his interest in the occult was purely academic, but the truth was that the insidious tomes stimulated his intellectual curiosity, and he often wondered what might be the outcome were he to test the abhorrent wisdom crouched within those nightmare tomes. He had never tried the spells, neither in *De Vermis* nor those described in the utterly depraved leaves of the *Necronomicon*, nor any of the other cryptic codices slumbering in the Miskatonic Vault. Not that he doubted the efficacy of the arcane conjurings contained in those repositories of demonic knowledge; he had lived all his life in ghoul-haunted Arkham, as had his father and his grandsires before him, and he had grown up immersed in the chronicles of the ghastly deeds performed by some of its less-savory inhabitants. As a boy, he had taken a shuddering pleasure in the whispered tales of Keziah Mason and the tall white stone in an unvegetated valley in the unwholesome hills behind Arkham where the witch reputedly communed with the Black Man. And of the old witch house on East Pickman where Keziah had lived and where, upon its demolition two-centuries later, a veritable ossuary of children's bones was found in the floor of a peculiar upstairs loft where old Keziah had performed obscene rituals. And, more recently, of the gruesome demise of Dr. Albert Quiller, Head of Antiquities at the Arkham Museum, in his South Hill brownstone, having run afoul of the Hounds of Tindalos in his quest to obtain the coveted Shining Trapezohedron. So many tales of strange disappearances and portals opening onto unknown and reprehensible dimensions: it was as if Arkham was one of those cursed abodes where the fabric of reality was tissue-thin; permeable, you might say, permitting monstrous egress to disrupt our insupportably complacent world. Or as the *De Vermis Mysteriis* had it: "Build the altars on the places where the skin of the earth grows thinner, on the edges of the swamp and on the tops of the rocks, and put on them your gifts." The very chronicles he had heard provided cautionary tales regarding the perils of crossing certain forbidden lines—lines that, once traversed, permitted no return. Regardless, call it a latent curiosity of the would-be necromancer that dwelt at the heart of the scholar, a desire to see first-hand if such contemptible yet miraculous wonders as contained in the Vault's obscure codices had any basis in reality or were, as detractors insisted, either the fabrications of frauds or the ravings of madmen—he itched, as he closed the computer window, with a renewed interest in trying his hand at the necromantic art.

A knock at his door distracted him.

"Come in," he said, at once relieved and annoyed at the interruption.

His graduate assistant, Jacob, entered with a hand truck hauling two document boxes. The lanky young man was smiling broadly above his sparse chin whiskers.

"Is that…?"

"Yes." Jacob stood the hand truck. "One contains the originals. The other, photographs you've been waiting for. The digitalization should be completed in a few weeks, but Dr. Lewellen thought you would prefer not to wait."

"The good doctor thought correctly." Halsworth rose from his desk. "Let's take our treasure to the Reading Room."

The box containing the original manuscript leaves remained unopened on the hand truck. The preserved pages would be encased in double-sided frames and floated between sheets of transparent Optimum Museum Acrylic. They would, however, also retain the overprinting that hid the treasure he had waited so long to unearth—the secrets of the Worm, if his premonition had any validity. The paleographer in Halsworth insisted he examine the photographs in order, but the dream was insistent. The page he wanted was about two-thirds of the way through the manuscript. Repressing the compulsion to rifle through the box until he found it, he assisted Jacob in arranging the folders containing the photographs in order over the table.

When the folders were spread in two rows the length of the table, he passed a hand above them. His hand tingled…. *As if with a cold fire*, he thought with a silent chuckle—as it neared a certain folder. The folders were labeled according to their printed contents. Sure enough, the label on the one that drew his hand included the Nineteenth Psalm. Trying his best to maintain an academic demeanor, he opened the folder, as if choosing one at random. The fifth through eighth photographs were the ones he sought. As they had in his dream, the spidery letters glowed with a supernatural light and seemed to rise off the photographic paper as if eager for him to begin translation.

"Shouldn't we go through them in order?" Jacob asked.

Halsworth gave his assistant a look that brooked no argument. "Humor me, Jacob. You start with the first folder. See what you can find. And keep meticulous records." He gifted Jacob with his best professorial smile. "You never know what you might unearth."

The specialists at the Rochester Institute of Technology had done an excellent job in revealing the undertext. Photographs taken at multiple wavelengths of light—visible, infrared, and ultraviolet—had been digitally stacked and subjected to algorithms that ignored the printed text and enhanced the underwriting.

The folder he had chosen included both sides of the leaf in question—the recto, or facing side, and the verso. Prinn's inscription continued on the verso, not quite filling the page.

Halsworth had checked the photos of the adjacent leaves and found they contained no trace of Prinn's crabbed hand but featured ecclesiastic texts in a clerical *textura* that included rubricated initial capitals and the letter "y." The absence of the letter "y"—which resulted in "Yog" being represented as "og"—was telling in Prinn's script, as the "y" did not appear with any regularity until the thirteenth century. There was no need to doubt the "Prinn document," as he had decided to call it, was not written at the time of the smuggled *De Vermis*. It might be that the long-lived warlock had learned his letters in the twelfth century and never bothered updating his style.

Jacob had taken the first folder to an adjacent table and, examining the photographs under a magnifying desk lamp, typed his observations into his MacBook, switching from time to time to dictation and murmuring in a low voice. The youth looked like a kid in a game shop with a gift card burning a hole in his pocket.

Sensing Halsworth's gaze on him, the boy looked up questioningly and asked if he had found anything interesting.

"It's all interesting," Halsworth answered. "But if you're asking if I've found anything of earthshaking importance, no. Nothing we haven't seen before."

Jacob's gaze traveled down the length of the table. "Maybe we'll get lucky."

"I like your optimism. But don't get your hopes up."

Halsworth put the photographs back and moved on to randomly glance through other folders, hardly registering what he saw, doing so only to distract Jacob's attention from the Prinn leaf—which he had no intention of sharing.

That night Halsworth dreamed again. He was home. He sat at his desk in his darkened office with the white glow of his magnifying lamp illuminating the photographs. He had brought them home, along with the frame containing the original leaf. He had left the folder. With Jacob proceeding in order, it would take the boy days to discover the missing leaf and its accompanying photographs. Before then, he would have what he wanted: the Secret of the Worm. He had decided he would keep the documents. He did not know what dread wisdom the leaf contained, but he knew it must be of immense importance for Prinn to have secreted it from his cell and not include it in the smuggled manuscript.

Yog-Sothoth. The name set his neck hairs to writhing. Whether or not the legends were true, he was loath to speak the name aloud. According to *De Vermis Mysteriis*, the outer god was reputed to be "the key to the gate, whereby the spheres meet." At once a single primordial entity, a supreme intelligence, the deity was also described as a nebulous, cosmic force that pervaded all time, all space, all dimensions, earthly and beyond. It was also said that, on rare occasions, the god might grant a favored worshiper the ability to slip the portal of the present and re-enter the earthly plane a dozen or a thousand years hence. Of course, such a granting came at a price.

Under the archmage's commanding gaze, Halsworth transcribed the crabbed Latin as one passage after another glowed with a preternatural light, the letters illuminating like Chinese lanterns above the page. At one point, he asked the apparition if he was indeed the Ludvig Prinn of legend. The wraith's reply was to point a bony finger at one of the photographs. Again, words glowed like neon in the darkness.

Audite me, tibi Magnum Innominandum, dominus nigrum stellae et inenarrabilis inanis, tu qui es ostiarius et porta, accipere sacrificium meum.

Hear me, thou great not-to-be-named, lord of the black stars and unutterable void, thou who art gatekeeper and gate, accept my sacrifice.

"What sacrifice?" he asked, turning to the warlock and dreading the answer.

An image appeared in his mind. Halsworth gasped and shook his head. His chair rolled back from the desk.

"No … I…that's …"

He waved his hand as if to dispel the apparition. The face he saw—the face his dream guide had planted in his brain—brown eyes, thin lips smiling above a scraggly chin, lips often wrapped around a lollipop—belonged to Jacob.

"I can't." Halsworth shook his head emphatically.

The wraith pointed to a photograph. A single word lifted off the page and hung in the air.

Longaevitas.

Long life.

Longevity.

The hairs on his neck prickled as he gazed on the eldritch sorcerer with dawning comprehension.

He called in sick the next day. In truth, he was ill. He had fallen asleep at his desk and his neck creaked like rusty hinges when he stood and stretched. Though he had not vomited, he tasted bile from the acid released by his churning stomach. His hands were clammy, and his head felt as if it was being squeezed in a vise. He realized his malady was psychological, born of the passions contesting in his gut. On the one hand, he found appalling the very idea of human sacrifice. It was one thing to read about it in an anthropological context; quite another to contemplate performing the act oneself. And Jacob, of all people! Not that he would feel differently were the sacrifice a stranger. (Or would he? His uncertainty over this quandary provided an additional source of unease.) On the other hand, the temptation of seeing the panoply of history unroll over the centuries—*longaevitas*—set his brain afire.

Despite his gnawing conscience, he kept wondering how he might draw Jacob into a trap. Purely an academic exercise, he told himself when he could not force the notion out of his head.

When he returned to his desk with his first of many cups of Earl Grey that day, he saw with a mixture of surprise and amusement that he had transcribed part of the text in his sleep. He set to work deciphering the rest of the document.

He found another reference to *longaevitas*. Then, with an adrenal rush that jerked him upright and made him stare at the screen with round, wonderstruck eyes, he came to the passage describing the ritual whereby the adept could achieve what mankind had sought for centuries. The ultimate quest. The end for which adventurers and scientists had labored for millennia. The search for eternal youth. Well, if not youth, nor eternity, then a substantial prolongation beyond the Biblical three-score-and-ten. He had often thought the human lifespan was ridiculously brief. All that study. All that reading. Years of papers and exams and youth gone, the ghost of a memory. Followed by the ever-accelerating middle years, flashing by so quickly you could hardly recall what achievements you had attained the previous year. No! To allow *vita brevis* to discard all his hard-earned knowledge and to turn his intellect to dust when he had the means to stave off that noxious consummation was insanity. The irony that following Prinn's instructions was even more insane was not lost on him. He read on.

The text described the setting in which the sacrifice was to be offered.

The summoning required the blood sacrifice of an intelligent being in the presence of a towering stone or a circle of standing stones. Only then might the words of the summoning be spoken safely and Yog-Sothoth present a favorable ear. Now that he thought about it, it was ridiculous to imagine the elixir of life could be attained without bloodshed.

The reference to a towering stone reminded him of the queer white menhir in the dark ravine beyond Meadow Hill. Nothing grew in the blasted heath surrounding the stone, neither grass nor tree. Animals shunned the area, and no bird ever serenaded the rising or setting sun from atop the repellent stone. He had visited the place on his youthful ramblings, trembling to catch a glimpse of Keziah Mason's Black Man, relieved that he had not. Yet he had felt a palpable evil pervading the place, as if the sky above the rugged stone might split open at any moment and disgorge something monstrous into the world.

Recalling the old conjuring adage—*Do not call up any that you cannot put down*—Halsworth returned to the words of the summoning. These he had to transcribe precisely. Not that he intended to use them. God forbid! But he was a perfectionist and took a professional pride in his work. Of course, if someone were to speak them and got the words wrong, a blow to one's professional pride might be the least of one's worries. What unspeakable horror might befall one speaking the wrong words, thereby provoking the ire of the Gate Keeper, did not bear contemplation.

That afternoon, the doorbell rang. Halsworth answered when his visitor persisted. Annoyance turned to consternation when he discovered Jacob on his stoop.

"Jacob."

"Hi, Professor. Geez, you look terrible. I mean, how are you feeling?"

The boy's Adam's apple bobbed. Jacob was four inches taller than him, so he got a good look at it bobbing. Jacob wore his faithful knapsack over his hoodie and clutched a white waxed paper bag. He held the bag up for Halsworth to see. "I brought you donuts from Holes."

Halsworth was partial to glazed donuts, providing they were gourmet.

Holes, located near the Student Union, made the best in Arkham. He often brought some to the office and shared them with visitors. He could not resist smiling at the boy's thoughtfulness.

With every fiber of his being urging him to send the boy packing, Halsworth said, "That's very thoughtful of you, Jacob." Though he was awake and standing in the frosty afternoon light of a gray New England day, he felt Prinn's gaze on his back. It was dangerous for Jacob here.

Sacrifice.

Though he could no more harm the youth than he could take his own life, he feared for the boy. And yet …

Longaevitas.

If his dream guide's revelation was true, his means to longevity stood before him.

The boy was itching to come in, shifting from foot to foot and glancing anxiously over Halsworth's shoulder into the house.

"I would invite you in, Jacob, but I don't want you to contract whatever bug I caught."

"That's okay, Professor. I never get sick," the boy said, white teeth flashing a big grin. "Besides," he reached over his shoulder and patted his knapsack, "I've brought something I want to talk to you about."

That's it! Halsworth thought. *He knows about the missing leaf.* But it occurred to him, perhaps—and he brightened at the perhaps—Jacob had made some other exciting discovery. The thought piqued his interest, and before he thought things through, he invited the boy in.

Before closing the door, he glanced up and down the block. The street was empty, the somber doors of the venerable town homes fortuitously shut. No one had seen Jacob enter his house.

❈

They stood in Halsworth's home office. The original leaf containing the Prinn text in its double-sided frame and between its protective acrylic sheets lay on his desk alongside the enhanced photos of the underwriting. The document on the computer screen showed Halsworth's translation. He had decided to come clean with his assistant. To a point, at least.

Jacob had not made a revelatory discovery. As soon as they entered the parlor and before Halsworth could offer the boy an Earl Grey to go with the donuts, Jacob had withdrawn a folder from his knapsack and set it on the coffee table. The very folder from which he had borrowed the photographs.

"What's so special about the missing leaf?" Jacob wanted to know. His tone was not accusatory but disconcertingly enthusiastic. "You've found something important, haven't you? You can tell me. I would never breathe a word to anyone. I swear!"

The boy had raised his hand in the Boy Scouts' three-fingered salute. Halsworth would have laughed, were he not dismayed to be found out so quickly. After that, there was nothing for it but to show Jacob the leaf. The graduate student was, after all, his assistant. Under the ruse of preparing a groundbreaking article on the palimpsest for the esoteric journal, *Oculus*, he led Jacob into his office and shared his findings. He made no mention of his dreams, however.

"Prinn … Ludvig Prinn?" Jacob scratched his head through his red-and-black Miskatonic U. baseball cap. His shaggy locks curled over his ears.

The boy was awestruck. His Adam's apple bobbed as his excited stare traveled back and forth between Halsworth and the screen.

"It would appear so. The style and dating of the script are consistent. My best guess is this would constitute a lost page from Prinn's *Saracenic Rituals*. At least, that would be the most exciting outcome, providing I can substantiate the claim."

"I'll say, it's exciting." Jacob got control of his enthusiasm. "It's a miraculous find, Professor. I know you've waited months for the photographs. You must have suspected this—" He waved a broad hand at the desk. "—before ever requesting the photography." His eyes lit up and he snapped his fingers. "You knew this—" Again he waved at the photos. "—was in the manuscript all along! And you kept it to yourself!"

"I don't traffic in speculation, Jacob. And neither should you. If you're serious about being a paleographer, you must be meticulous in your methodology. Work first, reveal later."

He caught himself wagging a professorial finger and put his hand in his pocket; he had always hated the habit but could not break himself of it. Jacob continued scanning the text on the screen. *As if trying to commit it to memory*, Halsworth thought.

"Go ahead and entertain yourself. My notes are on screen. Just click the mouse."

Jacob looked shocked. "Professor … I did not mean to pry."

"Of course you did, my boy. It's your nature. Do not be offended: it's the nature of all who search for knowledge. The urge to pry into man's and nature's secrets is at the root of our profession. I think we should have tea now, to go with the donuts and to celebrate our discovery."

"Earl Grey?"

"What else?"

⁕

Halsworth grabbed his sleeping pills from the bathroom on his way to the kitchen. While the tea brewed, his hands shook as he crushed two tablets in a small ceramic bowl. Part of him bristled at the thought of sharing his discovery with Jacob. How dare the boy intrude! Worse—what if he intended to steal the ritual for himself! The rational side of his psyche, however, was appalled by his actions.

What am I doing? Do I really intend to do this? I am no murderer!

His ambition, however, had its own agenda.

Longaevitas.

Was it not written in the *De Vermis*, "For He is *'Umr At-tawil*, the Most Ancient One, which the scribe rendereth, The Prolonged of Life'"?

Sacrifice.

Were he not to seize this opportunity, he would ever regret it.

Steel yourself, the louder side of his mind commanded, as he stirred the Ambien into the tea.

⁕

They sat in the parlor, Halsworth in one of the tufted leather armchairs, Jacob on the sofa, the service and box of donuts between them on the coffee table.

Jacob dabbed his mouth with the back of his hand. His knees jutted up nearly as high as his chest, so it was a bit of a strain to lean forward to set his cup on one of Halsworth's stamped leather coasters made to look like miniature manuscripts. "Did I read that right, Professor?" he said, sitting back. "A ritual to prolong one's life. You really think Prinn's the author? Wow!" The boy shook his head. "I imagine the old boy intended the ritual for himself … until the Inquisition interrupted his plans."

"I imagine you're right, Jacob. Tough luck, that … assuming the spell isn't the rantings of an unsound mind."

"Yog—"

Halsworth started forward in his chair, nearly spilling his tea. "Don't say the name aloud!" He immediately felt embarrassed. He was being silly. No way was speaking the name going to cause the dread god to appear in his parlor and blast them to some abominable dimension. Better safe than sorry, though; Arkham legend bore too many hideous accounts of unnatural visitations, disappearances, and unspeakable murders to take chances. Again, he was reminded how his beloved city was perched on the border between worlds.

Jacob silently mouthed the name Yog-Sothoth. The shaping of the name resolved into a yawn. The Ambien was working. That was one worry he could put to bed. The prescription was expired, and he had not taken one in over a year. Though the pills provided a refreshing reprieve from his bouts of insomnia, they tended to have a bizarre and potentially dangerous side effect—they made him sleepwalk. The last time that happened, he had gone into the kitchen to discover a half-made sandwich on the cutting board he had no memory of starting. The mayonnaise and a loaf of bread had been left sitting out, both open. Beside these, turkey and cheese packages, unopened. Two slices of bread, one with mayonnaise, lay on the cutting board. The worst thing though was the steak knife lying on the counter beside the sandwich, its serrated blade glistening with congealing mayo. Shuddering at the thought of cutting himself in his sleep and bleeding out in his bed, he had quit the Ambien.

Still, if he could sleepwalk and make a sandwich under the drug's influence, Jacob should be appropriately tractable. God forbid the boy should die from an overdose. He needed him pliable, not dead. The ritual called for the blood sacrifice of an intelligent being. Jacob was a 4.0 student, and his Latin was almost as good as his own. Surely the boy fit the bill.

Jacob yawned again. "Excuse me, Professor," he said covering his mouth.

Halsworth managed a soft chuckle. "Think nothing of it, my boy. All the excitement has tired you out."

Jacob raised a hand and started to say something. The hand dropped back into his lap.

"What is it you students say? 'No knowledge without sacrifice?'"

"'A small sacrifice for knowledge,'" Jacob corrected.

"Right." Halsworth helped Jacob to his feet. "Come along, son. Let's go for a drive."

"Where're we going?" The boy's words were slurred. He wavered on his feet as if a sneeze would topple him.

"It's a surprise, Jacob. You like surprises, don't you?"

Jacob looked perplexed as they made their way to the garage … as if he could not decide whether he cared for surprises.

Jacob came to while Halsworth was making his final preparations.

Halsworth had little trouble getting Jacob to their destination. He had considered loading the boy into the trunk of his old sedan, but Jacob proved compliant and had ridden shotgun, slumbering off and on as they made their way into the wild hills behind Arkham. The final half-mile from the road where he had parked under the trees had been more difficult. Though Jacob, assisted by Halsworth's steadying hand, proved capable of sleepwalking up the moonless path that wound through a dense tangle of hoary old willows and oaks, their bare limbs gnarled and arthritic, their trunks ashen and deformed as if from too-long clinging to unfertile ground, the going was slow, Halsworth further encumbered by the paraphernalia needed for the sacrifice. No owl hooted in the desolate trees; no nocturnal creature rustled the ancient matt of untrodden leaves.

They emerged from the wood into a blighted ravine where neither grass nor weed nor lichen grew, as if the very earth had been poisoned by the ghastly sabbaths conducted upon its stage. Over the gorge hung a haunted air, as if the horror of bygone atrocities lingered in the blasphemed soil like some ghastly palimpsest written in blood. Here, according to ghoulish legend, Keziah Mason had conversed with the Black Man, and the old warlock Edmund Carter, fleeing here from Salem in 1692, had called down terrors from the stars and monstrous entities from the bowels of the earth. In the moan of the chill night breeze, Halsworth could hear the ghostly shrieks of sacrificial victims, goat and, if the more lurid legends were true, human. According to the archives of the *Arkham Advisor*, infants were prone to vanish on Walpurgis Night.

Sacrifice …

Bound to the white stone by the rope Halsworth had carried draped over his shoulder, Jacob slumped against his restraints. A silvery thread of spittle dropping from his parted lips glittered in the vague starlight. Then his eyes fluttered open, and confusion, followed by an expression of dawning horror, spread over his face, as he struggled against his constraints and tried to get his feet under him.

"Professor…?"

"It's all right, Jacob. You're having a dream. You'll wake soon, and tomorrow you'll tell me all about it."

Jacob's expression said he was not buying Halsworth's version of reality. Then his gaze fell on the gasoline can at Halsworth's feet.

"No! Professor … you can't!"

The boy was clearheaded enough to catch on to what was happening. After all, he had read the ritual. Halsworth realized he should have put a handkerchief in the boy's mouth while he was under. He hated to do it. No one would hear him scream, but he might interfere with the ritual. He pulled his handkerchief from his hip pocket and approached the boy. "It's clean, Jacob."

Jacob thrashed his head and clenched his teeth, but Halsworth forced it in. The boy exacted a measure of revenge by clamping onto Halsworth's index finger and trying to bite it off. The wad of cloth saved Halsworth from amputation. "Damn, that hurt!" he growled through gritted teeth.

Jacob's muffled grunts were unintelligible as he fought against his restraints. His face glistened with tears. A bubble of snot popped from one nostril.

Despite his resolve, Halsworth's hands shook as he unscrewed the gas can. Again, he felt split between two camps—on the one hand, he hated himself for doing this to Jacob. The boy had done him no wrong; on the contrary, despite his garrulousness, he had been one of the best assistants he had ever had. And though his sense of humor sometimes bordered on the sophomoric, Jacob just as often said something that made him smile. Indeed, the boy had a bright future in paleography. Or *had* had, at any rate. On the other hand, the boy knew too much. Sure, Halsworth would have preferred to sacrifice a stranger. But he was no accomplished kidnapper, and procuring an unsuspecting patsy was a step above his pay grade.

He squeezed his eyes shut. Saw the single word float above the photograph.

Longaevitas.

He clamped down on his conflicting emotions, ignored his pounding heart. Will and determination would carry him through. His voice must not tremble when the words were spoken.

Halsworth approached the writhing boy. Jacob's wide eyes were delirious with terror. Careful not to get any on himself, Halsworth splashed gasoline over Jacob, soaking his clothes. He sprinkled the last of it over the boy's head. The petroleum fumes stung Halsworth's nostrils. His eyes watered. Jacob bucked with a renewed energy born of ultimate terror. Alarmed, Halsworth backed away, worried the boy might break his bonds after all.

Get on with it, a voice said. It was the voice that bid him *Observe* the night his dream guest showed him the palimpsest beneath the breviary's printed page.

Though the invocation was folded in his breast pocket, he did not take it out. He had memorized the words of the summoning. To read it he would have to use a flashlight and take his eyes off the sacrifice. To look away might be interpreted as fear. Everything he had ever read about conjuring, be it of demon, efreet, or eldritch god, demanded an unflinching resolve and a commanding execution of the invocation. Suppressing his qualms, Halsworth stared Jacob in the eye as he withdrew a matchbook from his coat pocket and tore three matches loose.

"Audite me, tibi Magnum Innominandum." His voice rang out, rolled eerily into the darkness, amplified by the unnatural silence and lack of vegetation to mute it. He struck the matches. *"Dominus nigrum stellae et inenarrabilis inanis."*

He touched the flame to the rest of the matches, tossed the blazing matchbook onto Jacob's chest. The gasoline flared, for a moment blinding him.

"Tu qui es ostiarius et porta. Accipere sacrificium meum"

Flames engulfed the boy.

"Leva velum et mihi petitionem dona!"

Jacob bucked and a high keening whine streamed from his nostrils.

"Audite me, Dominus Portarum! Apertor de via!"

A wind sprang up, whipping the flames that embraced the boy.

"Omnes in uno! Longinquus et longior vitae!"

The flames reached Jacob's face and engulfed his head. His flesh blackened, bubbled, split. The handkerchief in his mouth caught fire.

"Aperi ad portam! Tua devotus servus audi!"

The acrid reek of charred meat rolled over Halsworth like a greasy cloud, reminding him of the stench he had smelled when he brushed against the sorcerer's cloak in the dream.

Halsworth repeated the incantation, louder this time. His voice caught a rhythm, matching a ceremonial cadence to the words. It was far too late to retreat. He was committed. Jacob's sacrifice must not be wasted. Fail now and he was a murderer and society would deal with him. Succeed and with centuries to master the wonders contained in the library's vault and he would be the greatest magician the world had ever known. His deeds would outstrip anything Solomon or Faust envisioned.

"Audite me, tibi Magnum Innominandum. Dominus nigrum stellae et inenarrabilis inanis. Tu qui es ostiarius et porta. Accipere sacrificium meum. Leva velum et mihi petitionem dona!"

He had spent years at the lectern, addressing students while pointing out the subtleties of manuscripts shown on a smartboard with a light pen, and he had read aloud hundreds of Latin manuscripts in the lecture hall and in his study. Now his voice projected his words strong and steady as if they were material objects hurled against his burning assistant, feeding the fire, opening the way.

"Audite me, Dominus Portarum! Apertor de via! Omnes in uno! Longinquus et longior vitae! Aperi ad portam! Tua devotus servus audi!"

The wind gusted to a buffeting roar that drowned Jacob's muffled screams. Halsworth lifted his voice still higher. Dense clouds rolled in, obscuring the stars. Thunder growled over the rim of the ravine. His heart quickened. The spell was working. Surely the rising storm was evidence of its efficacy!

A great rent appeared in the massed clouds above the ravine, revealing not the old familiar New England constellations, but an immenset yawning gulf that might, should He Who Was the Gatekeeper and the Gate choose, engulf the numberless galaxies of man's material universe. Halsworth felt privileged yet infinitesimally small, beholding the Beyond.

*"Umr At-Tawil
Iak-Sathath
Yog-Sothoth Nafl'Fthagn!"*

Halsworth's eyes widened as he spoke the foreign words. Without meaning to, he had deviated from the ritual transcribed from the palimpsest and was chanting in a language he knew only from the cryptic books stored in the Orne's vault. His flesh crawled with wonder and dread as he felt a presence guiding his tongue to shape the guttural syllables. He was speaking R'lyehian, a tongue so incredibly ancient that by scholarly accounts it preceded the oldest Sanskrit inscriptions or Egyptian pictograms by tens of millennia. The guttural syllables were all but unpronounceable, prompting some authorities to propose an extraterrestrial origin. Though he had only a cursory knowledge of the language, he, somehow, understood the meaning of the words.

"Most ancient and prolonged of life
All-in-One
Yog-Sohoth, your servant calls upon you!"

He repeated the words, faster now, raising his voice to a near shout to be heard above the keening wind, sending his chant into the void.

Jacob was silent, his lifeless body sagging against his bonds as the flames continued to gnaw his flesh.

"Umr At-Tawil
Iak-Sathath
Yog-Sothoth Nafl'Fthagn!"

He thrilled as, out of the blackness, like phosphorescence darkly glittering on moonless waves, a maze of scintillating gossamer globes that flowed or orbited about each other in a sinuous and incomprehensible dance approached. A wash of awe and terror swept over him as he shivered in the numinous presence of the All-in-One. Yog-Sothoth had responded to his summons. The elixir of life was within his grasp.

But even as he repeated the eldritch refrain, straining his utmost to shape the alien syllables aright, he felt his will and his bodily strength fading. A static buzz filled his head. He wanted to attribute his sudden light-headedness, the blurring of his vision, to the physical and mental toll the summoning was exacting; but the apparition standing beside the white stone suggested otherwise.

Prinn stood pale in the lingering firelight, appearing not in his dreams but rippling before him like a tatter of mist resisting the gusting wind. As Jacob's body had withered and his own vitality had waned, Prinn looked paler than in his previous visitations. The old warlock leered as he addressed Halsworth, his words thudding like a judge's gavel through the cobwebs of his mind.

"Did you think you could steal immortality merely by reciting the summoning? You are unworthy. You know nothing of the mysteries of the worm. Did you think Yog-Sothoth would heed you were I not directing the summoning? You are no believer, but an opportunist. An undeserving dilettante playing with necromantic fire. Had the Infinite not granted me this body, he would have cast it, along with the mind inhabiting it, into the nethermost abyss where the devourers wait. As it is, that will be the fate of your consciousness. I thank you for the body.

"Umr At-Tawil
Iak-Sathath
Yog-Sothoth Nafl'Fthagn!"

A cold horror blanketed Halsworth. His consciousness, his sense of *self*, was being erased. He felt himself dissipating, as if his mind were mist blown by the wind. He groped for the words he had been chanting, groped to remember what he was doing in this ghastly place. His gaze fell upon Jacob's corpse and a wave of utter anguish crashed through him. He was responsible! He locked eyes with the apparition—Prinn!

DeQuincy had written of the countless handwritings of grief or joy inscribed upon the palimpsest of the brain, which, forgotten with the passage of time, nevertheless lurked under the strata of later memories. Layer by layer, the palimpsest of his brain was being erased, his consciousness scoured, not with gentle alchemical milk and oatmeal, but with a brutal erasure that would leave no trace of self. In despair, he shook the gas can over his head. Better to burn than to endure an eternity of being devoured. But only a few drops splashed onto his scalp; he had used it all on Jacob and he had no matches.

He turned his gaze to Prinn in anguish but could not summon the will to speak. He stared in horror at the leering visage. He was not just being erased—he was being replaced. Overwritten by the warlock. Prinn's ritual was never meant for him.

Halsworth's lips might have stretched in a bitter smile at the irony—were it not for the terror that consumed him as the last vestiges of his consciousness plunged through the gate into the midst of those scintillating globes that opened to receive his consciousness, then closed behind him.

Prinn stretched his arms. It was not the strongest body, more sedentary than ambulatory, but the flesh was malleable, and he would adapt it to his needs. And it had access to one of the world's greatest repositories of necromantic wisdom. But the greatest gift was freedom. He was back in the world!

Leaving the ravine and the smoldering corpse, he made his way through the wood and loaded the empty gas can in the trunk. He would have preferred to walk to his host's residence—the night air was exhilarating after so long an absence—but his previous incarceration had ended badly. It would be imprudent to leave evidence.

He opened the door and slid inside. Ran his hand over the steering wheel. The body retained muscle memory of how to operate the vehicle. He pressed the starter button, took satisfaction from the purring motor.

He drove slowly, getting used to the body. He lowered the window, inhaled deeply. The moist, clayey scent of earth was intoxicating. He stuck out his tongue to capture the acrid taste of desiccated leaves seasoning the breeze. So much to experience. So much to do. Meanwhile, to enjoy the night.

Ahead, the church spires and leaning gambrel roofs of Arkham rose into view.

A Prisoner of Dreamland

"Sleep which brings us our dreams fulfils the eternal need within us, the need of romance, the need of adventure; for sleep is the gate which lets us slip through into the enchanted country that lies beyond."

—Mary Lucy Arnold-Forster, Preface to *Studies in Dreams*

"He was an architect, you know."

They had finished their luncheon—Dr. Vesey, Assistant Superintendent of Bethlehem Hospital, had the steak and kidney pie, Professor Pierson of University College London's Experimental Psychology Department, the curried rabbit—and were waiting for port and cigars. Already a haze of smoke was gathering under the establishment's tin ceiling.

Pierson blotted his moustache, set his napkin on the table. "An architect, you say. Anything I might be familiar with?"

"You know the Acton Pumping Station?" Dr. Vesey was bleary eyed. He normally wore spectacles but didn't like wearing them while dining. Two deep red groves were worn into either side of his narrow nose.

"I've seen pictures. Quite ornate for its function." Though more modern, some said futuristic, the sewage pumping station rivaled the baroque splendor of Abbey Mills, Bazalgette's "temple of utility." The soaring arches and lightning rods disguised as spires drew the eye heavenward, away from the unpleasant reality traversing the tunnels beneath its foundation.

Vesey glanced at the approaching waiter, who sat their ports before them and trimmed and lit their cigars before retreating.

Vesey took an appreciative puff of his Montecristo and blew smoke ceilingward. "He is also quite an accomplished painter," he said. "Exhibited at the Royal Academy several years ago. Fittingly, mostly paints grand architectural vistas."

"Sounds like an interesting fellow." Pierson sniffed his glass before sipping. He let the port settle around the edges of his tongue and was surprised at the quality, detecting notes of blackberry, raspberry, cinnamon, and chocolate.

"'He hasn't spoken in the four years he's been with us," Vesey added. "Paints when he's not sleeping. I haven't been able to reach him. I thought maybe you could."

"With my device."

Vesey nodded. "He'd make an interesting subject. And with your help maybe we'll get some insight into what's going on in his head."

"From his dreams. You understand, though the DID utilizes Professor Rontgen's rays, it cannot detect any pathology of the brain." Vesey, a fellow member of the British Psychological Society, would know that. He just wanted to be clear. "All I can do is observe his dreams. Occasionally, if rapport is established and the subject a particularly vivid dreamer, the dream can be immersive."

"Oh, I would rate Greenwood as a particularly vivid dreamer. That reminds me." Vesey set his cigar in the ashtray, withdrew a sheet of paper from his coat pocket and passed it to Pierson.

Unfolding it, Pierson found it was a page from *The Cornhill Magazine*: an interview apparently conducted with the subject of their conversation.

> "I get my best ideas from Dreamland. It is sinful, really. I conceive the intricacies of a building's architecture, and when I wake, I hurry to my drawing board and illustrate what I've dreamed, and voilà—I have a building. It's as though my sleeping mind has a gremlin doing the heavy lifting for me."
>
> "Surely there's more to it than that."

"Well, I have to provide foundations, wiring schemata, plumbing. But the façade, the layout of the rooms, the ornamentation … they're a gift from Morpheus."

"You've stated previously that you truly believe in the reality of the dreamworld."

"Yes. I believe it is a place contiguous to our reality. I'm not the only one who holds this belief. The Australian aborigines, for example. The Papuans of New Guinea."

"Is it visions of Dreamland you paint, or do you draw inspiration from your imagination?"

"My dear fellow, Dreamland and Imagination are inseparable."

"I can relate to this." Greenwood returned the clipping to Vesey. "The idea for my imaging device came to me in a dream."

"You don't say. I find the whole mechanics and psychology of dreams fascinating." Vesey's cigar had gone out. He relit it and puffed to get it going. "I don't dream much myself."

Pierson heard the wistful note in his colleague's voice. He finished his port, set his glass down. "Well," he said, "I'm sold. It would be my pleasure to observe Mr. Greenwood's dreams."

"Excellent. Shall I send a wagon?"

"That won't be necessary. My equipment is portable. I'll just need an assistant to carry it in and help set it up."

Pierson and Vesey split the bill. Outside, they shook hands and parted company. Despite his limp—a souvenir from an Afrikaner bullet taken during the First Boer campaign—Pierson decided to walk home rather than take the cab waiting at the corner. From Piccadilly to Mayfair was less than a mile, and he could use the exercise, especially after a heavy lunch. His cane tapped the sidewalk as he proceeded up Great Windmill Street.

A man who believes in the reality of Dreamland.

If only that was true.

Pierson and Vesey stood over the dreaming man. John Howard Greenwood lay on his bed in his Bethlehem cell, his eyes fluttering beneath closed lids. Sandy-haired and square-jawed, Greenwood, no doubt, had been a vigorous, handsome man. According to Vesey, he'd never married. At forty-two, he had accomplished much in his brief span. What caused the drastic and sudden onslaught of his psychosis neither physician nor psychologist had yet discovered. Inquiries revealed no history of trauma and no family history of insanity. Nor was there evidence of tumor, encephalitis, or nerve damage. Barring psychological causation, Pierson speculated that there was a lesion in the temporal lobe, the temporal being the lobe that housed the hippocampus, which played a central role in dreaming. Vesey thought it best to exhaust all avenues of phycological inquiry before turning him over to a neurologist. Pierson agreed: surgery should always be a last resort.

Prior to visiting Greenwood's cell, Vesey had shown Pierson the gallery where the paintings of Bethlehem's patients, present and past, hung about the walls. Some were prosaic: water colours of flowers in the hospital garden, a poorly rendered and depressing portrait of the dayroom's desultory inhabitants, a remarkably realistic portrait of a foot. Others mirrored the madness of their artists: a screaming woman with bulging eyes rolled back in her head, an obviously dead child (judging by the green-gray hue of the flesh) sucking her mother's teat.

Vesey beamed with pride as he pointed out Greenwood's paintings. Greenwood, of course, did not paint as part of therapy but, apparently, out of some compulsion neither doctor understood.

"This painting is typical of his work prior to his affliction," Vesey said.

The painting was a grand affair, maybe four feet by five, depicting a broad mall replete with parks and plazas, fountains and floral gardens. Plane trees shaded a pedestrian promenade overlooking a canal. Rows of white Neoclassical buildings presented a broad sweep of façades that diminished with perspective. The artist's superb use of sunlight made the painting seem larger than it was.

Several smaller paintings surrounded this one. These were done in a style vastly different. Most presented architectural themes, although, unlike the uniformity of style and clarity of execution that marked the larger painting, these appeared hurried and unfinished. Adjoining buildings clashed in styles that jarred the eye. Another painting done in somber shades of green evoked a brooding forest. Another, in melancholy blues and grays, suggested the intimacy of the tomb. One of these depicted a barred cell. Curled on a cot reclined the figure of a pale woman.

"She appears to be crying," Pierson said, peering close to the canvas. Her face was indistinct, but the few brushstrokes captured sorrow, perhaps even horror.

"I noticed that myself," Vesey said. He adjusted his glasses and peered over Pierson's shoulder. "I wonder who she is?"

"With any luck, we'll find out." Pierson gestured for his host to lead on.

"You see dreams through these goggles?"

Vesey was holding the Dream Imaging Device's brass headset. In addition to the phosphorus-coated crystal lenses, the device consisted of an induction coil and a Crookes tube. The induction coil, a black cylinder mounted on a table on the opposite side of the bed, transformed the hospital's low-voltage current into high-voltage current that excited the electrons in the Crookes tube. The electrons, beamed through the dreamer's head, excited the special coating on the goggle's lenses, allowing the wearer to observe the subject's dream.

"Put them on," Pierson said.

Vesey donned the goggles. Pierson switched on the induction coil. The device hummed as the rotating cylinder picked up speed. He adjusted the two rods above the cylinder until a spark bridged the narrow gap. The front end of the Crookes tube began to glow a phosphorescent yellow-green. Vesey, sitting in a comfortable chair, leaned close to the sleeping Greenwood, as if he were examining the man's ear.

"I don't ... Wait. I see movement, but everything is dark and indistinct. Much like Greenwood's paintings."

"Congratulations, Doctor. You are seeing the patient's dreams. To see them clearly, however, requires the observer's brainwaves to be on the same frequency as the dreamer's. To this end, as an adjunct to my dream studies, I've practiced yoga, deep breathing, and meditation techniques. Once my heart rate and breathing match the dreamer's, I may enter his dream. To do so I require silent contemplation. So, I'll have to ask you and your assistant—" Pierson looked at the tall orderly who stood by the door. "—to leave so I may seek rapport with the dreamer."

Alone with the sleeping Greenwood, Pierson turned down the lights, set his cane on the floor beside the easy chair, donned his goggles, settled back, and began to inhale slowly through his nostrils and exhale through his mouth. At first, as his eyes adjusted to the near dark and the density of the lenses, all he saw was movement and somber colours. Then, as if his eyes suddenly adjusted to an altered state of perception, the camera obscura images on the lenses snapped into focus.

The beast was close. Its rank musk soured the air. The tall hedgerows of the labyrinth mocked him as he sweated his way through the narrow corridors. Each time Pierson reached a dead end and retreated, he found the way back blocked, and another avenue opened. It was as if the labyrinth was herding him. He fought the mild panic that fluttered at the thought. Panic was a distraction. An autonomic flight or fight reaction. He had learned that lesson in South Africa. In war, panic—losing focus on doing what you had to do to survive—could get you killed.

The beast was toying with him. His imagination painted a garish portrait of a slavering werewolf, all fangs and claws, rippling muscle, and fiery eyes. Of course, this was Greenwood's dreamworld. Who knew what creatures the man's imagination had invented.

Pierson recognized the labyrinth for what it was: a symbol of the unconscious. Considering his profession, he should be able to navigate its convoluted terrain. Trouble was, dream logic—the logic of the unconscious—was so far removed from the laws of classical logic that psychologists resorted to symbols to map it. Until he discovered the etiology of Greenwood's condition, he was walking in the dark.

Speaking of walking, he was doing so without his cane. That was one of the things he loved about Dreamland: you shed years when you entered its domain. A blind man could see, a cripple walk. For a moment he relished the suppleness of his limbs, the spring in his step.

The hedge rustled beside him, as if the beast was trying to break through from the next row. Despite his scientific aplomb and his awareness of the unreality of his surroundings, he quickened his pace. He imagined the beast's hot breath on his neck, its talons inches from his flesh.

The hedge rustled ahead of him. He started to turn but stopped when he saw a sword blade slash through the foliage. A moment later Greenwood, wearing a shirt of mail over a padded doublet, scarlet hose, and black leather boots, as if he were a knight stepped out of an illustrated book, stood before him. Greenwood smiled and, pointing his broadsword at the hole through which he'd emerged, said, "This way."

He turned and plunged through the gap. Needing no further invitation, Pierson followed. Exiting the labyrinth wasn't easy. The hedges grew back almost as fast as Greenwood's sword hacked its way through.

"Don't mind the beast," Greenwood called over his shoulder. "Its purpose is to hunt, not to capture or devour. Your fear is what it seeks. Why would it end the chase and forfeit the pleasure of the hunt? Lose your fear of it and it will abandon you for other game."

There it was again—dream logic. "Nevertheless," Pierson said, staying close behind Greenwood lest the fast-growing foliage separate them, "thank you for rescuing me."

Greenwood glanced back at him. His eyes were gray. "I wasn't looking to rescue you. I sensed someone following me and came to look. Who are you? I meet travelers from the waking world from time to time, but I don't recall one following me into my dream."

"So you're aware you're dreaming now?

"Am I? I believed I was. Thank you for confirming. Unless I'm dreaming you and you're telling me what I want to hear."

"I assure you, you are dreaming." Pierson told him how, in the waking world, he was sitting beside Greenwood's sleeping body. Listening for the beast despite Greenwood's words, Pierson told him his name was Eric Pierson, a psychologist. "Your physician, Dr. Vesey, asked me to help unravel your conundrum."

Greenwood paused his chopping for a moment to wipe the sweat from his eyes. "My physician. Then I'm in a hospital?"

"You are. Your injuries are not physical but mental. You paint but you do not speak."

Greenwood's eyes widened and seemed to glow as if something Pierson said had sparked a memory. "I remember painting." His brow creased as he tried to recall. "But I can't remember what." Greenwood laid into the hedgerow. His blade was sharp and sliced great swaths of foliage at every stroke. "I seem to have forgotten much. You wouldn't know my name, by chance?"

Pierson debated how much to tell him. It was always best for the patient to remember on his own. Information from an outside source was like a house with no foundation. Still, perhaps hearing his name would jog his memory.

"Your name is John Howard Greenwood. You're an architect by trade. A quite successful one."

Greenwood turned to face him. "An architect in the waking world. A knight errant in Dreamland."

But Pierson was no longer listening. He stared around in amazement. Without realizing it, they had left the labyrinth and entered a dark, foreboding forest. It wasn't night, because dim light filtered down through the dense, green canopy.

He looked behind him expecting to see the hedge wall of the labyrinth but saw only more trees crowding them. Dream topography, like its logic, was unpredictable and subject to change at the whimsy of the subconscious.

A dragonfly darted past, a silvery shimmer, then gone. He heard no birdsong, no scuffle of squirrel through dry leaves. He got the impression the forest went on forever. A wilderness of towering, ancient trees. And wasn't the wilderness, like the labyrinth, another symbol of the unconscious?

"Which way?"

Greenwood smiled. "It doesn't matter. One thing I've learned in my travels: in Dreamland any direction can take you where you want to go— or lose you in the wilderness." He spread his arms, encompassing the forest.

"Where do you want to go?" Pierson asked.

"That's just it. I can't remember. So one direction is as good as another."

Choosing a direction at random, Greenwood started walking. Enjoying his mobility, Pierson kept pace. As they passed through the narrow corridors with the great boles pressing on every side, his shirt grew damp, and he started to thirst. If he could find a stream, he could take an imaginary drink to quench his imaginary thirst. Listening for the sound of running water, he heard instead a buzzing. He couldn't tell where the sound was coming from, but it was getting louder.

Greenwood heard it too. He stopped and looked about.

A swarm of insects boiled out of the gloom between the trees. There was something peculiar about them. Pierson saw what bothered him about the insects when a silvery wing caught a mote of sunlight. The creatures were metallic.

He ran. Unnerved by the thought of being stung or eaten alive by the pursuing swarm, he sprinted into the woods. Though he was an avid hiker and, until recently, annually participated in amateur climbing on the Continent, he couldn't remember running since hanging up his football cleats.

The swarm was at his back. The buzzing eerily loud in the claustrophobic stillness. One of the winged automatons darted past his face. A razor wing nicked his cheek. Pierson stumbled, fell, clipped his chin on the ground.

He woke, removed his goggles.

Greenwood was waking too. Pierson shut off the current to the induction coil. The humming stopped. Greenwood rose, slipped his feet into his slippers, and headed out the door in his pajamas.

Pierson hurried after him.

Greenwood made his way to the dayroom where he took up brush and paint and got to work. Pierson stood behind him and watched in fascination as Greenwood replicated in dusky blues and somber greens and grays what could only be their episode in the forest. There, those silvery strokes must be the metal insects.

Pierson raised a finger to his cheek where a metallic wing had grazed him. His finger came away bloody.

When Pierson entered Greenwood's dream the following day, he found himself up to his thighs in tea-coloured swamp water. On either side of the sandy-bottomed stream, tall cypresses rose above their multiple trunks. It was night. A gibbous moon hung over the spectral trees, cast a pallid reflection on the slow-moving, muckish water.

The swamp was another manifestation of the wilderness, another representation of the unconscious.

Fear clutched the back of his neck. He had no idea what creatures lurked beneath the stream's dark surface. Snakes? Crocodiles?

The humid air was filled with the high-pitched chorus of frogs, crickets, and cicadas. A bat flitted by.

Greenwood stood near at hand, looking up at the moon.

"I seem to remember painting the moon," he said. He turned to Pierson with a sheepish grin that made him seem almost boyish. He examined the fingers of his right hand. "I can almost feel the brush between my fingers."

"Good. You're remembering." Pierson said. "And you were an architect. Do you remember anything you might have designed? Buildings? Bridges?"

Greenwood stared down at the water for a moment. "No. Not that I recall."

"It'll come. Have you remembered anything about your quest?"

"My quest?"

"You're a knight, aren't you?"

Greenwood thought, then shook his head. "I can't remember where I've been or where I'm going. Or what I'm supposed to do."

"Not to worry. Once you remember yourself, the rest will fall into place."

Pierson started forward, his trouser legs pushing through the sluggish water, his shoes sinking into the sand. Eyeing the darkness under the cypress roots, he imagined snakes gliding toward him under water. He was marveling at the power of the imagination to evoke unwanted emotion when a sinuous, muscular shape coiled around his legs.

The next thing he knew he was under water, thrashing. He came up, gasping, glimpsed Greenwood rushing toward him, went under again.

He woke. His clothes were soaked. He reeked of mud and primal slime. Again, Greenwood repaired to the dayroom and took up brush and canvas. This time the subject matter was clearer. There were the towering cypresses, dashed off in glossy browns, and there, one arm and a terrified face above water, was himself. And there, barely glimpsed beneath the dark water the sinewy coils of a great serpent.

The black castle stood atop a rocky prominence that rose steep and craggy above the broad plain. The pile's sheer walls and soaring battlements appeared unbreachable, the climb up the cliffs below impossible. Storm clouds covered the sky from horizon to horizon. Lightning flickered without any attendant thunder over the castle where the clouds were darkest.

The castle was a complicated symbol, Pierson mused from where he stood on a rise some miles away. The "black" castle represented chaos, that which is hidden, perhaps buried, as it also represented the entrance to the Other World. Pluto, Lord of the Underworld, lived in such a castle, as did the ferryman Charon.

Besides the castle, other architectural mysteries occupied the plain. These lacked the castle's basalt solidity and appeared as airy flights of fantasy or depression, depending where you looked. The buildings were ghostly and constantly changing. The white stone into gray, the gray into white. Neoclassical vied with Gothic. Soaring towers melted into squat rotundas. Classical gardens devolved into the worst excesses of romantic fancy. These glimpses of evolving and devolving cities reminded him of Greenwood's paintings in the gallery—clashing and unfinished. Like those, these were reflections of Greenwood's mental state.

Pierson looked at the man. Dressed in chainmail, his unsheathed sword gripped in his strong hand, Greenwood looked ready to face whatever challenge the dream offered. A brave front, he reflected, masking an amnesiac and a catatonic. Still, he admired his pluck in the face of daunting obstacles. The man had the heart of an adventurer.

"Are these of your making?" Pierson indicated the inchoate cityscapes.

"I ..."

"You are an architect. These look like an architect's nightmare. They suggest you are experiencing conflict. What do you see?"

"I see indecision. A lack of resolve."

Pierson gazed at the distant fortress. "Does this place jog your memory?"

"I've been here before. I'm sure of that. My quest has to do with yonder castle, and ..."

"And?"

"I see a face. Whose I do not know. She is beautiful. Did I know her? Or is she a vision conjured to mock me with a desire I cannot attain."

Pierson followed the younger man's gaze. Under the lightning flashes, the castle reminded him of a spider. Crouched. Ready to spring. To devour.

Greenwood's memory lay in there. But what else?

Whatever awaited them wouldn't be unguarded.

The attack did not wait for them to enter the castle. The sun had set, and darkness was settling over the plain as they neared the rocky outcroppings that formed the foundation of the precipice upon which the castle stood. They were trying to resolve the mystery of how they might climb the precipice without rope when they heard footsteps swooshing through the grass behind them.

Greenwood spun, sword ready.

The things that rushed them were loathsome parodies of man. There were four of them, Abhuman abominations like some blasphemous product of devolution, they towered over their human counterparts. Their fish-pale flesh and rudimentary simian features instilled such an atavistic horror in Pierson's breast that it was all he could do to keep from fleeing.

Weaponless, he balled his fists and crouched.

The long-limbed monsters loped across the plain. Now that they had no need of stealth, their bare feet thundered on the grassy earth.

Greenwood sidestepped the first attacker and raked his blade across its abdomen. The loathsome brute tripped and slid, its feet entangled in its own viscera. Before Greenwood could recover, a second brute slammed him a mighty blow that lifted him off his feet and hurled him against a boulder. Miraculously, he rose, shook off the pain, and charged the beasts.

Groping for a rock or branch, anything with which to defend himself, Pierson's hand closed over a stone. He hurled it into the loathsome face of the nearest beast. The half-human growled but came on apace.

"Run!" Greenwood yanked his arm as he passed. Pierson strained to keep pace.

A great fist struck his back, pounded the wind from his lungs. He sprawled, struck his chin on the ground, and lay stunned....

Remembering the abhumans, his vision snapped into focus. Greenwood was keeping two of the giants at bay with flourishes of his sword. A third scowled from a distance, nursing a deep wound that nearly severed its forearm. Blood reddened the earth at its feet.

Pierson found another rock and, equipped with the false bravery that came of knowing this was a dream and no real harm could come of it, joined Greenwood to do battle.

The circling fiends, wary of Greenwood's blade, looked up as a flapping like ship's sails in a gusty wind descended upon them. Pierson flinched as a shadow swept over him and a rising breeze almost lifted him off his feet.

The bird was vast. Larger than fifty eagles. Pierson recognized it from Arabian lore. In his youth, he had read of it in the tales of Sinbad in the *One Thousand and One Nights*. Yet so stunned were his senses, it took him a moment to recall its name.

Roc, from the Arabic *rukk*.

It didn't land but, spreading its wings to catch the air and slow its descent, it thrust out talons as long as a man's arm and, seizing an abhuman by the shoulders, snatched it high into the air before dashing it onto the rocks. It circled back. The roar of its passage provided thunder for the lightning flashing over the castle.

The last abhuman, seeing what happened to its companion, fled. The great bird folded its wings and dove. Again, it caught the wind in its spread wings. This time it landed. It raked the giant with its claws, shredding the brute as neatly as a seasoned butcher chops stew meat. The giant with the bleeding arm was still on its feet. The roc seized it in its beak, shook it till its bones were broken, and flung it into the gathering darkness.

Then it looked at Pierson. The psychologist staggered before the fierce gaze of that buckler-sized yellow eye.

"R'lil will not hurt you," Greenwood called. "We're old friends."

Pierson couldn't believe it: Greenwood stood beside the great bird, stretching to pat its massive shoulder. Each of its feathers was longer than Pierson was tall. The bird stood placidly, regarding Pierson but making no move.

"Once when I was traversing the Plateau of Tsang, I saved one of her young from the jaws of a manticore. I nearly died from the encounter. She took me to her nest and nursed me back to health."

Pierson, an avid student of mythology and folklore, had heard of the creature. Lion's body, head of a man, a scorpion's tail. An image of a fierce, sharp-cheeked face sprang to mind. It might have been handsome—were it not for the insane eyes and teeth-filled mouth. He shivered.

"Come," Greenwood said. "We won't need that rope after all."

R'lil set them down atop a watchtower. Pierson saw why Greenwood insisted they cling to R'lil's ankles. They would never have been able to descend from the bird's back to the rampart, as the crenelated tower itself was barely broad enough for the roc to perch upon. They dropped between her splayed talons to the flagstone deck.

They clung to each other as the bird took flight. The flapping of its mighty wings buffeted them with a wind that might have blown slighter creatures off the tower and into the night.

They waved as R'lil circled the castle, then disappeared into the north. When the marvelous sight dwindled to a dot, they descended an inclined ladder down to the steep spiral stair. The only illumination came from the lightning flashes at the narrow arrow slits spaced every so often on the outer side of the winding stair.

After many turns, they came to a door that opened onto a covered gallery. On one side, a series of arches opened to a view of the night and the inconclusive drafts of Greenwood's unfinished city rippling like gossamer tapestries in the air above the plain. Opposite this a long wall offered several doors.

"You said you've been here before," Pierson said. "Does anything jog your memory?"

"Not really. I have a vague impression that my feet know which way to go, but not what waits at the end of this or that path. Who knows what the Warlock has waiting for us.

"'Warlock'?"

"Did I— I did! I seem to recall a tall thin man, not an aesthetic but possessing the sinewy frame and dexterity of a fighting man. Or am I making that up because I said the word *Warlock*?"

Pierson ignored the self-deprecation. "Why do you call him the Warlock?"

Greenwood shook his head, and for a moment his look of fierce determination mixed with lighthearted deprecation faded, replaced by the vanquished gaze of the lost,

He spread his hands. "I don't know. Maybe my imagination suggested Warlock because the black castle looks like a warlock's home."

Pierson decided not to push it. Greenwood's memory would come when it would.

They chose the door at the opposite end of the gallery. Another stair. This one descended in a succession of right angles and was lit by more arrow slits through which lightning flashes intermittently illuminated the stairwell.

"Why are you helping me?" Greenwood asked.

Pierson considered how much to tell. Decided it might help if

Greenwood knew what his life had become in the waking world. "In your other life, you underwent a traumatic change. One day you were a successful architect, the next you were a catatonic inmate at Bedlam. You've been mute and unresponsive for four years. You sleep and dream. Apparently, you paint your dreams when you wake. Your condition doesn't appear to be physiological, and there is no evidence of any traumatic event that might have caused such a drastic change. Dr. Vesey speculates—and I concur—that the cause lies in your dreams."

"Is that possible?"

"Normally, no. Most people's dreams are ephemeral, a product of passive imagination. The associationists say most dreams reflect the day's events or what we had for supper. You, however, are at home in the Dreamlands and possess a particularly powerful imagination that exerts a creative influence on your dreams. So, yes, I think it possible whatever event caused your memory loss in Dreamland, caused your catatonia in the waking world."

A deep rumbling welled up from the darkness below. Rapidly, the sound grew louder. The stairs vibrated beneath their feet as if some tremendous beast surged up the stairs.

Not waiting to see what approached, Pierson raced behind Greenwood up to the door at the next landing. Before plunging through, Pierson glanced below and gasped.

Rats, as big as hounds thundered up the stairs. Their humped backs undulated like a greasy tide. Their black, cunning eyes glittered in the torchlight thrown down from the open door. Pierson shoved through, slammed the door, and threw his trembling weight against it. Of the few things that repulsed—nay, *unnerved*—him, rats were at the top of the list.

"Come on!" Greenwood was several paces down the hall. Pierson released the door and ran to join him.

They were halfway down the hall when the net fell. One second Pierson was running at Greenwood's heels, the next he was swept off his feet and found himself hanging in a net with his face pressed against Greenwood's shoulder. Greenwood shook the net in his efforts to saw through the ropes, but his arms were pinned.

"Got you!"

The gravelly voice carried an undertone of sadistic pleasure. Pierson twisted to see the speaker.

There were two of them. Each had four sinewy arms that ended in powerful three-fingered hands. The creatures had the thick wrists of born swordsmen; indeed, the lower hands of each wielded curved scimitars similar to the Turkish kilij, the blades single-edged from the hilt to where they flared wider into a double-edged point. Looking at their faces, Pierson was reminded of his earlier imaging of the manticore: mad eyes and rows of bristling carnivorous teeth. Their legs were thin like the hard, angular legs of a grasshopper and jointed opposite the way a human's bent.

The stairwell door crashing open interrupted the creatures' gloating as the rat horde spilled into the hall. The mammoth rodents surged toward them. One of the guards raised its hand. From its palm spewed a stream of fire that caught the lead rat in the face. The reek of singed hair filled the hall as the horde turned tail and jostled back to the stairwell. Pierson suspected sorcery, but then he saw the metallic insert in the guard's palm. A device, then. A weapon that shot flame.

The creatures were strong. Hefting the tightly twisted ends of the net over their shoulders, they carried Pierson and Greenwood, ignobly swaying between them, down long corridors then up a tower stair, until they stopped before a great oaken iron-hinged door. Ignoring Pierson's demands to be put down and Greenwood's further thrashing as he tried to maneuver his sword, the guards remained mute and unmoving. Anon, the door swung open.

A stench of sulfur and harsh alchemical smells stung Pierson's nose. The air in the cluttered room was hazy with smoke curling from a brick tower standing in the center of what he imagined was an alchemist's den. Phials, flasks, tubes, retorts, and jars of varying sizes littered a workbench alongside bellows, hammers, tongs, files, funnels, sieves, and crucibles.

The alchemist—or rather Greenwood's Warlock, for the tall wiry figure dressed in black samite that hugged his muscular physique could only be the master of the castle—stood by the workbench adding a measure of white powder to a bubbling retort. The man's beard and mustache were glistening black, as were the thick curls that fell to his shoulders. With his straight nose and cleft chin, the man might have been considered handsome, were it not for the hardness of his dark eyes and the lines at the corners of his mouth that, Pierson imagined, remained downturned even when he smiled.

"Put them there," the Warlock said, indicating a spot near an open casement window. His voice was deep and, like the purring of a great cat, contained an undercurrent of danger. Beyond the window, lightning flashed. Torchlight cast restless shadows in the corners. "And take away that damnable sword."

As soon as he was free, Greenwood lunged at his captor. The Warlock raised a hand and a beam of green light flashed from a signet ring bearing a hexagram surrounded by astronomical sigils. Greenwood froze; a catatonic gaze replaced his anger.

"Return to your cell," the Warlock commanded. Greenwood, slack-mouthed and gazing at nothing, left the room.

The Warlock wiped his hands on a towel and turned to Pierson. "Now you."

Hoping to sound bolder than he felt, Pierson said, "It's not my dream. I'm only an observer. You can't hurt me." Of course, he was mindful of the cut on his cheek and the soaking he'd received from the swamp.

The Warlock's smile let Pierson know the lord of the castle wasn't falling for his bluff. "Kill him," the Warlock ordered and returned to his work as if the deed were already done.

Eight dexterous limbs sprang into action. Four blades flashed in the torchlight. The first blade slashed his tunic and drew a thread of blood across his chest. The second would have nailed his arm to his side had he not twisted away.

If only he had a sword with which to defend himself.

The monsters came on. He willed himself awake.

Pierson started awake. Greenwood slept on. Pierson watched the sleeping man while his heart ceased pounding. Greenwood did not rise and go to the dayroom and commit his latest adventure to canvas.

After a while, Pierson rose and retired to his house.

At home, he dug his old saber out of a closet and ran through a drill of cuts and parries. The movements came naturally, quick and precise. The weapon felt good, an extension of his hand, a steadfast friend. Though the saber had been obsolete in the infantry by the time he took up arms for Queen and country and shipped off to the Transvaal, he'd fenced in university and taught saber while a sergeant prior to receiving his lieutenant's commission. But youth was behind him, and he was stiff from a sedentary lifestyle.

Don't fret it, he told himself, remembering how, in Dreamland, he'd not needed his cane.

How he would take on the Warlock's guards was another matter. He'd have to free Greenwood. Get a sword in his hand. They'd stand a better chance together.

He lay on his bed and, clasping the saber's hilt to his chest, closed his eyes and slowed his breathing.

⚜

He found himself on the stairs again. Lightning flashed through the window slits, illuminating the black stone walls. A savage wave of déjà vu swept over him. He gripped the saber tighter remembering the horde of rat hounds surging from below like some fanged and fetid tide. He glanced at the landing above: the Warlock's four-armed guards would be waiting in the hall.

Of course, the Warlock might have some worse horror in store for him. Dream logic was fickle. Still … he was a seasoned dreamer and believed in the power of the creative imagination.

Sure enough, a familiar rumble rose up the stairwell. He sprinted to the landing and grasped the door latch until he saw by the lightning flashes the heaving backs and hungry eyes surging up the stair.

He slammed the door behind him and charged down the hall. He stopped before reaching the net suspended from the ceiling. He traced fine cords down to the shallow alcoves of recessed doors on either side.

"You can come out now," he called. The guards stepped out of the alcoves. As before, their two lower arms wielded scimitars. Seeing he was armed, hideous smiles stretched over their faces as they advanced on their chitinous, backward-jointed legs.

Pierson ducked under the first stroke and severed a three-fingered hand as he rolled. He caught the hand as it dropped and came up behind the guards. Blood spewed from the shocked guard's stump. His comrade rallied and came after him, blades flashing. Pierson pried the flame weapon from the severed palm and slapped it on his own. Not a moment too soon, he thrust his palm at the mad-eyed creature. A column of flame consumed its hideous features. The thing cried out, dropped its blades, and, staggering back, raised all four hands to its smoldering face.

The stairwell door burst open. Instantly the hall was filled with rats. Their high-pitched squealing joined the screams of the guards. Lunging to either side of the hallway, Pierson yanked the cords keeping the net aloft. The net dropped over the flailing guards.

Not bothering to look behind him, Pierson ran to the door at the opposite end of the hall, leaving the shrieking guards to the rats.

Pierson's skin crawled at the currents of eldritch magic emanating from the cell. Within its confines, Greenwood stood staring slack-jawed and unblinking into a large oval mirror mounted on a wall. Pierson sensed movement in the mirror, but the architect blocked his view.

The mirror was slightly convex, its surface mottled as if from great age. Considering its provenance, Pierson did not doubt it was enchanted. As a psychologist, he recognized the mirror was a symbol of the imagination—and of consciousness in its capacity to reflect the reality of the visible world. As a reflection of the universe, the mirror contained the memory of all it had ever reflected.

Pierson raised his palm, aimed the fire weapon at the lock. A stream of flame shot out of the device and poured into the metal until the lock was white hot. Pierson grasped the door well away from the heated iron and jerked it toward him. The melting lock gave, and Pierson entered the cell.

"Greenwood," he said, hoping to rouse the man. As if mesmerized by what he saw, the architect continued to stare into the mirror. Within its murky depths, the conflicting fragments of his dream city dissolved and coalesced. Buildings spun from the gossamer threads of imagination began in one style then mutated into another wholly incongruous one. Here the façade of a magnificent gothic cathedral blurred into the squat arches of the Romanesque, then further devolved into a squalid hovel of wattle and daub.

It was as if Greenwood was having difficulty arriving at an aesthetic resolution. For some reason, Pierson thought of Penelope undoing her tapestry each night to put off her suitors. It came to him—why the Warlock had imprisoned Greenwood. The Warlock recognized the power of Greenwood's imagination, and as he was an architect of note, the Warlock was forcing Greenwood to build him a dream kingdom, as the legendary Kuranes dreamed into existence the celebrated city of Celephaïs. The constantly changing architectural styles was Greenwood's way of delaying the completion of the Warlock's desire.

Pierson stared at the man in admiration. What he was seeing was the equivalent of a man fighting with his hands tied behind his back. Under a spell, unable to move of his own volition, Greenwood was combating his tormentor in the only way left to him.

The mirror reflects all it has ever reflected. Pierson was on to something. He followed the thought. It came to him: the mirror was an extension of Greenwood's mind, the screen onto which he projected his thoughts. Greenwood might not be able to recall his memories, but perhaps he could project them onto the mirror and Pierson could observe them. It was a working hypothesis. To test it, he needed Greenwood's cooperation.

"Greenwood," he said, standing close behind the architect's shoulder. "John. Look into the mirror and show me the past. Make me understand how you came to be forced to do the Warlock's bidding. Four years ago, you underwent a psychic breakdown. Something prompted that breakdown. Make me understand. You're fighting the Warlock by delaying the design of his dream kingdom. You can also fight by remembering. Yours is a powerful imagination, but imagination cannot succeed without the foundation of experience supplied by memory. John?"

The scene in the mirror changed. The architectural grotesqueries faded. Before him London's familiar streets appeared. Pierson recognized the scene. Threadneedle Street. There at the intersection was the Bank of England. Greenwood had stopped to admire John Soane's impressive neoclassical façade.

Now he sat at the dining table in his posh West End home where he lived with his mother. At the head of the table, the handsomely dressed matron buttered a slice of toast. Eating an omelet, Greenwood sat to her right with his back to a window. With the images, Pierson perceived thoughts, impressions, and emotions, as if Greenwood was trying to communicate and make him understand. He had fame and fortune, but no one to share it with. The women his mother aspired to pair him with were lovely and rich, but none he met possessed the power of imagination he sought in a life companion. He was not interested in a trophy wife, one who showed him to advantage on his arm at the opera or ball. Indeed, though he loved the opera, he eschewed the frivolity, the narcissism of the ballroom. He sought the one woman with whom he could share sunsets and tea, perhaps even literature and architecture. In short, a soul mate.

Then, one glorious day he saw her in Dreamland. He'd traveled from fabled Xycansk, famous for its harbor where the red-sailed ships from still more fabled Kabatha arrived, their holds filled with silks and spices, to Salsanon, the Pink City. He had come for the city's opera, reputed to be the finest in all the seven realms.

Across a crowded bazaar, beyond a throng of merchants and shoppers, turbaned and tiaraed, he'd caught a glimpse of raven hair and moon-pale cheek. And in that moment, though he was at some distance and a crowd intervening, she'd turned her head, and he could have sworn her gaze met his and his heart lifted with the surety that she, that raven-haired, moon-pale beauty, was the one.

He started forth, weaving his way between the stalls and many-coloured tents, keeping ever on his toes to watch her passage. But the coach reached the end of the avenue and rounded a corner and so was gone from his sight. He despaired. Yet he was in Dreamland, and now that he'd spied his beloved's face, he knew he would see her again. He desired to know her name and learn if she was maiden still or—heaven forbid—wed.

He asked a kindly-looking merchant selling intricately carven combs and brushes and figurines of ivory and tortoise shell and jade who the maiden was and if she was wed.

"She is a rare beauty, that one," said the merchant, and Greenwood could see by the softening of the seller's gaze that he, too, was smitten by the lady. "Her name is Elora. Her father is vizier to his majesty. It is said that noble youths from far and wide, as well as several of Salsanon's own, woo her or petition her father for matrimony, but …"

"Yes?"

The old man looked upon the fair blue sky, kissed his bunched fingers, lowered his gaze, and pressed the kissed fingers to his forehead as Greenwood had often seen the Goddess's faithful do.

"They each met with a mysterious and painful death."

The news startled Greenwood. Was she a sorceress? Could he be so mistaken about the aura of innocence that glowed about her like sunshine? Surely the man jested.

"It is said," the merchant continued when he saw the doubt in Greenwood's eyes, "the Warlock who lives in the black castle in the mountain beyond the plain wants her for himself. She has refused him; therefore, he has promised death to any rival."

"Who is this Warlock?" Pierson asked, though he knew the answer, at least from a psychoanalytic point of view: the Warlock represented the id, Greenwood's self at war with himself.

What followed was a fevered blur of images and emotions played out in the mirror's depths like a movie on a cinema screen.

His return to the bazaar each day hoping to catch a glimpse of Elora. His learning of her abduction. His journey to the mountain beyond the plain. His entry into the black castle and subsequent capture.

He awoke in a dungeon. Manacles hung from iron rings set in the moist stone walls. A rack, its oak boards dark with sweat and blood, awaited its next victim. A bed of coals glowed in a nearby furnace, beside which a trestle table offered tongs, hammers, knives, and other instruments of torture. The air was thick with the reek of blood and excrement. He cried out when he moved and realized he stood on his toes, his wrists bound to an iron bar hoisted above his head.

Standing before him, the Warlock, fingering a short, hooked blade, offered to let him live if he would build for him a dream kingdom upon the plain.

He refused, and the Warlock used the blade to part the flesh across his bare chest.

Finding him obstinate still, the Warlock nodded to the hooded tormentor who took up a cat-o'-nine-tails and laid into his back. He passed out. Woke. A bowl of water stood on a table before him. The Warlock bade him gaze into the water and tell him what he saw.

At first, he refused, but curiosity, pain, and a terrible thirst drew his gaze to the water. In its depths he saw Elora chained to a narrow cot in a filthy cell. "My raven-haired beauty had thinned from refusing to eat," Pierson heard Greenwood say. "Her moon-pale flesh was gaunt upon her cheek. Her ruby lips faded to coral, the flesh beneath her eyes gray with exhaustion and sorrow. Her tears rent my heart. As I watched, the vision in the water changed. Years passed. Elora's despair succumbed to senile resignation as all hope died. Her emaciated flesh wrinkled, her hair grayed, until at last she lay dead, a shrunken mockery of her beauteous youth. This was to be her fate should I refuse the Warlock. I relented, swore I would do his bidding if he would return her to her father's house."

Pierson had seen enough. Surely Greenwood's memory would be restored if he broke the spell. He lifted his hand, aimed the flame device at the mirror, and blasted its surface. The fire's flow did not reflect off the mirror but drove into its depths. A heat shimmer danced over the surface. Then the glass shattered, leaving, when the smoke cleared, a black void from which emanated a terrible cold.

Out of the blackness into Greenwood's cell stepped a masked figure. The newcomer had the same build as Greenwood. His features were hidden behind a black veil that tented and fell with his breathing. He held a broadsword identical to the one the Warlock had taken from Greenwood.

"Your saber!" Greenwood shouted. Glad to see the architect restored, Pierson tossed it to him. Greenwood caught it in time to block his opponent's savage downstroke. The clang of steel on steel reverberated in the cell.

So began a series of thrusts and parries, of cuts and blocks. Greenwood and his opponent each fenced in the style appropriate for his blade. Greenway in a flurry of fast-paced advances and retreats, his blade ever seeking his enemy's heart. The masked figure, wielding a broadsword, circled and slashed. Though the fighters' skills appeared equally matched, the heavier broadsword took its toll on Greenwood. Each time he raised the saber to block a downward slash, he had to parry and sidestep to avoid being cleft.

Greenwood ended it. Tiring, he ducked under his opponent's blade, grabbed his sword hand, and, pushing the broadsword aside, ran the figure through with the saber. The masked man slid to the floor. He lay there in the spreading blood pool, holding his belly. His mask tented over his mouth as his breathing slowed.

He lay still. Greenwood lifted the veil and gazed on the swordsman's face. The two, the dreamer and the dead, could not have been more alike. Here was the same sandy hair, the same square jaw and identical gray eyes, the same broad chest. Pierson looked from one to the other in amazement. It made sense, however, that the figure that emerged from the mirror should be Greenwood's reflection, his doppelgänger. Like the mirror, the double was a symbol of the mind.

"I've killed myself," Greenwood said. The saber dripped blood onto the cell floor.

"This is Dreamland," Pierson said. "You've killed no one. Dreams are fraught with symbols. You've only cast off the mask of forgetfulness. What do you remember?"

"Everything," Greenwood growled. It did Pierson's heart good to see the man revitalized. "I remember the lashing the Warlock's torturer gave me and the indignities he has caused my beloved."

At their feet, the doppelgänger faded, then vanished, taking with it the sword and the blood pool so that nothing remained but bare floor. The cold of the void no longer emanated from the mirror. It was simply a broken mirror with shattered glass upon the floor.

Greenwood offered to return Pierson's saber.

"Keep it. You handle it well, and I have my weapon." He showed the architect the flame thrower concealed in his palm.

Pierson imitated the guards' knock on the Warlock's oaken door.

The master of the house bade them enter. The Warlock's dark eyes widened when he saw them unattended, then narrowed. His hesitation lasted only a second. He saw the blade in Greenwood's hand and the rage in his face and raised his signet ring to bind the architect. Doing so without regarding Pierson as a threat was his undoing. Pierson thrust out his hand and the device he'd taken from the guard shot a stream of flame into the Warlock's face. The reek of singed hair and burnt flesh overpowered the room's alchemical stink. The Warlock staggered back clutching his smoldering face. Greenwood stepped in. With a sweep of the saber, he severed the Warlock's pinky from his hand. Finger and ring fell to the floor. Bringing the blade up and around, Greenwood continued the stroke and, clasping the haft with both hands and putting his hip into the blow, severed the Warlock's head from his body. The head spun through the air, struck a cabinet, and thumped to the floor. The corpse's knees buckled as it dropped. The head lay on its ear. Its mouth moved but no words came out. Then the eyes glazed over, and the features froze.

Greenwood picked the Warlock's head up by its hair and hurled it out the window, where it described a bloody arc as it fell to the plain below.

Pierson joined Greenwood by the window and watched as Dreamland changed. The lightning over the castle ceased flickering. The storm clouds over the plain vanished. The sun emerged bright and warm. All through the air the ghostly tatters of Greenwood's disjointed city coalesced, transformed into a single, unified vision of beauty and splendor. An embanked serpentine river, overarched by many exquisite bridges, wound through the city. Buildings incomplete flew upward, floor after floor, till their turrets scraped the sky. Arches and towers soared. Parks and plazas sprouted as the city spread avenue after glittering avenue, district after breathtaking district to the distant escarpment. And upon the escarpment, a mighty fortress to protect the city should an enemy attack from that quarter.

They left the Warlock's den and searched the upper towers until they found Elora. Her cell was narrow and spartan, but not as squalid as the Warlock's vision had shown Greenwood. There were no chains, and the room was clean. However, the maiden was thin and, if possible, paler than before. Though her frame was slight, her mind was sound, and she thanked them profusely when she learned her abductor was dead. Though she looked fondly on the handsome architect, she did not cry on his shoulder. Pierson admired her for that. She would make a fine queen now that Greenwood had a kingdom to rule.

Pierson and Greenwood stood on a rampart overlooking the city. The castle, now white like the dazzling buildings below, had undergone extensive renovation. The dungeons and rats and the Warlock's alchemical laboratory were gone, relegated to whatever place dreams went to when no longer dreamed. Colorful pennants fluttered from the towers. The sky was clear, and the sun shone down on the wonder Greenwood's imagination had wrought.

"You've outdone yourself, John," Pierson said. News of the white city on the plain had spread quickly and people had been streaming into the city for days. A thriving bazaar had sprouted up in one of the central plazas. Schools were being organized.

"It is beautiful, isn't it?" Greenwood said with pride.

"What will you name your city?" Pierson asked.

"Elora, what else?"

"What else, indeed." Pierson tapped his chin. "However, it doesn't really ring when you pronounce her name and title: Elora, Queen of Elora."

The architect grinned. "It doesn't, does it? I'll work on it."

"Is it as real as you believe it is?" Pierson asked. "Dreamland I mean. Is it, as some cultures believe, as real as the waking world?"

"Look around you, man." Greenwood swung a muscular arm to encompass the world. "Do your eyes deceive you?" He plucked a seven-petaled lavender flower from a nearby pot and pressed it into Pierson's hand. "What does that feel like? Smell like?"

Pierson held the flower up to the sunlight, admired the way the velvety petals glowed. He brought it to his nose, inhaled. Its scent was sweet, not quite as heavy as a rose. "I take your point. I've long wondered. Most people glimpse Dreamland. You live it. I, too, as a youth, spent endless nights exploring its mysteries."

"What happened?"

Pierson lifted his brows. "War. University. Career. But you, sir, seem to have overcome the tyranny of adulthood."

"I have met travelers who claim hashish or opium gives them access to Dreamland. I've never had need." Greenwood cast a loving gaze over his dream kingdom. "I've ever felt the Dreamland is my home. Oh, I love London and the merry round world into which I was born. But where was I born from? And when I pass, where will I go?"

Pierson woke. He lay on his bed in his Mayfair home fully clothed and cradling his saber. He rose, excitement bubbling in his breast, washed up, and took a hansom to Bethlehem Hospital.

He burst into Greenwood's room out of breath. The bed was empty. Apparently, it had been for some time as it was made.

He hurried to the dayroom, expecting to find Greenwood painting their adventures, and, hopefully, fully cognizant. He found Greenwood's canvases and paints in their usual place, but no Greenwood.

Dr. Vesey rushed in. "I heard you were in the building, Professor. I was just about to send for you."

"What's happened? Where's Greenwood?"

"Well, that's just it. We don't know where he is. No one saw him leave. We've searched the grounds." Vesey pushed his spectacles higher on his nose. "It's as if he vanished. It's most perplexing."

"I'm sure he's about someplace," Pierson said to assure himself as much as Vesey.

"I hope you're right. But there's the matter of the note."

"What note?"

"The one he left for you."

Vesey led him to his office, showed him what lay on his desk.

A folded sheet of linen stationery and a flower.

His heart jolted at the sight of the seven-petaled lavender flower. It was a twin to the one Greenwood had pressed into his hand on the rampart. He picked it up by the stem and held it to the harsh electric light of Vesey's office. He remembered how the Dreamland sun set its velvety petals glowing, the heat releasing a sweet, exotic, unforgettable scent.

He set the flower down and unfolded the paper. The note was written in a florid hand dashed off in blue ink, as if the architect had been in a hurry to return to his kingdom and his lady.

Dear Eric,

Without your aid, I would surely be languishing in Bethlehem Hospital, perhaps until the Warlock tired of me. And my beloved Elora condemned to die in her cell.

I have many plans for my city on the plain. I am something of a perfectionist and keep making changes. Elora thinks it beautiful as it is and kids me about my obsession. My latest addition is the inclusion of a dozen grand fountains.

You are a friend indeed and are already sorely missed. If ever you find yourself in my part of Dreamland, please stop by and stay as long as you like. Know that you will always be welcome and will be lauded at a banquet in your honor and called upon to make a speech.

(Kidding about the speech!)

Your friend in perpetuity,
John Howard Greenwood

But Pierson never found his way back. Over the years he traveled wide in Dreamland. Even took up cartography to help him map his travels. Not that any map of Dreamland was reliable—dream walkers were fiercely independent and too few to form a consensus reality. He'd made it to far Kabatha with its white ships and fine port wine. In Dhul he heard rumours of a white city on a plain with a noble and munificent king and a gentle queen whose beauty was said to be without peer in all the kingdoms of Dreamland. And once he viewed through a spyglass across a green valley on the shore of a shimmering lake the soaring arches and tall towers of Greenwood's fabled city. But ever he woke and took up journal and pen and with the memory of his latest trek clear in his mind recorded his travels.

In Tanth, he talked to an innkeeper who heard from a traveler only last month that King John had waged war on a tyrannical neighbor and freed prisoners, lowered taxes, and began an ambitious plan to establish trade routes with other cities. And he was bringing something called electricity to Luxavia. The innkeeper said the traveler described the electricity as lights. "Bright as the sun," he said and wagged a finger. "Bright as the sun."

Pierson smiled at the memory. It would be like Greenwood to bring electricity to Dreamland. What next? He hoped it would not be traffic.

Leaning on his cane, Pierson took up the book lying on his desk. He'd had it privately published for circulation among friends and collogues. It was the record of his Dreamland travels, as well as a history of his Dream Imaging Device. Though he'd invented the DID as a tool to help psychologists reach unresponsive patients, it had in recent years begun to be used for entertainment purposes. Dream parlors had opened in Paris, Manhattan, and London, and it was said that the Edison Company was working on a way to project dreams onto movie screens.

A wave of nostalgia washed over him as he traced his thumb over the embossed title done in gold against a black field:

A Prisoner of Dreamland.

He opened the book to its center where Greenwood's flower and note lay in the crease. He took up the flower. Though flattened, its lavender petals remained as fresh and supple as the day Greenwood left it. He'd once shown it to a friend from the Royal Botanical Garden who exclaimed he had never seen its like. His friend wanted him to donate it for analysis, but he couldn't part with it. He held the flower to his nose and smelled it. After all these years it retained its exotic fragrance that never failed to remind him of the faraway fields of Dreamland.

He set the flower down beside the book and unfolded the note. He'd long ago memorized every word, but he enjoyed seeing Greenwood's exuberant script. He imagined the architect hadn't changed much. A distinguishing touch of gray at his temples, a streak or two in his beard. Time ran differently in Dreamland.

When he was feeling melancholy, the note filled him with an ache of unfulfilled longing. Other times he flushed with gratitude at having played a part in a grand adventure.

Tonight, he was melancholy. It was his seventieth birthday. A few surviving colleagues had treated him to dinner, but their company had failed to lift his spirits. Sleep, ever his friend in youth, had deserted him. And along with sleep, his sojourns in Dreamland waned. Lately, he caught only fleeting glimpses of those fabulous lands beyond Dreamland's gates. Insomnia was a widening moat separating him from his heart's desire.

Replacing the note, he took up the flower again and held it to his nose. He closed his eyes and sought in its sweet summer scent the faraway fields of Dreamland.

ABOUT THE AUTHOR

GARRETT BOATMAN is the author of *Stage Fright* (Paperbacks from Hell), the hooligan nights novella *Floaters*, and the dark fantasy trilogy *Night's Plutonian Shore*, *The Clocks of Midnight*, and *The Mirror of Eternity*. His stories have appeared in *The Valancourt Book of Horror Stories*, *Penumbra* and *Weird House Magazine*, among others. An experienced oneironaut, he writes from that liminal space where Dreamland meets the waking world. A member of HWA, SFWA and the British Fantasy Society, Garrett lives in coastal North Carolina.

About the Artist

Steeped in the enthralling fantasy and science-fiction illustrations of the 1960s, '70s, and '80s, artist and illustrator **K.L. Turner** brings a bit of old-school painterly style to today's methods. With more than 30 years of experience in the arts, he expertly brings an expressionistic style into his illustrations to create compelling works which captivate and draw the viewer in. His works are found in media and galleries around the world, and celebrated in pop culture.

A versatile creative type, Turner is also accomplished in the mediums of photography, sculpture, and the fine arts. Choosing to live and work on the beautiful front range of the Colorado Rocky Mountains where he was born and raised, he continues to derive inspiration from nature as well as cultural influences both at home and in his travels.

www.ingramcontent.com/pod-product-compliance
Lightning Source LLC
Chambersburg PA
CBHW032210030726
47494CB00020B/944